# THE M... AMERICAN REVOLUTIONARY

## BY JON FOYT

Andrew Benzie Books
Orinda, California

Published by Andrew Benzie Books
www.andrewbenziebooks.com

Printed in the United States of America

First Edition: July 2015

10 9 8 7 6 5 4 3 2

ISBN 978-1-941713-23-5

*Cover and book design by Andrew Benzie*

For My Fad Friend Cece
September 2015

Jon Foyt

One of the fun events about writing a novel, in addition to the historic research, paying homage to the mindfulness of the characters, and the daily hard work, is dedicating the work, which I now do to Helen, and especially to the Founding Fathers who signed the Declaration of Independence, and to the men and women who today defend it with their lives, their hearts, and their minds.

# TABLE OF CONTENTS

# ACKNOWLEDGMENTS

Especially, I wish to acknowledge the thoughtful assistance of Roy E. Goodman, Curator, the American Philosophical Society, for his research into primary sources about Robert Morris, and to the Pennsylvania Historical Society, as well as to the many historical markers of the City of Philadelphia that take a stroller back into the life at the time of the American Revolution, allowing one to get into the mind of the time. To Claire Pingel, Associate Curator of the American Jewish Museum, for her kind tour of the Haym Solomon Collection. To Norma Van Dyke for her introductions and B&B hospitality. To the Green Library at Stanford University. And to Dr. Martha Losch, Talia Barach, and Jennifer Bielenberg at the Veterans Administration Clinic in Menlo Park, California.

# WHAT WAS SAID

*"Is life so dear, or peace so sweet, as to be purchased at the price of chains and slavery? Forbid it, Almighty God! I know what course others may take, but as for me, give me liberty or give me death."*
—Patrick Henry, March 20, 1775, St. Johns Church, Richmond, VA.
Speaking to 120 delegates to the re-convened Convention.


*"We do not fight for a few acres of land, but for freedom—for the freedom and happiness of millions yet unborn."*
—John Jay, Address of the Convention, December 23, 1776.


*"To Pennsylvania's two most distinguished citizens, Robert Morris, a native of Great Britain, and Benjamin Franklin, a native of Massachusetts."*
—Massachusetts Justice Rufus Choate's toast


*"The American Revolution embodies a multiplicity of implications rather than a single preeminent 'truth'."*
—Ruth Bogin, Author, *Abraham Clark and the Quest for Equality in the Revolutionary Era*, 1982

# SETTING THE COLONIAL STAGE

By 1776, Philadelphia, affectionately known to some as "The Quaker City," to others as the "City of Brotherly Love," had become home to a kaleidoscope of immigrants speaking a multitude of languages. They had crossed the Atlantic Ocean on arduous voyages in ships sailing from ports in England, Scotland, Germany, Ireland, and the Caribbean. Their numbers were augmented by slaves from Africa, free Blacks, and remnant members of Native American tribes who had avoided small pox and who had not fled West to join their fellow survivors.

And taverns. For the water was unhealthy to drink. Besides, cider was buoyant, whisky conductive to debate, as the noise, the food, and the barmaids coalesced, coming together to become the Colonial catalyst, the whole scene edging ever so tenuously, yet with historic certainty, toward Revolution from the long-prevailing Mother Country.

Meeting houses for Quakers, and places of worship for Protestants, soon for the Jews, and some Catholics, each with their welcoming entries, lined the city's dusty streetscapes. These congregations, with their religious services and social functions, fulfilled the basic human need for sober venues in which Colonists could congregate, talk, vent, listen, and gather mutual support as the 13 English Colonies struggled to exist, to prosper, to grow, to expand, and, yes, to unite against the decrees of a non compassionate King and the oppressive laws passed by his Parliament. King and Parliament attempted to reign from halfway around the globe—a distance and a time measured in weeks, sometimes months, but for people on both sides of the Atlantic, undertaking the trip embodied a formidable voyage aboard a crowded, stinking, tossing sailing ship, its successful arrival never assured.

# AUTHOR'S DIALOGUE NOTE

In a novel, to capture a character's actual dialogue in a historical period some 250 years ago is a daunting, if not impossible task for today's writer. For sure, one can read primary sources, including journals, letters and speeches and form an idea of the language of the period, but none of us can listen in to the actual spoken words. We cannot absorb the innuendos, the subtle hints, the voice tones, nor can we see the gesticulations punctuating the voices. Moreover, in that long-ago period, no dictionary existed. (You should see some of the weird and, worse, inconsistent spellings.) Nor was there a style sheet for grammar or Capitalization, as Words were arbitrarily and indiscriminately capitalized. As a result, a novelist of today, attempting to write period accuracy, can easily become engrossed in the minutia of endless attempts at creating an authentic lexicon while never finishing the manuscript.

This novel is a work of fiction as seen through a present-day looking glass—a modern perspective—yet set during the formation of the American republic with characters, some real, some imaginary, living in 1776, before and beyond, experiencing and trying to cope with real and imaginary (but quite likely) scenarios.

# CHARACTERS DEPICTED AND EVENTS NARRATED IN THIS NOVEL

Most characters depicted in this novel, but not all, were real people playing vital roles in the American Revolution. (The character of the Hesse-Kassel prince is based upon an actual royal personage in that German principality.) Many events narrated, but not all, did take place. The dates and the sequence are not historically lineal, for after all, this is a work of fiction, not an historian's chronology of events. Yet the combination of characters, emotions, and events cast a curiously correct compendium of our country's creation.

To further sketch the role of an historical novel in its relationship to a non-fiction work, I cite the review of Jerome Charyn's novel, *I Am Abraham: A novel of Lincoln and the Civil War*, written by Andrew Delbanco in *The New York Review of Books*, in which Delbanco comments: "In the effort to say something new about Lincoln, novelists would seem to have an advantage over historians. As the philosopher R. G. Collingwood wrote in *The Idea of History* (1946), 'the historian stands in a peculiar relation to something called evidence,' which leaves him free to interpret but forbidden to invent. The novelist, on the other hand, can take liberties—suppressing this, embellishing that, even inventing situations, characters, and words that were never actually spoken. He has 'a single task only: to construct a coherent picture, one that makes sense.' A novel is beholden to no external measure of truth; it must only be true to itself."

# AUTHOR'S TALK THERAPY OBSERVATION

The dawn of what we today know as psychiatry and its psychological companion, talk therapy, emerged in Bavaria in the late 18th Century at the time of the American Revolution. Down through the years, this psychology of exploring the mind made missteps, many of them monstrous. That is, until present time. Studies of the mind are beginning to explore its multiple complex neurological cartography. (The author's observations are derived from his sessions with talented therapists.)

# CHAPTER ONE:
# THE GENTLEMAN IN THE CITY TAVERN

Of the 178 places of drink in Philadelphia in 1776, the most popular was the City Tavern. On this cold and icy midwinter evening, the City Tavern was lit by candles set in wall sconces and augmented by candles in brass candelabra set atop the stained and pockmarked wooden trestle tables. The edges of these tables and their accompanying benches had been rounded from the strength of firm handgrips as, night after night, emotional patrons forcefully proclaimed their heartfelt dogmatic political arguments.

The heart-of-pine wide plank floors were soiled, parcels of lamb, mutton, bread, and potatoes having joined the spills of cider, ale, and whiskey, the blend creating artistic abstractions. Only the snow, stomped off hand-tooled leather boots, melting into puddles, offered a cleansing to the floor filth.

Cats crouched, waiting to pounce upon any available edible tidbit. Begging for their share of sustenance, roving dogs whined, nuzzling male patrons' silk pant legs. The array of animals acted much the same as the mix of patrons, as human and animal alike seemed to be awaiting some development, food for the animals and for the people a statement, perhaps a decisive event, or for sure a populist declaration calling for action. For fresh in the patron's minds was the afternoon incident on Market Street where the King George III Tavern sign had been pulled down by a rag-tag group of Revolutionaries.

All of a sudden, as if on cue, a group of tavern patrons, rising in rowdy camaraderie, hoisted their tankards in celebratory gestures. Boisterously toasting each other and possibly the day's events, they broke into Benjamin Franklin's 1739 drinking song:

*Then let us get, like bees lay up honey*
*We'll build us new hives, and store each cell*
*The sight of our treasure shall yield us great pleasure*
*We'll count it, and chink it, and jingle it well.*

*Oh! no!*
*Not so!*
*For honest souls know,*
*Friends and a bottle still bear the bell.*

*Then toss off your glasses, and scorn the dull asses,*
*Who, missing the kernel, still gnaw the shell;*
*What's love, rule, or riches? Wise Solomon teaches,*
*They're vanity, vanity, vanity, still.*

*That's true;*
*He knew;*
*He'd tried them all through;*
*Friends and a bottle still bore the bell.*

Watching, and yes, even participating in song and toast, although his voice was less melodious than deep, one well-dressed gentleman's boosterish gesticulations joined in the musical beat. He smiled as, from time to time, groups of men rose like ocean swells to toast a prominent Colonial patron. Many are still acting out their arduous sailing ship journey from across the Atlantic, he thought as he relived his own—six endless weeks on his father's frigate from Liverpool—years ago as a frightened yet eager teenager.

Robert Morris stood out among the tavern's mix of socially elite Philadelphians, his presence noted by most. While he realized that by now in the Colony he was accepted as a "Prominent Patron," his status did not preclude him from listening to and empathizing with those patrons regarded as "Ordinary Lower Orders." For in the City Tavern the "prominent" and the "ordinaries" shared conversations that derided the oppressive English laws, of which he often noted, no one in any of the Colonial social classes had a say in their passing by the ocean-distant English Parliament.

Our gentleman of note was rather plump, especially in the jowls, and partially balding. Women loved it when a dimple in his left cheek subtly revealed itself when he smiled at them. While handsome to their eyes, unlike many other men, he wore no wig. What remained of his natural brown curls served as attractive male adornment to what to him were the lovely ladies of Philadelphia attired in their London and Paris finery, much like his dear Molly, whom he was proud to love as his wife. In his mind she outshined them all.

As had been the case for days, weeks, and even months, impending political sea change permeated the City Tavern's smoke-filled atmosphere, which was filled with the olfactory sensations of Colonial cooking, which Morris loved to partake. Yet in his sixth sense rang a subliminal and omnipresent clarion call. Some might fearfully describe it as a pending catastrophic war being imposed upon the Colonies. Others might hail it as a national greatness waiting in the wings for its clue to come on stage. When asked his opinion, which was often, Morris forecast that this call, if and when heeded, would serve to shape the future of America. If there were present in the tavern a clairvoyant sage, as many drinkers thought they themselves indeed were, their predictions would foretell of unpredictable—yet surely predictable—events that would go even farther and turn the world upside down.

To some in the City Tavern it seemed to matter only that there was someone or something to toast. Meanwhile, other patrons gambled away their fortunes in the game of Bragg, betting on the random dealings of the 20-card deck. As the evening wore on, outbursts from Colonial separatists contrasted with the subdued statements of those still loyal to the distant King George III, by now a monarch to only a dwindling few. Yet, Morris reminded himself that, regardless of revolutionary ideologies or fading royal allegiances, the Colonists, their parents or grandparents had each shared the grueling experience of sailing across the Atlantic Ocean. They had survived the journey to settle the Pennsylvania colony. As he began his second tankard of ale, he reminded himself that the Colony had been founded more than a century earlier by the revered English Quaker, William Penn, who was loyal to the monarchy. What would that leader think of the array of ideas being expressed this evening as to independence from that same monarchy? Tonight, as every night, Morris concluded, the visions of patrons expressed a thread of consistency. Yet a consensus as to when and how was still jelling.

Robert Morris was not a hero-looking knight astride a white horse, nor did he intend to be so, the thought never having crossed his mind as he went about his ocean-going merchant business. Nor was he the image of a military commander forging through snow, waving a banner, rallying with his sword and his shouts the troops under his command to advance no matter the enemy's volleys. Nor was he a leader you might visualize rallying rowboats to cross the Delaware River on that year's future snowy Christmas Eve.

In that regard, the dedication and determination expressed by his countenance, in his gesticulations, in his mellow deep voice seemed in command of a personal, societal, and patriotic mission as much as any military commander. His actions, not to mention his mind and wit to those with whom he conversed, were as quick as any swordsman, rifleman, or artilleryman. His gaze locked on his own mental targets, announcing to those who studied him that his personal course was charted through the battlefields of merchant commerce, day-to-day scenes envisioned only in his duty to enhance his personal wealth. By now in his life, Morris was, simply, a merchant, and a wealthy one at that, a status that brought even more prominence to him and to Molly's social standing.

Morris did not flinch when, at a table nearby, what began as a loud harangue between two men was approaching fisticuffs. Suddenly, one inebriated patron removed his glove and slapped the other's face, challenging him to a duel. Not unusual in Colonial America, Morris thought, but still undesirable among presumably civilized men. Our gentleman promptly rose and moved to their table. Intervening, he advised each in turn to come to his senses and look to a cooler moment. Alas, his effort was not needed, as one of the men slumped to the floor, whiskey felling him in place of a pistol shot. The friend of one thanked the gentleman and offered to buy him a cider, a gesture the gentleman declined with a smile and a curt tip of a forefinger to his brow in what Morris meant to be the recognized salute of male Colonial respect.

Comfortable back at his trestle table, his tankard of ale again in hand, Robert Morris glanced at his dog-eared copy of *Common Sense*, signed with the scrawl of its author, Thomas Paine. Taking a break from the pamphlet's inflammatory words and looking up, Morris nodded a greeting toward Paine, who was seated at an adjacent table.

To Betsey, the ever accommodating barmaid who served his table,

Robert whispered in a confidential tone, "As usual, Bets, Mr. Paine's facial and wig powder with his over-the-top perfumes are wafting toward us and, indeed, toward everyone." Betsey pinched her nose and tittered her agreement.

Projecting his voice, Morris spoke to Paine. "Thomas, my esteemed friend, tell me what took you so long to complete your most provocative essay, which I might describe as the rallying shout for independence? I have been an elected member of the Continental Congress for more than a year, and we have debated this question of whether to separate from the Mother Country and take command of our own destiny."

The author smiled and started to reply, but was drowned out by Morris's deeper voice. "Thomas, Sir, we do not all agree on the precise action to take. Many profess loyalty to the Crown and hope for some form of reconciliation, in which we would enjoy a major degree of self-determination over our political and trade affairs. That is to say, for our near future. Maybe even for the long term. But, had your seminal work been published earlier, you might have rallied the cries and helped define the concept of independence a year or two sooner."

Paine replied, "Mr. Morris, Sir, as one of the worthy and esteemed leaders of the Colonists, you may be right. But first things first. You see, I was in Lewes, in Sussex, clarifying my thoughts and scribing them on paper."

Morris interrupted to ask, "Where did you get your ideas? Were you reading the English historian Catharine Macaulay? She advocates freedom and self determination for people, do you not agree?"

"Yes, I do, and there are others in history. For example, Baruch Spinoza, the Jewish lens grinder from Portugal who lived in the Netherlands and advocated 'the operation of necessity'—the same 'necessity for independence' I advocate in my pamphlet."

The two men tilted their tankards toward each other and drank. Wiping his mouth with his sleeve, Paine said, "As to your question about timing, you see I could not leave Lewes because of my entanglements. Over there, I was forced to undo a bad marriage, pay my debts, and clear my name and honor. I came to America as soon as possible. Besides, no one would publish my work in England. The one offer I did receive would not come close to compensating me for my accomplished writing skills."

Morris said, "Here in Philadelphia, since the printer Robert Bell agreed to publish your work, I presume you have taken in a treasure of coin. Even so, our Assembly has so far refused to join other colonies in championing your cause célèbre of independence from England."

"It is the people's cause, not mine alone, Sir! While my tardy timing may be a pity, it is not too late. That royal brute, King George III, will never enter into any compromise. His mind is not open to reality. He is following, or so in England I was told, his mother's royalist advice."

"His mother?" Morris exclaimed.

"Yes. What real man, I ask you, Sir, dares to go against a mother's advice?"

"I wouldn't know, as I never knew my mother, only a grandmother." Morris changed the subject, "But there is a rumor recently published in *The Williamsburg Gazette* that the unwelcome and unpopular English laws are soon to be repealed."

Paine let out a hearty laugh. "Forget it, Sir! Remember, the Colonies are alive with rumors. Would that it were true, but my friends back in London tell me the king's dear mother compels him to pursue preservation of empire by declaring that all Colonists are traitors. He refuses to change his decrees or countermand any of Parliament's laws, including the forced billeting of English troops in our homes. He is driven to even more rigorously enforce the laws against us. Worse, Parliament is not investigating the situation on its own, only acquiescing to his Lowness. Our only course, Sir, for our own good and our own future…" A profound Paine pounded the table with his fist, "…is complete independence from England!"

Declining to agree unequivocally with Paine's proclamation, Morris countered, "Yet the adverse fallout from our revolutionary activities is jeopardizing our Colonial commerce, inviting retaliatory actions by the Royal Navy in blockading our ports."

Paine's voice rose. "Exactly what I am advocating, Mr. Morris, Sir! The only solution for healthy commerce is for the 13 Colonies to unite and fight for collective independence! That way, we shall be rid of the Royal Navy."

Morris countered, "But during the time of our fighting the war for independence that you advocate, My Friend, the Royal Navy will strip our Colonies of our lifeline of commerce, cut us off from our export markets. We will be unable to receive imported goods from Europe or even the Caribbean, as the British Navy will increase their blockades, intercept our ships and confiscate our goods. We merchants will go bust if the Colonies enter into a war for independence."

Insisting, Paine said, "Sir, if in this revolutionary episode we are indeed victorious, your merchant ships will sail in freedom from being intercepted by English patrols, boarded, and the captain and crew hung as traitors. Independence, I assure you, Sir, is the sole solution to worries about profitable commerce on the high seas." With that, the author rose and, clutching a copy of his book, marched up the stairs to the tavern's second floor.

"Where is he going?" Morris asked Betsey.

"To read to a guild of illiterate longshoremen dining in a private room." Looking into Robert's blue eyes, Betsey sheepishly whispered, "Robert, everyone in Philadelphia is talking about *Common Sense*. What's in it? The words, I mean. Oh, Robert, I wish I could read."

Not long after his arrival in the Colonies, Morris had come to realize that the lack of letters among the King's subjects was more common than not. He had found that many intelligent people were unskilled in reading and writing. That didn't detract from their curiosity, their ability to think, or the performance of their trade. He said to Betsey, "As Mr. Paine argues, it is common sense for our Colonies to be independent—free of the English monarch and his Parliament. As you know, Bets, they are each many, many miles away in London across the vast ocean. In reality, neither the King nor his Parliament is capable of governing from such a distance and ruling the diverse collection of Colonies that have sprung up here in America."

"Independence." She repeated the syllables in slow succession. "My Mum and Dad in Ireland would rejoice at the sound of that word, or so I have been told by Irish settlers. 'Aye,' they say, to some day be out from under the yoke of them oppressive English."

Morris smiled. "Please remember, Bets, independence for the Colonies is the goal of many men, but not all men."

Betsey asked, "What does the women in the Colony think?"

Morris puzzled, suggesting, "By prevailing gender custom they are inclined to follow the men."

"Must they always think like their men?" Betsey asked.

Morris smiled at the barmaid. "Not always, I suppose. What about you?"

Betsey was quick to respond. "I thinks for myself." She gestured to a Negro slave making his way through the tavern collecting dirty dishes. "Do our slaves think for themselves?"

Morris clicked his tongue dismissively. "Some believe the Bible says they are inferior, and in God's plan will always be our slaves."

"Destined to benefit the white men? But if we—that is you white men—wants independence, why don't the Negroes wants their freedoms, too? And why not also our savage Indians, the Delawares?"

Morris mused. "I suppose you could so argue."

"Suppose I does so argue?" She smiled. "What would you say?"

"Then I would tell you to wait."

"For what?"

Morris gazed up toward the smoky tavern's beamed ceilings. After a moment, his reply formulated in his mind, he focused back on Betsey and said, "This new land of ours—whether we remain part of the British Empire, or forge a new country—perhaps off into the future beyond my years—offers new vistas, new ideas, and new intellectual horizons. Everyone who is fortunate enough to have immigrated here, even those natives who were here before we Europeans, like the Delawares, will benefit. That is what I mean by time passing." He smiled at her. "Time will bring freedom and visions of making one's personal fortune, or so I hope and believe. That is my objective in having immigrated here in these opportunistic times."

She raised her voice to ask, "But now...today...what is it you wants most to achieve?"

Morris suppressed a chuckle, then thought such an expression rude. Instead, his answer conveyed conviction, "I want to make my fortune...and, of course, keep my hard-earned capital from being taxed away by a distant King to be used in the maintenance of his empire at home and off in some distant part of the world."

"But, Robert, why does you want to make more money? I mean, you have a lot of riches already, don't you? Your country house and your trading firm. Why does you wants more? You greedy?"

Morris shook his head. "No, I do not call it such. I look at our Colonial situation as my trying to take advantage of a rare God-given opportunity. I mean, I would not want to shirk an assignment from the Almighty."

"You mean, God is telling you to do what you is to do?"

Morris sighed a dismissal.

Betsey would not let up. "I still do not understand why you needs to make more money?" Waiting through a no reply, she carried on with her questioning. "Do you wants to know what I think?"

Having switched his attention back to his copy of *Common Sense*, Morris looked at the barmaid, trying to conceal his annoyance. Feigning inattention, he said, "About what, Bets?"

"About why you men wants to build fortunes. I mean, we women don't think about such a matter, does we?"

He replied absently, "I would not know."

"Men don't care what women think. Men think only of themselves, not of us destitute poor folk. If you rely solely on your selfish motives to build up more riches you is overlooking the rest of us people. And I says that is selfish."

Morris scowled, his rising temper evident.

Betsy said, "You are taking on that upper class superiority of yours—being a leader among the men running the Colony. Are the decisions you men make solely for your own benefit, no way aiding folks like me and my two run-away children?"

Morris felt a hint of concern, but not enough for compassion. Was she going to needle him more? In what he deemed solely to be for argumentative purpose, her mood replacing her required barmaid role of pleasantness, she said, "Here's my take on men and money. I'm going to give you my wisdom whether you cares to hear my words or not."

"Uh huh." Morris replied in an uninterested tone as he put down Paine's pamphlet and looked at her, waiting. "For you rich men clutching your stashes of capital, money adds prowess to that thing of yours. The more of it you packs into your belt, the bigger—"

"—What?"

Betsey laughed. She had indeed gotten his attention. She went on, "Wealth makes you, Robert, attractive to us women by adding the prestige of sexual prowess to your reputation—not only in your business status, but to your male desirability."

Morris seemed stymied for the moment. Taking advantage

afforded by his silence, Betsey whipped the horse one more time. "Your making money for yourself means you are taking advantage of everyone else. Does not your game of riches..." she paused, seemingly proud of her description of his business... "if it is to flourish, demand fairness for everyone—even simple folk like me?"

Morris laughed, what at first he knew the barmaid could easily discern as a disturbed laugh, but what he hoped would be a dismissive expression, for he then gave what he hoped would be a closeout puff on his pipe, allowing the ensuing ring to hover over, darkening his mood. Abruptly he shooed her away, decreeing, "Bets, please bring my favorite pork dinner...and another cider. He raised his personal toasting glass engraved with the emblem of the Society of the Sons of St. George, a club he had told her he had formed to support fellow British immigrants. Musing over the embossed schooner, now empty, pride in its ethnic affiliation showing on his face, he looked intently at Betsey. With intimacy, he took her hand and squeezed it. In a warmer voice, he said, "You know, my Molly expects me to be true to her...much as I do admire your...."

Not showing offense, but laughing as she re-assumed her tavern role, Betsey admonished, "Robert, your Molly will never have to know, you know." The barmaid stood provocatively in front of the gentleman, the fluff of her breasts enticing. She pointed. "Room's upstairs. I'd like to see if my pontification has substance."

Morris blushed. He shook his head negatively. "Bets, I have changed from the young man I was back in those long ago days. I became a different man when I married my lovely Miss Mary White."

Smiling salaciously, Betsey said, "Some say you are...or were...quite the rake around town. One of the girls who worked here a few years ago told me you had every fair-haired lady in Philadelphia flocking around you. Is not that right?"

Morris reminisced for only a moment. "Guilty, you might say, but as I explained, that was back before I met Mary, my 'Molly', before each of us recited our vows of fidelity. You see, we were properly married in Saint Peter's Episcopal Church by her brother William."

Betsy chuckled. "I didn't think you talked like a Quaker."

"Quakers are a different sort—is that what you are saying?"

She shrugged her shoulders. "How would I know?"

"You know, I know," Morris stated. Many Colonists here are English Quakers because the Puritans went to Boston. And, Bets, you know a lot of the Quakers…the men, I mean."

The barmaid smiled. "That may be. But tonight and for the next weeks, your Molly's away at Hill House—miles out of town. She'll stay put there through the long winter!" Betsey drew out her pronunciation of 'long,' adding, "With your seven dear little children."

Robert Morris smiled as he visualized his family ensconced in his comfortable country home on his farm astride a bluff overlooking the Schuylkill River. The Lenape, or Delaware Indians, so he had read, called the river something that translated into English as "hidden away" because of the dense trees and bushes that concealed its watery presence at the point where the tributary flowed into the Delaware. Hidden away is how he visualized his family's elegant two-story home with its complex of smaller buildings that included a coach house and several greenhouses—hidden away from the complex issues and assortment of people and medley of revolutionary ideas circulating in Philadelphia.

The gardens of his Hill House were laid out in the Tudor manner with meandering walks and ponds set amongst groves of fruit trees. He replayed in his mind some of the delightful times he had spent with his children walking, sometimes running after them for short distances. Although, to his regret, given the pounds he had put on by eating the cuisine of Colonial Philadelphia, he was quickly out of breath. As a family they had explored those paths, skimming pebbles, watching the fish swimming in the ponds, listening to the songbirds and, in season, plucking fruit from the orchards.

Happily he recalled that from their veranda, Molly and he could gaze across the miles to see the spires of the churches in Philadelphia and beyond to count the topmasts of the array of ships in the harbor. Proudly he could identify those belonging to his firm of Willing and Morris. In more normal times, Hill House had been their weekend retreat, until the political and merchant situations became so complex and critical, as it was this night, requiring him to remain in Philadelphia. As always, he was endeavoring to earn more profits by attending to his company's complex merchant business demands.

Standing, Robert nodded at Betsey and threw the conversation back at the barmaid. "Tell me, Bets, what has become of your two little children?"

Betsey backed away. He saw her tears. For the moment, Robert felt regret that he had touched upon such a tender personal topic for her.

Growing upset, Betsey demanded to know. "Why do you ask? Do you men care about anything other than making money, strutting round in your fancy clothing while bragging about your accomplishments, whether it be women or wealth?"

Morris thoughtfully surveyed the crowded tavern and looked back at Betsey. "I care about everyone here, Bets, especially you." His voice lowered. "You and I have talked...often."

"But why do we talk and not...?" Her voiced drifted off before she answered about her boys. "To the frontier...left one day with their father. He took them away from me, their mother, saying he'd find land, clear it, start a new life...plow the land and, well, farm it for himself and for them, make their living in this new land. Said he didn't want his boys growin' up raised by a barmaid mother—his judgmental punishment of me."

Morris said, "But surely you do not agree with him!" Observing her slow negative shaking of her head, Morris reminded himself that Betsy was a caring human being. He acknowledged that her husband, having abandoned her, was an adventurer who was looking out for his sons, and, of course, himself, but not his wife. He reflected about how, in this New World, this new continent, this British Colony, male roles were unlike back in his native England. Back there, a man's role was cast in stone at birth, determined by class custom, by the constraints of tradition, by a strict social creed that had little changed over the centuries. Few men ventured into new territories. For a moment he clung to empathy for Betsey's husband, even as he consoled her. "As a man, I share your husband's desire to seek opportunity in the new lands out there in The Westward." Recognizing her remorse, he reflected, "At the same time, I feel regret for you and your boys. Families ought to stay together. By my design, my family stays as a loving unit here in Philadelphia."

Betsey frowned. "I don't think I'd dare go out there to the frontier...that untamed wilderness. I'm deathly afraid of those savage Delawares. The frightening stories you hear tell. Them natives want revenge for our taking their land, for our bringing the smallpox down on them."

He nodded. "I understand your concerns."

Smiling, she drew physically close to Robert, adjusted her frock to expose more of her breasts, brushing against his tailored jacket. He felt her closeness as she said, "It's easy for you to keep your family together. Your wife comes from wealth. Some say she's the richest woman in Pennsylvania. Her brother is some high-up preacher. You dare not go against her wishes."

"—Bets, enough girl!"

Ignoring him, she went on, "It must be nice. You're a rich merchant, maybe the richest in these parts. You own sailing ships. You trade goods in Europe and—"

"—The Caribbean—"

"—In cotton, tobacco...slaves, too, sometimes, or so a man told me."

Robert smiled. He held up a finger, nodded and said matter of factly, "We deal in many sorts of cargo. My partner in our trading house, Mr. Thomas Willing IV...."

Betsy spit out the word "partner." The volume of her voice disturbed several patrons nearby. "My so-called partner left me, took up with some Delaware squaw, so I was told by his brother. I spit on partnerships."

Being an advocate of partnerships, in both marriage and merchant shipping, Morris reflected on both his marriage and his commercial partnership with Thomas Willing. From its very inception, Willing & Morris had been profitable and personally satisfying, albeit demanding of his time and requiring the investment of his capital. Vows and capital, how they went together here in the Pennsylvania Colony.

There was a certain cohesion, he had come to believe, among the people. Call it a Colonial camaraderie. Whether they admitted it or not, he felt most of the Colonies were divinely destined to chart their course in a united direction—severing political and emotional ties with the British Empire sooner, maybe later. Yet in the anguishing and likely bloody process they would launch their own American Empire. If he were to label the mood, he would say the 13 had become despondent provinces of the British Empire. For better or for worse. For him and his personal wealth, he would make certain it would be for the better.

Watching Betsey as she moved off toward the kitchen, and warmed by her closeness, Robert reflected on her future in this New World. He wondered if, despite her fears, she would give up her barmaid life and venture west to resume mothering her two children. And what if she did? What of her husband's acquired Indian—maybe Delaware—squaw? For Betsey, was finding and re-joining her family to be her life's reward? Or was she, instead, to go through life as an independent woman, perhaps starting her own drinking place? Many women had done so. Licensing to open a tavern was not complex— an appeal to the City Board. Appearing before the all-male Board, Betsey could plead successfully.

Thinking of the future, Robert asked himself what was to be the course for the Pennsylvania Colony? Was it to go off on its own, separated from the other 12 Colonies? Were we to see 13 separate and independent countries develop along the shores of the Atlantic? But what if each colony, instead, went its own way, setting its own separate form of government, its own coded laws, that is, if there was to be law and order following the disruption of the age-old allegiance to the King and his laws. That bond had been an accepted decree binding the people to their King by divine prerogative from God Himself. He mulled the thought until Betsey returned with his dinner and more ale and then asked, "If we throw off England and its King, what will be the new rules for law and order?"

She didn't reply. He watched her shrug her shoulders. She knows no answer, he told himself. Nor do I, he appended, as he gestured toward a trestle table on the far side of the room. He said to her, "See the man with the scar on his cheek? Bets, can you tell me who he is?"

Betsey followed his gesture. "A Hessian mercenary from Germany—a major."

"I suspected as much from his demeanor. But how did he get here? See, his appearance seems non-military, as if that lifestyle was an afterthought in his life."

"I...ah...know him...well. I mean, he's a fencer—his scar, you see...they all fence, or so he explained—military training is their way of life—it's a coming of age ritual, makes you a man, or so he believes. All the officers does it, he says. Strange people, those Germens, the men, I mean. He's from some little German state. Tells me they gots kingdoms—tiny royal holdings—some no bigger than a city and the farmland surrounding. Not like our Pennsylvania—goes west hundreds of miles—some say to the Pacific Ocean, wherever that is."

"But what is he doing here, Bets? Why is he not with his fellow

Hessian troops whom the British have hired to fight our Colonial militia? The Hessians are up in New Jersey…Trenton. Billeted there."

"He was invited by some doctor here among the German immigrants in Philadelphia. Two doctors from the same hometown, somewhere in…what'd he call the place? Bavaria, or something like that. Although he said he's now from another place called…I think he called it Hesse-Kassel."

"Bets, how did he get here?"

"He's a pass signed by General Washington himself. He showed me the wax seal—Washington's personal signature, so he boasted."

"Speaks English?"

Betsey nodded, "Good, too. Educated, he is."

Robert pressed, "What sort of doctor is he?"

With an incredulous smile, Betsey said, "Says he wants to get into people's minds—soldiers, others, too. He tells me he asks questions about what they are thinking, how they feel about fighting, and what they think of this far away from home continent of America. When he's with me, he wants to know what I'm thinking. He asks what I'm feeling about him, about life in general, intimate questions. Once I told him it was none of his business, and he soothed me with some explanation I didn't understand."

"I have never heard of such a doctor, or such personal questions being asked." Morris mused. "Intrusive, it seems to me." Morris looked confused. He added, "I have always believed that one's feelings come from the heart, not the head." With uncertainty he asked, "Does not everybody know that?"

She looked toward the Hessian, "Yeah. He's strange. He told me the mind was what mattered to both him and his Prince." She tittered and said, "Well, Mr. Continental Congress member Robert Morris, Rich Merchant of the Colonies, how does you feel about some German mercenary telling you he cares about what you think and wants to know what you really feel, deep down, about this American Revolution?"

Morris troubled over the idea of being asked to explain his private thoughts. No way, he said to himself. His mind went to thoughts about Betsey's boys, and he acknowledged he had concerns for her and for them. He had not asked their names—two boys—now without a mother, two boys like him and his half-brother, Thomas, TM—himself without a mother and a father, while TM had a mother.

At least Betsey's boys had their father. Robert did not ask more, for Betsey was no longer by his side.

# CHAPTER TWO:
## FLATBOAT TO THE WESTWARD

The wooden flatboat seemed to be a victim, almost helpless in its struggle for progress against the steady current of the descending Schuylkill River as it carved its wandering and downward way east from out of the Appalachian Range, intent on making its watery way toward its almost hidden confluence with the Delaware River. There, the combined waters would unite and, continuing on, eventually flow into Chesapeake Bay.

The Colonial civilization of Philadelphia with its suburban farms, from which Betsey's husband, the father of her two sons, along with an attentive Indian squaw had left behind, faded into distant memories. For the group, accompanied by their guide, having portaged the spectacular falls where the river cascaded with awesome force down into the Delaware basin, rowed on, intent on confronting the unknown of the vast western Pennsylvania wilderness.

Up ahead, the omnipresent crenellated Appalachians rose to challenge them with a seemingly insurmountable blockade to their hoped-for new and prosperous life beyond. Yet in their minds, offering new opportunities, based on the much-touted horizons, The Westward offered tracts of fertile land waiting for one's occupying and taking, even if taking from the natives. That is, if only one could get there. Then all in their lives would be milk and honey.

As if judging the little river craft with its adventuresome mission, the tree-covered range seemed to challenge those on board by daring them to try to cross its summits, challenging them in their efforts to seek new lands, and daring them, once there, to seek their fortunes in the face of insurmountable odds. The westerly wind could be heard to whisper, "Go back! It's dangerous out here! Go Back!"

The river took them past a log cabin hugging the land a short distance up the shore. In an adjacent field, a farmer was falling a tree. On the ground rose a pile of rocks laboriously pried from out of the soil. No longer would these rocks be annoying impediments to a mule-driven plow. Sawed down tree trunks were stacked lengthwise next to the rocks, awaiting the axe to permit their burning in the cabin's stone fireplace, or else to fulfill their role in the construction of a barn to shelter the farmer's two cows grazing nearby.

"That's the work we will be doing soon, boys," their father explained, "when we get farther west to the plot I bought last week when that friendly land salesman came through Philadelphia."

"But why didn't Momma come with us?" asked the youngest.

Their dark bearded father, rowing on one side of the craft, opposite the mustachioed guide pulling hard on the other side, tried to explain between deep and arduous breaths, "Out here—" In a sweeping motion of his arm, briefly taken off the oar, the father gestured at the never-ending wilderness—"is no place for a woman."

Pointing to the Squaw next to him on the craft, the older boy said, "But Spring Robin is a woman."

"An Indian woman," their father corrected, his tone a tad demeaning as he added the appellation of "Delaware," as if it were a label connoting a lesser level of human importance.

Spring Robin sat passively, surveying in turn the slowly passing riverbanks. On occasion, she directed the boys' attention, once to a stag grazing, then to a mother deer with two fawns close by. Soon she pointed to a bear fishing among rocks along the river's shoreline. Spring Robin made certain the boys saw and watched the actions of the wildlife. "Good hunting," she said, her English broken as she simulated pulling an arrow back through a bow and then letting it fly away toward a target as she simulated an archer's "zing."

The guide's resultant look of approval triggered the father to laugh heartily and exclaim, "We won't go hungry tonight, boys."

"But I want to see Momma," the younger boy insisted. He started to cry. Instinctively Spring Robin hugged him, but to little avail, as his angst lasted into the night's campfire until he fell asleep, hungry and fearful of the unknown of the morrow, and the morrow after that.

# CHAPTER THREE:
# EARLIER IN HESSE-KASSEL

Major Wilhelm von Lowenstein, proudly wearing his Hessian Mercenary uniform, his salad bowl of medals glistening in the bright sun, led his battalion of fighting men in the festive parade in birthday tribute to his hereditary ruler, Landgraf Friedrich II von Hesse-Kassel. Upon his command "eyes right," the Major initiated his outfit's precise salute to his Prince. Column after column followed as the principality's marching band played traditional Teutonic tunes. Marching in formation always stimulated the Major's thoughts, especially today as he recognized the Prince awarding his salute with an acknowledging smile.

No surprise, the Major thought. Seeing himself akin to German royalty—albeit a stretch, for "von" meant "from," suggesting that somewhere along his hereditary Bavarian line, the Major hoped someday he might discover a bloodline to some king, queen, duke, or prince.

His Landgraf Prince often cited his lineage dating back into the distant days of the Medieval Holy Roman Empire, making him a member of the exclusive Uradel, the ancient German nobility begun four centuries earlier. Undaunted by his Landgraf's royalty, the Major treasured his close conversational relationship with the Prince developed over the time of dutiful service to him.

Given their close contact, the Major had begun to align his own inquisitive thought process with his ruler's incessant curiosity. The Prince kept questioning him as to why men joined the Hessian Army to fight in far-off wars. Now these mercenaries were going off to America to fight for the British. The Prince had asked why these men would go halfway around the world to fight, and maybe die. Truth be told, the Major was also asking himself why he would want to sail off with his troops and leave his wife and two children behind, for maybe he, too, might never return. Perish the thought!

Later, the troops filed back to their barracks. The horses were cared for in their stalls. The loyal crowds were either at home or celebrating in beer halls. The pomp and ceremony, the music, the pride in their Prince was now an inspiring memory for another year.

It was then, by mandated invitation, the Major joined the Prince in sipping sherry in the castle's royal quarters. Amidst the hereditary banners hanging from the ceiling and the ancestral portraits decorating the stone walls, the Major reflected on how he had come to enjoy this coveted princely camaraderie. Years earlier, seeking new horizons in both military adventures and medical discoveries following university, he had been attracted to the mercenary forays of Hesse-Kassel and its aggressive but benevolent ruler. He had applied for the position of regimental chaplain and surgeon. Now he was on the inside of planning the care of the troops going off to fight the Americans.

The Prince, clad in his royal attire, a bandolier draped across one shoulder and wrapped around his slim waist, his golden epaulets brushing his shoulders, smiled and said "Major, when my men come home to our Hesse from fighting some war in which I have contracted them, a number return wounded from bullets, canon fire, even bayonets. For the rest of their lives, they remain physically disfigured from battle scars you surgeons attend to with your perfected methods. They live out their lives, hobbled in their gate, restricted in their work, yet still able to do some farming with assistance from sons and siblings." The Prince went on, "But some, or so I have observed—as you have, too—while physically able to farm or work, seem distracted, go moping about, unable to work while evidencing a distraught attitude. Why is that? Their behavior has moved from the strict discipline my commanders impose in training and warfare. What are these unseen battle scars inflicted on their minds, Major?"

"Your Highness is bedeviled by curiosity about what may take place in the human mind which, in your opinion, is apart—that is, different—from traditional feelings presumably coming from the heart. I mean, Sire, your heart is big when it comes to your subjects."

The Prince smiled. "Yes, I am the first ruler to build an art museum to display works from not only Hesse-Kassel craftsmen and artists but from other German states. Anyone in my realm may view the exhibits—not just the nobles, the important people—but everyone, important or not."

The Landgraf continued, "And a medical clinic with a surgeon, to which any of my subjects can go for treatment and hopefully for cure. Except for these mental wounds."

"And your new library, my Liege, as well."

The Landgraf glided on. "You have seen the books. Anyone can go in, even soldiers. But, back to your question. Heart or mind? You see, as Prince, I may explore wherever my mental obsessions lead me. Think of me this way: a fruit tree blooms once a year, promising a harvest to come. In the same manner, I bloom once a year—and that is right now—promising a fruit of a new variety. That, my loyal subject, means a fresh idea each year, and with your support, every year to come. You do agree?"

Not a question, of course. Nodding, the Major said, "But Sire, come fall your leaves will turn color and drop. In those shortening days, will your idea still be alive?" Telling himself he was a valuable cog in the Landgraf's Hessian Army, why should he not test the strength of his Liege's respect?

"Ask me in this year's fall season, Major. By then I will have become more resolute in my desire to know what goes on in men's minds, even yours, and then I will respond to your dried leaf remark."

The Major thought his ensuing explanation would close-out his Prince's ongoing query: "My Liege, may I suggest that being a mercenary is a good rewarding job for young men at a time when there are few, if any, jobs available. Soldiering pays more, especially for a young man, or even someone older, who is likely a drifter, perhaps a bankrupt, clearly unemployed, maybe because of his criminal record, likely uneducated, probably unattached to anyone or to anything at all—a man needing a cause, an identity, seeking camaraderie and adventure."

"Ja, ja, ja," the Landgraf acknowledged. "Those are the reasons the soldiers tell you, but they are not a man's inner emotions. Go beyond that, please, for me, your ruler, Heir Major. Find something deeper. What is in their thinking?"

The Major took a conversational chance. "In addition to your query, I also yearn to understand the American Revolutionaries."

The Prince frowned. "What is there to understand? They are rebels, are they not, Heir Major? And they are rebelling against God!"

Gesturing to the heraldry banners. The Major said, "Yes, my Prince. You, as well as the King of England and each of the rulers of countries and principalities, have been designated by God to rule over your subjects. Isn't that the age-old royal prerogative imbued in each of today's rulers?"

"Quite true."

"All royalty are related. King George III is your nephew."

"And my English wife, Lady Gwendolyn, is a duchess from Yorkshire."

"That makes the American Revolutionaries heretics, going against God."

The Prince clenched his fist and pounded the table. "Yes! Indeed they should be punished." He grew silent. After a moment he said, "No people have acted this way before. But we do need to know what is in their minds, so we can stomp out such misguided thoughts. Such heresy must never happen again...anywhere." The Landgraf surprised the major by blurting, "Major, let us move our two selves into my secluded den."

Leaving the royal chambers, the Major followed his Prince, who opened a concealed door and led the Major along a corridor. After a dozen steps, the Landgraf extracted a brass key and unlocked a door.

Inside a dank room with only one small window, the Prince lit two candles. The room seemed little used, or was it? The Major detected the fragrance of cinnamon. The Major guessed the Prince and his nobles were frequent occupants.

From off a stained pine table, the ruler handed the Major an elongated pipe with a ceramic bulb at its end. "I here offer you good opium, Major. Appreciate it. Given to me by one of my generals who confiscated it when we fought the Turks on behalf of the Emperor of Austria-Hungary in some battle we won. I forget where. You, Major, are special to me for having promised to feed my inquisitive mind. This is your reward."

The Major filled the pipe with the brownish powder and then ran it across the flame from an oil lamp, which the Landgraf had lit. Our prim military man inhaled the pungent fumes. Something about his Prince—the incessant probing, the new idea about men's minds, and

One Thousand Dollars

1000

Thirty State

Washington

One Thousand Dollars

1000

15592

8 2 95 off

— "R. Morris"

now stimulated even more by the elixir from the pipe, the Major's inquisitiveness escalated.

Meanwhile, the Landgraf had shed his royal coat and was now in his undergarment. He put his arm around the Major and commented intimately to his military man, "You want answers?"

The Major loosened his military necktie, nodded, and wondered what his ruler had in mind...surely not.

Speaking as if he was delivering a God-inspired declaration, the Prince proclaimed, "Sex is short-lived, while my ideas can and will last a lifetime—yours and mine—beyond into the distant future. And my idea of finding out what is in the minds of these American rebels is vital to preserving world order."

"Some of our soldiers have deserted on their march toward the embarkation port. Why is that?"

The Prince held up a finger, waving it unsteadily, and suggested, "Not so with the second division under Lt. General Freiherr von Knyphausen. His regiments are disciplined. Any deserter would be hung." The Landgraf inhaled more from his pipe. The Major followed suit. The Prince admitted, "I do not understand. Seems to me that once you have experienced death, watched as it happened to compatriots, how can you relish more such experiences?"

"But Sir, as ruler, you have personally decreed sentences of death."

"In the line of duty as ruler. I have never watched the sentences carried out."

The Major puffed again and felt compelled (but did not) suggest, "Maybe had you done so." But after some thought, he did voice his quick observation.

The Landgraf stared off into space.

The Major asked, "The officers do speak of their personal lives— boasting of their land holdings, their estates, their stables and horses—and their royal ties to you? Does it trouble you, Sire, that most of your subjects are much less fortunate?"

"Royalty, Major, is indeed a lofty status. No question about that." The Landgraf nodded several times to signal profound endorsement of his own statement. "Wars give my subjects purpose in life. The men espouse war. They must idolize their rulers, their officers, don't you see?"

The Major interjected, "Are you saying, My Liege, that peace is counter productive to stability amongst your subjects?"

The Prince's facial expression lit up in agreement.

"But, Sir, a few weeks ago there was that rumor of an unexpected peace with the American Colonies. Maybe we won't be going there—"

"—Disturbed me and my ministers," the Prince was quick to comment. "Shocked us! Ever since the American Revolution broke out, my government has been bargaining—successfully, I might emphasize—with the English King and his ministers to furnish tens of thousands of mercenary fighters. That's what we do here in Hesse-Kassel—we breed soldiers! We fight! Germans are warriors. Not like those wimpy French or those stuck-up English. We offer all nations our hired military—I mean, we fought the Turks on behalf of the Austrians, and we...well, you know the many governments our soldiers have gone into battle for. As a small principality, we have come to count on these contractual payments to supply...call it contracting out...our fighting men. Now we are again being hired by the English Parliament. My dear principality is being monetized by the English King's silver, bringing me funds to pay for the benefits I provide for my subjects."

"If there is no peace treaty, we will be embarking to America to fight the rebels and quell the Revolution started by misguided Colonists."

The Landgraf voiced a sharp reply, "The meaning of revolution. I wonder if war is the only activity men can pursue these days."

His words slurring a bit, the Major said, "Sir, I will need authorization from you to interrogate the Revolutionaries. Do you not agree?"

The Landgraf nodded slowly, his head weaving as he said, "Major von Lowenstein, as your ruler, I order you to find out what goes on in the minds of my mercenary soldiers. Discover the meaning of war to them, the justification of their killing Colonial militia, even women and children, and risking their own lives on far-away battlefields. Tell me how they deal with the possibility of being shot, bayoneted, falling wounded or lying dead on the cold, wet battlefield. Moreover, find out what is in the mind of these heretical American Revolutionaries."

The Major clicked his heels, although the precision of his movement was not quite what it should be given the opium's effect.

"That is a large order, Sir. I must advise that no one in my medical profession has heard of nor ever undertaken such an assignment. What goes on in men's minds remains an unknown."

"Break new ground."

"Yes, it is time for those of us in the medical field to explore what is in men's minds...perhaps probing into emotions, thoughts, and the whys of actions."

Before he fell asleep in his royal chair, the Prince mumbled, "Yes, Major, find out what is the mind of those Revolutionaries—especially their leaders."

The Major waited for the Prince to lapse further into oblivion. Anticipating the special opportunity offered by his new orders, yet dreading the good-byes to his wife and two sons, Major von Lowenstein gathered his opium-frayed faculties and removed himself from his Prince and the domain of royalty.

# CHAPTER FOUR:
## WHEN THE MAJOR ARRIVED IN PHILADELPHIA

Wearing civilian dress, Major von Lowenstein made his way through the morning's fresh snowfall for his appointment with Dr. von Hogarth, the leading physician in the German immigrant community.

In this cold winter of Philadelphia, the snow clung like leaves to the branches of the oak trees lining the narrow cobblestone streets. The Major marveled at such a tranquil setting. Yet, reluctantly, he resigned himself to the coming chaos from the Colonies' misguided war for independence from their God-given ruler. What could they be thinking? The question roiled his mind in the same way the gusts of wind shook the snowy limbs overhead as balls of snow pummeled him.

He asked himself what unknown forces were at work shaping the politics of Pennsylvania and the other Colonies? Don't they see that they are immersed in a mess of mindless acts and dissident writings that urge them to conduct an act of war against their King? He thought of his Landgraf and vowed again to honor his orders.

To his delight, a cozy warm fire blazed in Dr. Hogarth's stone fireplace. The Major felt a mood of Teutonic camaraderie between them. The pleasurable moment caused him to feel as if he were back in Hesse-Kassel with his wife and children. Above two bookcases hung a portrait of Louis I, Duke of 12th century Bavaria. By its side a less grand portrait was crookedly displayed as if there by royal decree—King George III.

The doctor pointed to the royally uniformed British King and said, "At least 30 percent of the settlers here in my adopted Colony are German. Each of us wanting to settle in Philadelphia had to swear a loyalty oath to England and pledge to speak only English. Otherwise, or so the English fear, our town would be speaking our beloved Germanic tongue." As the two medical men sipped Cognac, Dr. Hogarth mused, "Instead of being called Pennsylvania, our Colony might be known as 'Germanvania'."

The Major said, "So long as the winter ice doesn't block the ships, the receiving and sending of goods to and from Europe will continue to increase, so it seems from my walks along the wharf."

"Yes, the wealth of a continent is sailing away on brigantines and frigates to the Old World."

"What, Sir, do you make of the rumor of a Peace Mission from London?

Dr. Hogarth poured another round of Cognac. His German guttural groan indicated disagreement. "I fear we have moved past the realm of reason. Colonial normalcy will never be restored, as it was following the French and Indian War." He thought for a moment. "We are not to be spared suffering and death."

Recalling his own tedious ocean crossing, the Major wondered out loud, "Why have so many of our countrymen migrated here...enduring that endless ocean voyage—for as long as 12 weeks confined in a smelly sailing ship? Not a pleasant experience."

"Freedom!" Dr. Hogarth was quick to reply. "Here, there are no Prussian troops lording over us, even imprisoning us, especially if our sons don't comply with conscription. Oh, maybe there are some English troops being billeted in our homes—by decree." He sipped the Cognac. "This is a vast New World without regulations, without taxes, without some lord of the manor dictating our daily lives, milking us for funds to support some ruler's lavish lifestyle, pay for his castle, and fund his excesses of luxury."

Dr. Hogarth added with pride, "We Germans are hard workers, enterprising. Given our ethnic energy and determination, we can make our fortunes. The opportunities are many." The doctor savored his Cognac. "Yes, Major, we are going to make this New World into a showplace of achievement. Mark my words."

The Major reflected.

"So, tell me, what is your military mission here? You are not wearing your uniform."

Reaching into his greatcoat, the Major extracted an official parchment.

Examining it closely, Dr. Hogarth showed surprise. "Why, this is a pass through the Revolutionary lines signed by General Washington—with his official and personal wax seal. It is good as gold here in this colony. If you are at liberty to explain, Major, how did you arrange such a clever ruse?"

"As I mentioned, there are rumors of a peace delegation from Parliament."

"Your cover?"

"So to speak," the Major said. "There cannot be a peace settlement without the British military's consent, or so I suggest to anyone who questions my pass, although few do so after seeing General Washington's seal. My division leader, Count von Faucitt, secretly wants peace, not war, in spite of the fact that he is trained to fight. Like me, he displays the facial scar across the cheek received during our coming-of-age fencing bouts. The Count has told me that since he arrived here he has seen things that the King of England, constrained by his royal blinders, either has overlooked or refuses to acknowledge—economic opportunity."

Doctor Hogarth raised his glass, "Skoal!" As the two men toasted, the doctor said, "But I sense, Sir, that you have a deeper interest in what is taking place here."

"Do you mean apart from the...ah...barmaids?"

The doctor laughed. "They do need training in the ways of the Continent."

The Major chuckled. In a confidential voice, he said, "Doctor, my orders are to get into the mind of one of the rebel leaders. Doctor, I would like to know if you, or any other medical person, are exploring issues having to do with...ah...mental problems.

"Such as?"

"Emotional disturbance, abnormal mood, unusual behavior? I think those sorts of problems torment the minds of these Revolutionaries."

"Well, I have talked with Dr. Benjamin Rush, a graduate of the University of Edinburgh. He has designed a special chair for those unfortunate people whom he terms "mentally disturbed." He straps them into this chair—I have seen him do it. But, you know, I don't think his chair makes any difference. He does profess the benefits, but he also advocates bloodletting—a practice that makes no sense to me. I say, Major, let your soldiers do that on your bloody battlefields.

Yet Dr. Rush is respected for having written the first study on dengue fever. Mosquitoes, you know. Another of his procedures that I do not agree with is prescribing calomel—powdered mercury. He tells patients to sprinkle the stuff on bread and eat it with meals. Dr. Rush claims his patients who follow such advice improve their moods. Some of us laugh, while others laud him and say he is a father of some new medical field having to do with what takes place in a patient's mind."

The Major scoffed, "It is not the same as what I am seeking, Doctor."

"Please define your search more precisely, Sir."

The Major leaned closer. "Just between us, Doctor, and this has to be in the strictest of confidence, my mission is to seek out one of the leaders in the American Revolution and delve into his mind through conversations, questions, verbally probing why he is a Revolutionary. I hope to understand his thought process. I am to report my findings to my Prince as part of his research into the minds of men."

"You have a most unusual Prince, Major." The doctor raised his glass in a salute to an admired far-off ruler.

The Major toasted his Prince by name. "He takes guidelines from the Florentine Prince Niccolo Machiavelli."

"He was a long time ago—how many years?"

The Major calculated, "Two hundred fifty some." He wrote that they who are appointed by the Almighty to govern ought to rule for the benefit of their subjects. To do so, my Prince wants to understand men's thinking. In that way, he feels he can better provide for his subjects."

"He is a revolutionary ruler indeed."

The Major chuckled, "Yes, maybe you and I are partaking in two quite different kinds of revolution underway here in Philadelphia."

Dr. von Hogarth looked into the remaining amber fluid in his glass and suggested, "In that case, if you will accept my assistance, given my drinking establishment contacts, I will arrange a meeting with the most perspicacious among the notorious American Revolutionary leaders."

CHAPTER FIVE:
YEARS EARLIER—GROWING UP QUAYSIDE IN
LIVERPOOL WITHOUT A FATHER OR MOTHER

A lad growing up in Liverpool in the 1740s could not help but be enthralled with the commerce buzzing about on the docks of one of England's major ports. As he read in Daniel Defoe's 1727 book, *A Tour Thro' the Whole Island of Great Britain*, young Robert Morris marveled at the forests of sailing ships' masts rising up to populate the horizon. He watched their cargoes being unloaded. His eyes followed the hordes of sailors rushing to sign onto yet another seagoing adventure. He wondered at the constant cacophony of chatter coming from the shore-side taverns. For this young Liverpudlian, the port scenes painted a picture of global trade. He imagined what surely what must be the moneymaking opportunities in ocean commerce, and his ambitions began to crystalize.

Yearning to share his imagined goals, he voiced his thoughts to his grandmother "Nanna." Yet, deep down, he wished he could express himself to the mother he had never known. Even more to his desire, he wanted to share his observations and ideas with his long-absent father, hoping somehow to earn his father's guidance and the endorsement of fatherly encouragement.

As he grew into his teenage years, Robert no longer nagged his grandmother with questions, such as, "Where in the New World is my father, Nanna? When will he send for me, or will he ever do so?" For Robert was trying to understand Nanna's explanations, which went something like, "Your father, Robert Senior—remember, you are his junior—years ago sailed off to the American Colonies as agent and factor for the firm of Foster, Cunliffe & Sons."

Nanna, a proper English widow, was caring for him in some small degree of comfort near but safely distant from the rowdy dock area. In their conversations, Robert came to realize that she loved her son, his father. He sensed she missed seeing her son as much as he yearned to talk to his father. Yet he had almost forgotten what his father looked like. How many years had it been? How many more would go by? Meanwhile, Robert was growing, maturing, and seeking answers to life and its meaning, while exploring the tide of thoughts and dreams about his future. He kept asking himself where the years ahead would lead him?

Nanna would write to the Senior Robert Morris, narrating his son's ideas and explorations. Whenever she received a letter in return, she would read it to her grandson. Before long, he was reading the letters on his own as she unfurled the maps she had acquired for her small library. Spreading the maps across the kitchen table, she would point to their locations and name the 13 American Colonies. Enthralled, Robert would watch as she identified the Caribbean Islands and then the west coast of Africa, whence came the Negroes. He listened intently as she described the flourishing three-cornered slave trade: English and Dutch ships calling into African ports where they would collect black slaves, which they would chain below in the hold and then, after crossing the Atlantic, unload them in the Caribbean or at one of the American ports.

He'd jump in and say, "And in Jamaica, the ships load rum for the Colonies." Nanna would nod, telling him she was pleased with his growing knowledge of commerce. All the while he would visualize the muscular dockworkers and their often whipped slaves on the docks of some American Colonial city packing aboard cargo for the ship's return trip to England. With a knowing smile, Nanna would remind her young charge, "Everyone's making money with every ship docking in every port,"

"Except the slaves," Robert would quip.

*     *     *

On his birthday, having turned 14, Robert was strolling the Liverpool docks. Approaching a schooner being unloaded, he stopped to closely examine the cargo. Seeing a properly attired gentleman posting numbers on a sheet of paper, Robert summoned his courage and asked, "Excuse me, Your Excellency, what is in those bales? Are they all the same?"

Surprised at the interruption and looking at the boy, the gentleman smiled slightly. "Tobacco—from Virginia—bales of tobacco leaves, boy, grown on huge plantations off there in the New World."

Always curious, Robert asked, "Sir, what does a gentleman do with these bales of tobacco?"

Sensing young Robert's genuine interest, the gentleman replied, "Inside each are bundles of tobacco leaves. You take one of the dried leaves and smoke it. But first you crumple it up and then stuff it into your pipe. Let me show you." He demonstrated the English pipe-smoking procedure.

Watching as the gentleman struck a match, Robert caught whiffs of the fragrant puffs of smoke as they broadcast their medley of new and special olfactory flavors. Robert asked to try smoking the pipe. The gentleman handed him the pipe. Inhaling, Robert was quickly coughing out his lungs. Watching, the gentleman laughed and patted Robert on the back. "You will learn, my young man. It takes practice. All the gentlemen in England are doing it."

Without warning the wind from off the River Mersey picked up. Soon rain began to pummel the dockside. His hand resting on the boy's shoulder, guiding him, the man quickly led Robert into the shelter of a nearby tavern. "You need a beer," he said, "to clear your throat." He ordered two pints from the barman.

Robert drank and within moments was reeling from side to side, though the alcohol content was not high. But Robert had never consumed an alcoholic drink.

"Off with you now, boy, home to your mother—"

"—She's dead," Robert managed, slurring his words. He tried, "I never knew her, really. It is my grandmother, you see, who takes care of me, Sir."

"And your father? Where is he, boy?"

"He is off to the New World."

"Run away from his family, a seaman perhaps...maybe a Royal British Fusilier?"

"No, Sir, Nanna tells me he is a merchant's agent."

"From a firm here in Liverpool?"

Robert nodded, naming the firm, but mispronouncing the name, the beer's effect troubling his tongue. He also found it difficult to pronounce the Colony of Maryland.

To Robert's surprise, he heard, "I am Cunliffe." The gentleman added his full name, "Forest Cunliffe. Tell me, son, are you Robert Morris, the junior?"

The boy nodded. "Yes, Sir, Mr...." Again he mispronounced the man's name.

"Yes, Oxford, Maryland. Your father is transforming that little seaport into a major source of tobacco and, of course, profit for us."

Robert's curiosity rose as the gentleman's smile turned warm, mentor like. But the smile vanished as Cunliffe observed young Robert eying a buxom barmaid. "Master Morris, my man, you may look all you want at the women in here, but to stay healthy—which you must do as you grow older—my advise to you is not to get intimately involved with any of the barmaids. They are for the sailors, the longshoremen, the men who do the physical work of trade."

Seeing further query in the boy's face, Cunliffe quickly advised, "These sorts of women are likely to carry syphilis. Even English royalty can contract it from having sex with one of them who is infected. And you cannot tell ahead of time, so contain your urges and use your head, not your tool." He waited, watching the boy's face intently. "Do you understand me?"

Robert contemplated the gentleman's advice, the beer's effect slowly being mitigated by the strength conveyed by the gentleman's intense serious gaze. Trying his best to comprehend, he nodded. "Yes, Sir."

They sat at a table where the gentleman finished his pint as Robert's eyes visually roamed the room, taking in the patrons, the barmaids, the lowlies picking up the dirty glasses and dishes, while shooing away the dogs and cats.

Handing him an engraved business card, Cunliffe said, "Tomorrow morning at 9 sharp you come to this address. I will show you around, tell you more about what a merchant's agent does, that is, if you want to learn. You will find out why Great Britain, given its vast empire, rules the seas." He added, "And the world."

Robert wanted to know, "What about China, Sir? I've read about that place. They have lots of people. Perhaps it is a market for your tobacco, as well."

"You are a most unusual young boy to raise such a question."

Cunliffe spat on the dock, his act seeming to dismiss the idea, Robert thought. But then he followed with what Robert sensed was his need, in spite of their age difference, to explain and not appear to be rude. "They are of little importance. You see, son, China has no colonies. We British are a stronger world power. We have colonies—like the 13 in America—plus India, Australia—well, you know some geography, don't you? The colonies provide us with the raw material and they buy our finished goods. It is all about trade and building your fortune on the seagoing trade made possible by the sailing ships you see along the wharf." He gestured right and then left.

Robert wanted to ask, and then did, "Sir, can you tell me more about what my father does in this place you call Maryland?" This time he correctly pronounced the Colony. "How does he make money?"

Cunliffe looked surprised at Robert's question. Waiting a moment, he said, "I will tell you what he has done for our firm. Your father has improved the tobacco trade. Thanks to him, standards have been agreed upon by those of us in the trade—grading of the tobacco, that is, appraising the quality of the leaves. And he is translating the accounts of trade into actual money—real money, pound sterling— not in pounds of tobacco, so that we here in Liverpool can finance our growing tobacco trade through our bankers. In short, your father has made a lot of money for himself and for our firm."

Robert listened, his pride and curiosity growing about the life of his far-distant father.

With eager hope, Robert watched Cunliffe closely as the gentleman added, "I sense you want to learn more."

Excitedly, Robert said, "I do, Sir, yes, very much!" He observed the gentleman's body language, hoping for and anticipating their next meeting.

"Tomorrow?"

Robert repeated with hope, "Tomorrow, here on the docks?" He was ecstatic with the gentleman's confirming nod.

Robert told Nanna, who happily instructed him to attend the meeting. The next morning she made sure Robert was washed and well dressed. She went with him to the edge of the docks where they could see the door of Cunliffe's establishment. "Be respectful, listen and ask questions." With tears of happiness in her eyes, she instructed, "Robert, make your father proud."

\*　　　\*　　　\*

For days thereafter Robert sat in the offices of Mr. Cunliffe. He listened. He observed. He garnered sense after sense of what ocean commerce entailed. He felt the uncertainty of the high seas. He perceived the risk of loss: men, ships, money, and even fortunes. Even at his young age, Robert glimpsed an insight into how he, too, might make his fortune. He yearned to share his thoughts with his own father off in the New World Colony called Maryland.

One day Cunliffe told Robert he should have a job. "The pay will be small. You will work hard in my warehouse helping to monitor our firm's cargoes—keeping the ledgers for ships docking and sailing. You know, Robert, I sense you have a keen mathematical mind and that this will be your opportunity to further develop that skill."

Excited, Robert told Nanna, who was delighted. For more than a year, 10 hours a day, 6 days a week, he applied himself assiduously. The reward was an expanding sense of ocean commerce. At night he returned to Nanna, tired, hungry, yet smarter and, best of all, happy in his work.

\*　　　\*　　　\*

Fantasizing about his future, wherein, he hoped, would be the opportunity to accumulate his fortune, Robert rejoiced one evening when Nanna announced, with a mixture of grandmotherly glee and cautious foreboding, that she had received that morning an important letter from his father. With reserved happiness in a voice tinged with remorse, she told him, "Robert, dear, you are to sail for the New World!"

Excited, Robert smiled with the anticipation of adventure, fortune, and the thought of once again seeing and talking with, and, yes, learning more about commerce from his loving father, who would no longer be distant but close by.

"The ocean crossing will be difficult," Nanna told him. "And dangerous, very dangerous!" Tears in her eyes, she hugged her grandson. "You might not complete the voyage…the ship might not…." She looked away. Robert saw distance dominating her countenance. Her voice grew weak. "Like your grandfather's ship.

You know, he never came back. His frigate disappeared, along with the crew and its cargo. We never knew what happened to him." A dark silence surrounded them.

Hesitatingly Robert asked, "But is it not too soon for me to go to the New World?" Ignoring her warning of the dangers in sailing across the Atlantic, Robert said, "I mean, Nanna, I am not yet 17 years."

She bid him stand against the special spot on the wall where, during the years of growth, she had regularly marked his height with a small piece of charcoal. Standing tall, he complied. She read the current mark and said, "You are six feet tall, and may still grow taller." He nodded as he looked at the mark. She went on, "You are a smart lad. You want to learn more. Your father will teach you—"

"—What about Thomas, my little half-brother, who I seldom see as he lives on the other side of town? Does my father want him to come, too?"

He saw the disturbed look on Nanna's face. He recalled snippets of conversation as he was growing up, wherein he had come to sense her disapproval of the morals of the Morris family—her occasional rare criticism of his father. Trying to put family into perspective, Robert asked more about this half-brother, who Nanna called "TM," maybe, he speculated, out of disapproval or her disfavor.

Curtly, Nanna advised, "TM's mother will take care of him. He is different from you, and your father knows it." She shook her head. "No, Robert, it is not to be TM. Your father wants only you."

"But sooner or later, Nanna, do you not think I will be beholden to take care of him? After all, he is my younger half-brother. That does not mean he is the same as a full brother, or that he is a bother only half the time. Is that not right?"

"Some day, Robert, that Morris family matter as to the fate of TM will become yours to decide."

Robert wondered at her prediction. Yet that night and in the days ahead as he focused on his future and mentally prepared to leave Liverpool, he dreamed about what life for him would be like in the far-off vast and unknown land of America. Would that western wilderness welcome him?

# CHAPTER SIX:
## BETSEY WANTING TO FIND HER BOYS

Though she looked more erudite than the fact, though her hair seemed coiffeur, though her dialect was becoming more or less cultured from picking up the Philadelphia manner of speech as she listened to and then tried to emulate City Tavern patrons, Betsey the barmaid effectively hid her illiteracy. So, she felt neither embarrassed nor out of place to ask Robert Morris to help compose a letter to her two boys, Luke and Mark, in the hope that somehow a carriage driver or a boatman might some day deliver the letter to wherever her boys might be living out there in The Westward. She reasoned that wherever they were, surely someone would receive and then read her loving message to her dear Luke and Mark for, like her, neither could read or write. With consuming emotion, Betsey was counting on Morris to help her express her love to her two boys, who had been too many months away from her. She asked him to write that she was inquiring of their health and asking about their wilderness adventures and, of course, expressing her motherly wishes.

After Robert penned the letter on Colonial paper, it was delivered to a trustworthy westward-going boatman. Weeks and agonizing months went by without a response. With the growing uncertainty that her words—actually Robert's dear words—might not have reached them, given the uncertainties of Colonial mail delivery, Betsey's nights at the City Tavern became longer and longer. Her anxiety rose as each night without her offspring became lonelier. Eventually, with motherly concern consuming her, she made up her mind to undertake the journey west. Certainly, if she were to seek out her boys, she would find them for, with certainty in her mind, a mother's instincts would guide her search.

Over time, Betsey had put aside some English coins, along with a stack of paper notes issued by different Colonies. Counting up, she figured she had enough to pay for a seat in a carriage that would take her along John McAdam's new Turnpike, even though construction was still underway as it carved a route west toward the borough of Lancaster. There, she could pay a boatman on the Schuylkill River who would be paddling and poling a flatboat west through the first layer of mountains to where she felt her estranged husband and her boys must by now be working their family farm.

She bid farewell to her barmaid friends, they all wishing her well, packed what clothes and personal belongings she had in a cloth bag, the one with spring flower buds sewn in. Betsey then set off in the next carriage headed west. The ride was absurdly rough across the log planks laid by McAdam and sequenced in a lateral pattern to make up the pike's rough road.

Weary and exhausted, almost longing for her usual barmaid duties, albeit demanding, yet at least to some degree pleasurable, given the interesting men she met and perhaps briefly befriended, Betsey began to question herself as to the wisdom of her journey. The more land that passed by her carriage, and which days later floated by on the shores of the river, she began to realize the vast and seemingly unending extent of The Westward. She became fearful of the multiple unknowns that lurked, the passing Indians on shore that eyed her, or so she imagined, the crude and frightful men that approached her, the callous, rough, uncivilized, illiterate men of the frontier with their rifles, their knives, their animal skin clothing, all unlike the attire she was accustomed to and admired among the cultured city men of Philadelphia.

Betsey asked herself what life was like in England, where, so she had heard from immigrant patrons in the City Tavern, everything was civilized, codified, ordered, structured, and fit into a social structure accepted by all. Life there was devoid of revolution and turmoil. It was supposed to be a family-oriented lifestyle. Or was there, in reality, such a place as that anywhere in Old Europe or even in New America? If it did exist in the Colonies, it would be in Philadelphia. For, Betsey she came to realize, that was the only lifestyle with which she felt comfortable.

Her savings nearly gone, consumed by carriage and boat fees, she decided to hold onto as much money as she could while making her way back to the City Tavern. Her two boys and her departed husband had made their choice of lifestyle, and now she must make hers.

Nearing the Quaker City on the carriage, her money almost gone, Betsey mulled over the men and the few ladies she had waited on and talked with in the City Tavern. Once, a few months ago, she recalled having talked with a Mrs. Gates—Elizabeth, she had said her name was. As they talked, it came out that she was the wife of a Continental general. Strange, Betsey recalled, for as their female bonding grew, Mrs. G had told her to never use her real name or for sure even her first name, saying that she regretted the slip of her tongue. "Just Mrs. G is acceptable."

At their last meeting in the tavern, Betsey recalled Mrs. G giving her a gold coin—since spent on her aborted trip—and told her to keep her name a secret. But before they parted, Mrs. G had asked Betsey to tell her as much as she could about Robert Morris. She had offered to slip her another coin when and if Betsey could fill her in on the man. She had given Betsey the name of Arnold, her slave—actually the General's slave because women couldn't own property. Betsey, she instructed, should contact the Negro when she was ready to disclose to her any information about this particular revolutionary leader.

As she re-entered the City Tavern, Betsey knew she was ready to disclose to Mrs. G everything she knew and could learn about Robert Morris.

# CHAPTER SEVEN:
# WHEN ROBERT MORRIS, JUNIOR
# SET FOOT IN THE NEW WORLD

Nanna's warnings about the ocean crossing had been set aside by young Robert as frivolous grandmother worries—not to be taken seriously by a strong and adventurous young man. But the actual seaborne experience brought her concerns rudely back. Aboard the ship Atlantic Star, seasickness, boredom, and the feeling of a possible lost-at-sea disaster—these emotions and fears were often dominant in his mind. Yet he made himself put them aside as he regularly experienced excitement about the life he perceived, and hoped, was ahead. Filling his mind were soaring thoughts and dreams of a virgin rich land lying somewhere out there—ahead, that is, if the ship would simply continue sailing west—and only if soon he would hear the oft-described and welcomed vibrant cry from the lookout atop the crow's nest, exciting all on board ship, "Land ho!"

After long weeks of daily exercise on deck, of the crew trying to keep the ship clean with swabs of vinegar-enriched rain water, of food running low, of the beer and rum having been consumed, of tempers flaring among the crew and also among the passengers as boredom took control over normal emotions, and tensions rose, of illness, growing despair of being lost at sea began to dominate talk and feelings on the seemingly endless voyage. All these negatives caused Robert to come to question the entire endeavor of the New World.

Then, at last, the welcome call-out from the crow's nest was heard and celebrated by all. Robert watched as the captain broke out his secretly stashed rum, which was rapidly consumed by crew and passengers. With full sail, the ship seemed to guide itself around the intervening peninsula and enter the choppy Chesapeake Bay, soon enough cruising into the port of Oxford, Maryland.

Greeting young Robert was the sign above a large dockside warehouse, "Cunliffe & Sons - Robert Morris Agent." Instantly, Robert's feelings bubbled with a sense of comfort along with hopeful excitement. At last he had arrived at his new home. He hoped it was destined to shape his life and allow him to make his fortune.

A young boy-messenger came up to him and perfunctorily greeted Robert as he stepped off the sailing ship and onto the dock, his feet welcoming the firm footing of Mother Earth. Yet in his stride he was still weaving back and forth with the more than a month-long motion of the ship. It had been a long disorientation to the familiarity of solid land. But at last it was the end of an unforgiving and unending hellish experience. Each forward firm step restored his sense of both mental and physical balance.

Robert observed the quayside hustle: black-skin slaves hoisting huge bales of tobacco onto ship after ship; others unloading ships by carrying crates of goods whose content he knew not. He sensed the flow, not so much of only tobacco but also of other goods coming from and going to Europe. He could also feel the fortunes being made before his eyes with the backbreaking labor of the cadres of dark-colored human beings, some free, he supposed, but how could he tell those who were not slaves?

Watching, he told himself that each bale hoisted, each crate unloaded, assured the merchants—men like his father and Mr. Cunliffe and their partners off in distant Liverpool of their on-going profits adding to their accumulated personal wealth. Their fortunes were growing daily with every bale of tobacco added to the cargo manifest on the waiting ship, the demand for the leaves being so great as to assure continued consumer demand—the new fad of smoking or chewing by English gentlemen who would pay almost any price to experience the heady stimulus, while exhibiting their social status that this fashionable new product from America bestowed upon them.

Admiration for his father's business acumen flooded young Robert's mind. He longed for a series of conversations with Senior to learn more—as much as he could—as he molded himself into the image of his father. Therein lay the hopes and dreams for his future here in Oxford.

Well dressed and trying his best to be polite, the boy-messenger was waiting for Robert's full attention. Robert smiled and heard him announce in rehearsed style, "Your father has asked me to tell you that you are to call on him tomorrow night at the India House Tavern." As the message quickly sunk in, Robert's emotions spun downward. He despaired. His father. Not 'til tomorrow!

The messenger went on, "Tonight you are to stay at one of your father's houses—the one over there." Before he disappeared into town, the messenger pointed toward a large yellow house with three dormer windows overlooking the harbor and its mid-day bustle.

*       *       *

As afternoon faded into evening, Robert Morris, inhaling the all-too-familiar fragrance of the Chesapeake Bay salt water, walked the docks, automatically counting bales of tobacco waiting to be loaded aboard brigs—all soon to be on their way to Mother England, its monopoly on the trade and its import duties assuring the Crown of bountiful monetary harvests, as well as merchants making profits on dispensing tobacco.

Curious about this first town in America, Robert strolled the narrow, sandy streets, his way eerily lit by the moon shining from a cloudless sky. He stopped to examine a sail maker's workshop. The huge sails were mostly rolled up, yet some were left unfurled in the open, the moonlight rendering them as ghostly as the town itself. He saw piles of tall, thick masts, trunks of lodge pole pine that, so he assumed, had been harvested from the virgin forests. He wondered how much of this new land had been explored, and how much was still to be surveyed and platted. Yes, for sure, he told himself, vast fortunes lay in wait for the taking.

Raucous voices drifted out from behind a stable, disturbing the peace of the evening. Their pitch rose like ocean waves, only to subside briefly, then billow up again, cresting like sea foam. Exploring, Robert dared go around the corner of the building. There he saw something he had never seen before. It appeared to be a cockfight with men betting on one rooster versus another, staking money on one cock being the winner in a fight to kill the opposing one. Robert wondered what other life and death incidents lay ahead in this unruly frontier.

Turning away from the wagering, he transferred his thoughts to what he sensed was New World opportunity. He insisted to himself that he must formulate his plans as to how to accumulate his fortune.

Lost in thoughts, he soon smelled cooking—onions frying, meat roasting, all augmented by subtle flavorings of spices. Following the fragrances, he found the delightful sensations were emanating from a tavern. Roasting coffee confirmed his hunger.

He was quickly caught up in the bustle and boisterousness of barmaids bellowing out their customers' orders, of drinkers hoisting tankards, and go-for-it gamblers placing bet after bet, some winning, he supposed, but most likely losing to the house or to their table mates. Right there and then, he decided he did not want to spend his life gambling. The merchant business was not gambling, or so he had come to believe. But was he certain of that? He would learn the difference for sure when he met with his father. And in their many conversations to follow.

To his surprise and immediate interest, in an alcove toward the tavern's back, a candelabrum illuminated a trio of young women. They were talking intimately to each other, smiling to each other, and laughing softly. He wove his way across the room, dodging barmaids and rowdy customers, drawing closer to them. Now he took more hesitant steps, quietly observing. One by one, the comely young women looked toward him, their chatter subsiding, curiosity about him, or so he imagined, capturing their attention.

He thought the dark-haired girl smiled at him—slightly. But no. His self-important imagination was playing tricks. Embarrassed, he stood, studying each of them with quick and clandestine, but likely obvious to them, glances. Sheepishly he turned away. Few women, none young, except for two children in their father's tow, had been passengers aboard his ship. How many weeks had it been since he had seen a beautiful young woman, let alone talked to a girl near to his age.

Their custom tailored dresses, he concluded from his first impressions, were stylish, matching the latest fashions he had seen in Liverpool. But it was their alluring feminine figures that excited him and urged him on toward them. From beneath their little designer hats, their hair flowed in curls, luminous in feminine radiance. He speculated as to the soft female bodies concealed beneath their attire. His nerve buoyed by male drive—yes, by a young man's desire to explore the other gender, he approached closer.

Their collective silence, their gazes suggesting curiosity, the strength of their numbers seemed to embolden their visual inspection of him. He sensed they were critically and excitedly examining him, looking into him in the same way in which he had been, secretly—no, openly—looking at them.

He made eye contact with each girl as he said, "I am Robert Morris, Junior, from Liverpool. I arrived today." Without waiting, he queried, "Do you all live in Oxford, or are you passengers off the clipper ship docked harbor side?"

The girl with red hair in pigtails falling across her breasts laughed in a titillating expression of femininity. It had been a long time since he had been so excited by a lilting female voice—from one so young and so pretty. A smile followed. "Well, Mr. Junior, freshly-arrived Liverpudlian." She laughed at reciting his town's nickname. "Welcome to our Oxford, our Maryland."

"Ah...Robert, please." He smiled. To each in turn, he said, "Call me Robert."

"We live here, Robert" the blonde said, adding, "in our respective sea captain's homes—our father's homes."

To Robert's surprise and pleasure, the brunette motioned coyly for him to sit between her and the redhead. "I am Sally, Sally Smythe." She shifted slightly to allow him barely enough room.

"And I am Rosemarie," the redhead said softly, her voice enticing, so he felt. Quickly he obliged, his coat and silk stockings brushing against each of their dresses, his adrenalin rising with the touches. The blonde purred her name, "Annie."

As he looked closely at their faces, their carefully applied makeup, their soft skin, Robert couldn't immediately decide which girl was the most beautiful. Perhaps it was her lithe body movement in making room for him, or was it the lilt in her feminine voice? Or maybe it was the hint of seduction hidden in her smile, all traits melding together, giving the edge to Sally. Trying to divert his mind, he asked, "Is there music in this town of yours, maybe a place to dance?"

The three looked at each other. In unison they slowly nodded. "Yes," said Rosemarie. "But not tonight. Are you staying a short time, or are you here for good?"

"I do not yet know—that is, until I meet my father tomorrow night at the India House Tavern."

"And, pray tell us, who is your father?" Annie asked.

Robert found himself absorbed with the gossamer of her twirling curls. It took him a long minute to focus on her query and compose a reply. "Ah...he is Robert Morris, Senior."

Sally, surveying Robert, loud enough for him to hear, whispered to redhead Rosemarie, "You know, Rose, he is that wealthy merchant who runs the Cunliffe tobacco warehouse."

Her gaze fixed on Robert, Rosemarie nodded.

Embarrassed at their attention focused on him, Robert heard himself blurt, "Why is there no music tonight?"

Sally replied, "Because two nights from now the barmaids will put on a show here in this tavern. There are usually a couple of sailors with guitars who strum along. We sing sea-going ballads. That is when we dance—that is, if there are any young men we want to dance with, which there usually are not, but now, with you having arrived, we will each take our turns, Mr. Sea Legs Junior Morris." The three maidens laughed as if they had captured a pirate's prize. They watched as four ciders were delivered, the result of Robert having beckoned to a barmaid.

In his most cultured Liverpool voice, trying to avoid the derided Liverpudlian dialect, Robert told them, "You have made me feel welcome here, and I am obliged to you each." While titters ensued, questions crossed his mind, leading him to ask about their fathers and the ships.

"My father is always sailing, so it seems to me." Sally said, snickering.

"Yes, regularly," Rosemarie said.

Annie said, "My father is in port awhile, that is, loading another cargo, and then he is to be off...I think it is to Portsmouth this time."

Examining Robert and the quality of his attire, Sally asked, "And you, Mr. Morris, Junior, will you be playing a role in all this ocean-going commerce that keeps this town alive? Like sailing a ship? Or will you be an investor in the cargo aboard one or more ships? What will you do here, Master Morris, to make your fortune?"

Annie said, "Yes, tell us what will be your role in our little Oxford tobacco colony."

"Do tell us more," Mr. Morris, Junior, Sir...Robert, Sir," Sally said, her smile as inviting as her gaze that fixed on him as she patiently waited in silence, inviting him to reveal more of himself and his intentions.

*     *     *

Amidst their female company and their collective closeness, and eventually overcome with physical exhaustion, Robert savored the energy and the beauty of the three young women. From them, individually and collectively, he sensed the strength driving the direction of this virgin continent. Exciting emotions of adventure, of fortune, filled his mind. Energy. Was the strength he felt a gift from the Noble Savages that seemingly forever in time had ruled this land—a land only recently familiar to Europeans? But bit by bit, the savages were yielding their homeland to the westward onslaught of settlers from afar. Was it the wonder of a new continent, its reaches so remote, and its economic value not quantified, yet so promising? Or was it his own male prowess that he wanted to celebrate? What did it mean to be here, to participate, to contribute? Consumed by uncertainty, he concentrated on the direction he should follow to make his fortune.

Finally, after midnight and back in his own bed in one of the dormer window rooms of his father's boarding house, both his young age and what he hoped was his growing wisdom having imbued him with excitement, yet physically exhausted, Robert lay awake. His unswaying straw bed was welcome after the shipboard nights back and forth in a rocking hammock, trying to drown out the snores of sailors and passengers. Here, in privacy, he was beginning to anticipate the possibilities that could design his future—from being with beautiful young women to displaying the wealth he would build for himself in the tobacco trade. For sure, he was going to learn more from his father on the morrow. But could he ever equal or exceed the monetary success his father was accumulating?

Speculating wildly, the night's pleasures emboldening him, his mind soaring, Robert imagined vivid pictures of what these 13 New World Colonies could grow into. He had set foot in only one. What were the other 12 like? And then there were the westward lands stretching to a great beyond. And the women…

# CHAPTER EIGHT:
# FATHER AND SON MEET

The following night, inside the crowded and boisterous main hall of the India House Tavern, sitting at a table-clothed corner of a long trestle table, to which young Robert was directed, Robert Morris, Senior, looked up from his tall tankard of cider and extended his arm, hand outstretched toward his newly arrived 6 foot two inch tall grown son. The father waited, impatience showing, for his hand to be firmly shook, the ritual seeming to Robert to be the formal greeting practiced in Oxford, Maryland. Once this male procedure was completed, having been executed with promptness, the elder Morris motioned for Robert, Junior to sit opposite him.

Stunned by his father's curt avoidance of his hoped-for warm and emotional greeting, the father not standing in recognition of his son's arrival, absent his longed-for paternal embrace, certainly to be returned, young Robert's feelings being deeply hurt, his emotions slumped into a depressive state. His mind went back to his feelings since sailing out of Liverpool. He had wanted, and fully expected, to throw his arms around his father, the father-son gesture being readily reciprocated. He had hoped to hug his father, kiss him on the cheek, perhaps shed a tear of joy, and relate to him intellectually, mind to mind. Yes, and having successfully sailed across the Atlantic, express his thoughts to Morris, Senior, and describe his feelings during the arduous crossing. And especially tell him about his meetings with Mr. Cunliffe and his having worked there with such vigor. And, of course, tell of Nanna's love and motherly greeting. Oh, and present him with the small gift Nanna had so carefully and prettily wrapped in special English paper. After all, he himself had never known his own mother, so surely his father would want to hear about Nanna, his dear mother, learn of her health and be happy with her wellbeing.

Here in the India House Tavern, before Robert could compose himself and deliver his planned filial greeting, as if on cue, a plump painted barmaid approached, bundling up against him, her fingers flowing through his curls. "I'll wager you are good," she purred. She looked to his father for approval of what, so Robert assumed in assessing her moves, would go down as a quick encounter, likely perceived, albeit mistakenly, as an introductory boy virgin learning the sex experience for this father's handsome masculine specimen.

The father chuckled impatiently and looked intently at his son. Waving off the barmaid with a flick of his wrist, he told her, "Not now. Not here." To his son, he advised, "She is not for you. Trust me."

"I do, Father," Robert was quick to proclaim. Trying to advance closer emotionally to his father, he blurted, "I trust you and I want very much to learn from you, if you will so kindly oblige me."

"No!" was his father's stunted reply.

Robert was stunned by his father's decree. His emotions, his feelings of belonging, his hopes for this new land, all descended downward into dark dismay as his father went on, his explanation not comforting, not mitigating young Robert's growing void of what he had hoped would be a joyful reunion, especially after so many years apart.

Senior continued, "I am involved here in making money. I have no time to teach you." Verbally rushing on, the father did not seem to care that he had shocked young Robert with his abruptness, his candor, and his got-to-get-on-with-it tone. It did not matter to him that his son now appeared dejected.

Then, somewhat to Robert's relief, his father told him, "While you are here in Oxford, I have arranged for a tutor. Hale is his name. He is fluent in mathematics. He will teach you, show you the skills you need in order to understand money, what it is and what it represents—the trust and abstractions that support its value. I have instructed him to explain how money and trust work hand-in-hand to make fortunes. He will explain how agents make the merchant trade function, not only for their own benefit but for the good of everyone."

Robert's spirits rose. Hope for his future began to rekindle. He managed, "Thank you, Father."

The barmaid returned, her gaze on the father, who motioned for her to bring cider for himself and his son. Soon, winking seductively at young Robert, she set a glass of cider down in front of him and one for his father. Robert sipped, then gulped, then gulped again as he groped for a glance into the future his father had just described. Robert wanted to fortify his love affair with this new land.

Robert Senior was speaking again, not as father to son, but more, Robert concluded, as a leader who should be followed in lock step. "I will be monitoring your progress. Your tutor, Mr. Hale, will report regularly to me."

Robert was puzzled by his father's next words, feeling they were surely prophetic. The senior Morris looked at his son and sternly delivered a gruff fatherly directive. "Your future is up to you, My Son, if you want to fill my shoes, manage wealth, and grow in stature in the eyes of your fellow man. Only you can explore the world and its commerce and act on behalf of your personal financial benefit. To do so, you must learn all you can from others who are in the business. I am giving you that opportunity. Do you understand me?"

Robert nodded, verbally enforcing his understanding. "Yes Sir. Yes, Father."

Yet family questions flooded Robert's mind. He wanted to query his father about his family, their family. Questions, such as who was his mother, but more immediate, who was this father of his, a father he had not known before coming to Maryland and a father he did not seem to know even now, sitting with him this evening in the India House Tavern. With tonight's abbreviated conversation, he was not learning much. Waiting no longer and venturing into the subject of family he so dearly wanted to talk about, Robert impatiently said, "Father, who was my mother? Please tell me about her."

Robert Senior's facial expression appeared to reveal annoyance at his son's query. Watching his father closely, Robert was almost sorry he had asked, yet knew that for his own peace of mind he must learn about his mother—at least something, her love for him perhaps, or maybe not, and where was she buried—yes, he must know something about her.

"Jane," the father stated. "That is…was…her name," he added as if that tidbit of information closed out the topic. But then, after staring off at the tavern's high ceiling for a few moments, the father turned reflective. His gaze coming back, he said, "We were together those nights in that port in Normandy. She was staying with her aunt in the village. I was there as a factor for my Bristol firm's ship. We were loading the cargo. I was to complete the manifest and have it cleared through customs so we could sail back across the English Channel."

Robert perceived the scenario and quickly asked, "She was pretty, Jane, I mean, my mother?" He answered his own question, "Of course she was. She was my mother. Yes?"

His father nodded. "Oh, yes, she was a beauty." He was silent for only a moment before going on, "She described to me her love of ships, of watching them sail into harbors, both in the Normandy ports and back in Liverpool."

Hesitatingly, Robert asked the question to which he had already sensed the answer, "But later on, I mean, you didn't—"

"—Marry? No. Ours wasn't...was not." The father paused, seeming to recall a relationship, perhaps with some pain. "A while later, after that...those few days...she wrote to me from her mother's home in Liverpool, giving me the news that she was with child."

"In response, you—"

"—Yes, I agreed to pay the midwife's and the doctor's fee and to care for the child, raise it after it was born. That is, raise him...ah...of course, I mean you, My Son." For this once, Robert felt his father's eyes focus on him, and he realized his father was looking intently into him, lingering on his face, his body, examining—perhaps for the first time—seriously considering his son and calculating, perhaps, what his son meant to him. Robert hoped that deep within his father there was love, at least a love of sorts. What was paternal love? What was maternal love? Then he heard his father say, "You look a lot like her...Jane...your curls, your eyes...your dimple. Yours are her eyes, their color, their intense, deep, meaningful look." The father downed his cider in one tilt of the tankard.

"And she, my mother, where, what...?"

In a voice low, even soft, reflective, pensive, so Robert sensed, his father said, "Complications during childbirth." Then the senior fell silent, perhaps a regretful silence, Robert thought. A silence seeming without end. Until, hesitatingly, Robert posed, "Later, you knew other women, did you not?" Of course, he reflected, there was his younger half-brother, Thomas, back in Liverpool.

His father nodded, supplying new information, "Several. In addition to Thomas, I did father your two younger sisters."

Surprised, Robert exclaimed, "Two sisters...plus Thomas!"

"Yes, you have two half-sisters, and a half-brother. I have paid for their births, their upbringing, each one, and they...and you, Robert, are each mine, my offspring, my family." Robert's father laughed the laugh that surrenders to a fate beyond one's control, a fate that had shaped one's life.

Then suddenly, without any hint of a warning, Robert Morris, Senior, stood, straightened up and walked briskly out of the India House Tavern without so much as a good night or even a good-bye gesture to his son.

\*       \*       \*

Standing, awestruck for moments, Robert almost cried. Then he began to ask himself what values, what memories, what motivations, and, yes, what knowledge had gone through his father's mind with all these affairs with women, one his own mother, without any of them ending in marriage, without...or perhaps with...love, or some degree of love? He thought again of his father's tryst with his mother in France. And he thought about the later trysts with several other women, or were his sisters and brother progeny from just one other mother? But not his own mother, for, he reminded himself, she had died in childbirth.

This evening with his father's abrupt departure from the tavern, Robert wondered what had gone through his father's mind. Was his leaving tonight so abruptly the same as leaving a woman after completing the act of sex? Robert reflected how he had left the three young women the previous night, after being physically fully expressed.

Later on that second night in the upstairs bedroom of his father's elegant house in Oxford, as he was falling asleep, Robert speculated as to what his father was really all about. Was he uncaring, selfish, clever, smart, callous, or simply a wealthy merchant? Did being rich excuse his other traits, or was being rich a product of those traits? But did those traits, some or all, negatively or positively, characterize his father? He asked himself if, as his own life developed, would those traits become his traits?

# CHAPTER NINE:
# ROBERT'S STUDIES

"As a factor...." Mr. Hale began and stopped. "Now, tell me again, Robert, what is a factor?"

In the fourth month of his tutoring adventure, Robert was standing tall in his tutor's library in the office of his house on the main street of Oxford. He recited, "Sir, a factor is an agent who buys and sells on commission on behalf of principals who are usually in another country, or even across the ocean on another continent."

Mr. Hale asked, "Assuming you are in business as a factor, are you at liberty to act on your own behalf if, by circumstance, a personal money-making opportunity should arise?"

Robert ruminated on his tutor's question. He sat down in the red leather wingback chair reserved for Mr. Hale's students and contemplated the library books as a backdrop for both pupil and teacher. Robert yearned for the acquired wisdom of the commercial market place, yet with that wisdom overlaid with a viable code of ethics. He wondered if any of the books displayed harbored answers to life's seemingly unending important questions. If so, did they offer clarity to this ethical question posed to him by his tutor? How would the learned authors of the books answer?

"Well?" Mr. Hale was showing his impatience at not hearing a response to his question. After all, Robert speculated, in Mr. Hale's teaching mind, a tutor is a tutor, not a reservoir of morality, not an answer book of ethics. Make the student think, that is his job, or so in his mind he must justify the questioning of his pupil.

Robert ventured his reply. "Keeping one's word, maintaining one's personal reputation with business partners—those are life's important guidelines, so it seems to me, Sir. Although I have not been tested by such a merchant situation, all I can do is to guess."

To Robert's discomfort, the tutor said, "The answer is important, Master Morris, for, as you have pointed out, your reputation is all you have. When you have lots of money, or none at all, either way, your reputation, what people think of you builds overriding and guiding values."

"Nanna told me once that my father follows such guidelines."

The tutor nodded, "Indeed he does. He is a man of his word."

Robert asked, "But, Sir, can not business situations change and, without warning, become adverse due to events that are beyond one's control? In which case, a factor might become helpless against the strong winds that can blow guidelines and behavioral rules off course. Is not that so, Sir?"

"Yes, if you are a pragmatic person, which it appears to me you are. Then I would agree that a factor is obliged to adapt to any and all changing situations, providing, that is, your honor is not compromised."

Robert said, "To return to your question, Sir, I believe the guiding axiom calls for the factor to honor his word, even if the situation changes. Maybe that calls for his word to be re-defined and re-stated, given any new set of circumstances."

Mr. Hale smiled. "That is an acceptable answer."

Hearing the tutor's response, Robert felt relieved, but then he was immediately confronted with a different, even more difficult requirement of his teacher, who said, "Now I want you to define for me the word, yes, it is a concept—that being finance. Please tell me what that idea, or concept, means to you."

Quickly Robert replied, "Finance has to do with money."

"Of course. But tell me what does the term finance conjure up in your young and, I believe, ethical mind?"

Robert did not hesitate, replying, "To me, finance is arranging to pay for something when you do not have the funds in hand, but know, or are confident you know the source of the money to pay for it, and that sooner, preferably, or later, for sure, you will indeed pay for whatever it is you have contracted to purchase."

"And if you do not know the source of funds?"

Robert thought for only a moment before saying, "That would constitute fraud."

"And what makes the difference between fair and fraud?"

"Sir, my word, my honor, my reputation."

From his facial expression, Robert felt the tutor showed pleasure with his pupil. Relishing in his teaching results, Mr. Hale smiled and said, "Good, Robert." The tutor then said, "Soon you will have many opportunities to address these same questions in real life on an everyday basis, for your father has told me he is sending you to Philadelphia."

Surprised at the news, Robert quickly asked, "Sir, what will I do there?"

"You are to stay with a Mr. Greenway and work for him in his trading business, where you will learn, learn, learn...."

Excited, Robert asked, "When do I leave?"

"Mr. Morris told me there is a coach leaving Oxford tomorrow. The journey will require several days—the roads, well, we can't really call them roads, muddy this time of year. Travel is slow going to Philadelphia or anywhere in the Colonies for that matter."

Puzzled, but not wanting to show annoyance at his father, Robert asked, "But Mr. Hale, Sir, why did my father not tell me himself, why not in person?"

"He has sailed out of Oxford. Off to the Caribbean on one of his ships—left instructions with me to arrange for the coach."

Robert's disbelief surged into anger at his father. No longer able to hide his feelings, Robert said, "He did not speak to me, explain matters to me, wish me well before he sailed off for the Caribbean. Why?" Robert's emotions spilled forth. "I mean, I am all alone here. I have no one to—"

"—Mr. Greenway will take care of you, provide for you. Your father has arranged for your care, Robert. Do not despair. I remind you that your father is a man of his word." Mr. Hale placed both his hands on Robert's shoulders and looked him the eye. Slowly he said, "Never forget what I have just told you, but especially remember what I have taught you in our many sessions. Robert, do these things for me, your tutor, for your loving father, and especially for yourself."

# CHAPTER TEN:
# ROBERT IN PHILADELPHIA

In his visual sweep of Philadelphia's waterfront, having studied the variety and quantity of the unloaded goods on the docks, and observing in return the Colonial goods stacked for export, Robert Morris concluded that this Colonial port scene rivaled that of Liverpool. As he strolled quayside, looking north and south along the west bank of the Delaware River, he calculated that the wharf stretched at least a mile in each direction.

With his mathematical mind registering the number and types of ships anchored in the harbor, along with those docked at the wharfs, Robert counted the silhouettes of 134 sailing ships. Breaking down the mix, he mentally tallied 31 brigantines, 13 schooners, 44 sloops, 9 snows, plus 37 vessels of mixed design and varied sailing purposes. Some ships, he reflected, were easier to identify as they fit a more or less standard design, while others appeared to be creations of shipbuilders back in English ports whose craft was freeform, following that particular craftsman's own whims. As he had learned in Liverpool, there were no standard ship designs, only those handed down from a father shipwright to his son, each of whom were likely illiterate and unable to record their designs or describe them to others, except verbally with hand motions and charcoal drawings on a wharf's wooden planks. Robert noted how some of the ships were meant to carry cargo; some were built for speed. But all, Robert concluded as he focused on his own future, were meant for making money for the owners. Oh yes, he had to admit, sometimes the captains benefited and, as added incentives, there were possible bonuses and port city perquisites for the crews.

Taking it all in, Robert felt the heartbeat of trans-ocean commerce and was excited he was located here in what he deduced was the New World's commercial heartbeat. He observed all the commercial activities and yearned to learn more about each. Yes, and to calculate the potential profits. Impatient to begin, he realized he must find this Mr. Greenway, who offered the apprenticeship arranged by his father and verified by Mr. Hale.

He asked a ship's captain for directions to Mr. Greenway's warehouse, which he had been told by Mr. Hale was in the epicenter of the port. But the captain, who was more interested in conversing with the parrot astride his shoulder, dismissed the query saying he was unaware of each warehouse location or where to find a Mr. Greenway.

Wandering among the waterfront's bustling activities, his valise with his belongings over his shoulder, Robert looked about for a tavern, which he reasoned would be a center of information. To his surprise, after asking another passerby, his gaze was directed to a series of caves extending into the bank of the Delaware River. From out of the first, noisy chatter floated across the wharf, along with multiple flavors of cooking. "Taverns in caves," he commented to himself—so strangely different from Liverpool. Robert marveled at the peculiarities of Philadelphia.

Daylight was left behind as he entered the smoky light of the first of several cave taverns. Its flickering illumination was provided by clusters of candelabra that increased in number deeper inside the busy establishment.

Robert was suddenly gaze to gaze with an older fashionably dressed woman.

"You, Sir, are new in town. Welcome to my drinking establishment, Mr....ah...?" She smiled. Not waiting for him to supply his name, she said, "I like to know the men who come to me, especially one so young as you." Her arm encircled him and drew him close to her breasts. "I am Matilda Motherhouse," she advised, a name he instantly questioned, but decided to let the matter alone as, wiggling, he tried to extricate himself from her strong embrace. "You may call me Mother, Mr....ah?"

"Mother," Robert began, looking at her intently, yet choking up at his having voiced a loving name he had never before been able to say out loud to any woman. He visualized his grandmother. Despite her guiding light during his growing up, "Nanna" was Nanna, never

"Mother."

"Yes," she answered him, relinquishing her hold and demanded to know, "What is it you want here, My Son?"

In his most polite voice, trying to speak like a Colonial gentleman and not an immigrant lad with a Liverpool accent, he said, "I am looking for Mr. Greenway. Can you direct me please?" He added, trying for the tenderness that the caring term implied, "Mother."

"Tell me first who you might be." He felt the insistence in her voice and realized she was in charge, perhaps even the owner of this cave tavern.

Robert looked into her eyes longingly. Almost affectionately, he replied, "I am Robert Morris." He quickly appended, "Junior."

To his relief, she smiled. Nodding knowingly, she said, "I know Mr. Greenway quite well." To his delight, her precise instructions followed in rapid staccato. "Go back onto the dock, turn left one block, then left again. You will see his name over the door. You may tell him that Mother sent you."

The time not being too late in the afternoon to present himself to Mr. Greenway, Robert bid a somewhat reluctant good-bye to Mother and left the tavern-in-the-cave. Following her directions, he came upon a painted sign above a large wooden door, advising Greenway & Sons. He pulled upward on the brass knocker—the head of an English lion—letting it fall against its companion brass plate. No response. Then again. Silence. Trying to control his impatience, he repeated the routine a third time.

Soon the door cracked open and, to his delight, the face of a young woman looked out at him. Her darker skin suggested she might be Delaware. Timidly she lowered her gaze, then, looking at him, she said inquisitively, "Yes?"

Smiling, he told her in his most friendly tone, "I am Robert Morris, Junior, from Oxford, directed by Mr. Hale to introduce myself to Mr. Greenway."

Examining him, she stared intently for an agonizing moment. Finally she opened the door and bid him enter. Walking away from him into the dimly lit and cluttered warehouse, she swirled her dress that he saw was woven in native fashion with hoop-like stripes, characterized animals, and strings of beads here and there. Her whirling motion created a medley of pleasant sounds as beads hit upon each other. Following her captivating performance, he entered a room whose function he had learned from Mr. Cunliffe and Mr. Hale was a counting room. Its tables were topped with green felt and piled with ledger books, quill pens, and inkwells, all awaiting their assignments to make appropriate account entries. With delight, as he surveyed the ledgers, Robert recognized the essential tools used to tabulate the merchant commerce of ocean shipping: shipping manifestos detailing cargos of tobacco bales; ledgers of accounts not yet paid; others, so marked that tallied amounts due owners of brigs and snows; still others were labeled for payments received. These last ones would show—he had learned the system—money to be added to the personal wealth of his new tutor, Mr. Greenway.

The young woman stopped in front of him, her beads quieting. She stood on her toes and, her lips alluringly close, whispered, "I am Melissa."

Reluctantly diverting his gaze from the comely girl, Robert made himself think about his role here in the Greenway firm. But who was this damsel? She remained so close he could touch her. Abruptly she turned away and disappeared from the counting room into the recesses of the warehouse. Yet he could still hear the swirl of her skirt. Apprehensive, left standing there, he called out, "Melissa, where have you gone?" No answer. A growing sense of loneliness, of isolation overcame him. Where was this Mr. Greenway, in whose hands Robert Morris, Senior, had entrusted his nascent career?

After a long interval, a strong male voice boomed, "Where are you, Master Morris? Show yourself!" Robert heard footsteps and the rustle of a man's clothing. Before he could speak, he was suddenly face to face with a large man in tails whom he assumed was Mr. Greenway. Without any preliminaries, the man announced, "I have work for you, Robert Morris, Junior." He added with the force of a verbal pistol shot, "Now!" In the dim light, Robert noted that the man's untrimmed reddish beard, contrasting with his name, jounced back and forth with each spoken word. His clothing seemed proper for a merchant, but his tails were unkempt and revealed a stature slightly bent. To Robert, the man's large head seemed to be storing his own set of records augmenting the ledgers atop the tables.

Robert ventured, "Mr. Greenway, I—"

"—First, you will take the broom in the closet. Sweep the floors, and second, when you are done, go to the warehouse and do the same. It will take you quite a while, I should think. This is a spacious place."

"Yes, Sir," Robert managed.

"There is a bunk for you in the back." Greenway gestured to a far door, which Robert could discern through the dim light. "Outhouse, of course, out back. My wife will prepare food for you from time to time. She is Melissa who let you in. Her kitchen is also out back—meals served at Indian time, her time."

"Thank you, Sir." Robert's voice was weak as he tried to acclimatize himself.

"Oh, I almost forgot."

More duties, Robert thought.

Instead, Greenway said, "Your honorable father has asked me to one day introduce you to Mr. Charles Willing."

Robert repeated the name in a questioning tone.

"Our wealthiest trader," Greenway explained as Robert detected a tone of male business envy.

Robert asked, "In Philadelphia?"

"In our 13," Greenway corrected. "To meet him you must first qualify. That will be my decision, based upon your performance here in my firm. In the event you do please me with how you carry out your duties, I will make your next apprenticeship—with the Willing firm—official, subject, of course, to his consent. Mark me, Robert, if you satisfy me and Mr. Charles Willing, your future in commerce here in the Colonies will be all but assured."

Robert extended his right arm, offering a handshake. "Mr. Greenway, Sir, I will shake on that!" The two did. "You have my word, Sir, that I will perform to your satisfaction and that of Mr. Charles Willing."

"Spoken like your father's son," Mr. Greenway said. He smiled and patted young Robert on his back. "He is a man of his word, and I expect you to be, as well."

"I shall prove it to you, Sir," Robert said, his firm handshake and sincere words sealing his promise.

*     *     *

Late evening, settling into his bunk in the rear of the warehouse, Robert heard the rustling of beads and the swirling of fabric. She didn't knock, instead entering. "Welcome to this place," Melissa said sweetly, her eyes lingering on Robert's curls. Coming closer, intimacy hinted, she allowed Robert to reach out to her in desire.

Melissa was indeed a beautiful Native American woman. Her father, so she later explained to him, was a Puritan who had gone back to Boston, her mother Lenape, her word for Delaware.

Afterward, as she left, she told him, "We...I want you to feel at home here."

"At home," in Philadelphia. Repeating the words, Robert's loneliness was left in his past.

# CHAPTER ELEVEN:
## THE LETTER, DEATH, AND BIRTH

A few months into the apprenticeship, Mr. Greenway entered the counting room and called out, "Robert, I have a letter addressed to you...came on the weekly carriage from Oxford." Hearing no reply, Greenway repeated his message in an even louder voice, calling out to young Morris wherever he might be, either sweeping or learning the ledgers.

Quickly Robert emerged from amidst the counting tables, quill pen in hand, unable to hide his questioning look.

This time, to Robert's surprise and abrupt worry, Greenway spoke in a soft and, for a Colonial male of the day, almost a caring, father-like tone. It was, Robert concluded, a compassionate voice. But why? Greenway looked away, offering the letter over his shoulder. As he walked toward the door, the big man said, "Robert, if you want to talk, I mean afterward...I will be in my office."

Robert rushed to grab the letter. Right off he noticed that the sender's red wax seal on the flap had been broken. He had come to realize from his New World residency that letters were important. They could carry requests for goods, promise payments for amounts due, tell of important personal news, express advocacy for a person or a cause, or report a denial of such support. Apart from tavern talk, after-church conversations, and an occasional newspaper, Colonial letters were the only means of conveying information and ideas.

Robert opened the flap. In the practice of the time, a letter was folded with the name of the recipient and the place he or she was most likely to be found written across the front before it was handed to whomever the carrier might be—ships' captain, coach driver, boatman—the name and address having been written in iron gall ink that soon turned to brown in the practiced and accepted penmanship of the day. To retain privacy, the letter's message was hidden inside. The broken wax seal meant Greenway had read the contents, Robert concluded, thus the explanation for his deeply personal tone of voice. Examining the envelope, he saw the sender's name imprinted into the wax seal, "Captain Seaborg Smythe," a name familiar to him. Robert's thoughts were suddenly as far reaching as the destinations of the warehouse shipments surrounding him. With trepidation, Robert began to read:

"My Dear Mr. Robert Morris."

No "Junior," Robert noticed right off. Why not his full name? He read on:

"I have the unwelcome duty, as a ship's captain and devoted friend of your father, Robert Morris, Senior, to advise you, Sir, of his untimely and tragic death."

"My father is dead!" Robert exclaimed, repeating in an even louder voice the finality of the word "Dead!"

Stunned. For support, emotionally and physically, Robert sat atop a tobacco bale, one hand clutching the epistle as he tried to circle his mind around the news. But the bale and the news were too overwhelming to be contained. "How, why...my father was...ah...not old yet." He calculated the math and told himself out loud, "Thirty-nine, or so, I make my father's age to be. How could he be dead?"

He felt a soft hand on his arm and looked up to see Melissa offering him a cup of tea. "Drink this," she softly advised. "My herbal Lenape tea will help you."

Gratefully he thanked her. Tenderly she kissed his lips, swirled her skirt and turned to leave. Absently, glossy-eyed, almost crying at the news about his father, Robert watched her billow her skirt. He listened to her beads softly hitting each other as the letter's news continued to hit hard. Her fascinating movements mimicked the swirling of his mind. Forcing himself to focus his turmoil and redirect his eyes to the letter, he sipped the stimulating tea and read on:

"As I am certain you will agree from my recount of his passing, narrated herewith, the events having to do with your father's untimely death are indeed most strange. For you see, young Robert, Sir, your father related a dream on the night previous to his unfortunate demise. In this dream, so he told me on that fateful morning of his death, he was stepping off one of his frigates that had just anchored in the Oxford harbor when one of the cannon, in celebration of the ship's successful ocean crossing, fired a salute to the harbormaster—as you know, a customary practice marking the completion of a ship's ocean crossing and its return to home port. In his dream, the discharge, while not a real cannon ball, of course—simply a wad of powder, yet harmful if you were to be hit by it—struck your dear father in the back of his head. He dreamed that as a result of the hit he died.

"In relating this nightmare, your father told me he was so disturbed that he wanted to share his dream with someone. We discussed it as one might do with such a nightmare, seeking its possible meaning. Together we hoped it was not a premonition of an event that might occur sometime in the distant future.

"The next day, and this is what is so strange, so eerie, so dreadful, we were celebrating the return of another brig from England. On board, he and I and the captain drank a toast, and the captain fired a salute celebrating the completion of what was a successful voyage. Your father then boarded a small boat to return to shore. That was when the second in command of the brig accidentally fired a deadly second salute, the wad of powder striking your father, knocking him out of the smaller craft. He tumbled into the bay. There, I am so sorry to tell you, Robert, that before we could rescue him, he had either drowned or else was sent to heaven by the wad itself hitting his head."

Robert sat for a long time, reliving again and again what he imagined were his father's last moments—celebration turning abruptly into death. Living becoming emptiness, life, in its full bloom and perfection existing one moment, then in an instant changing into whatever it might be in the hereafter.

Suddenly Robert became enraged at his father for allowing this terrible incident to take place. Yes, it was his fault! How could he have been so inconsiderate—inconsiderate of his son, of his partners, of himself? Robert's rage continued unabated. He lamented, asking why could father and son not have had a long lasting relationship, a loving relationship, a family relationship? He heard himself damn his own father.

In the silence of the ensuing moments, Robert struggled to understand. Haunting him were the details of such an event: a father no longer there, a certain emptiness in his life, now matched with thoughts of the mother he had never known. With his emotions unleashed, Robert's rage rapidly changed into sadness, regret, and a longing for never having experienced family love, except for his grandmother Nanna in Liverpool. Desolation, seemingly as vast as the continent, consumed him.

Robert eased down from the bale and, as if in a stupor, walked around the warehouse. His discomposure growing, he perched himself atop a counting table where, after delving deeply into thoughts, he vowed to never let such a fate happen to him. When (and if) he ever had a family, a wife, a son, a daughter, he would always be with them, protecting them, caring for them. The mission of family, of protection, of caring, should it be assigned to him by the will of the cosmos, would be his dedicated goal in his life on Earth.

Returning his attention to the document, Robert saw that Capt. Smythe's letter continued. However, reeling with the devastating news about his father, consumed with discordant emotions, he laid the letter down. He had never had a mother's affection, and now, without warning, he was left with no father to provide guidance, to construct arrangements, to—yes, maybe—love him. Discordant emotions overcame him. His grandmother, Nanna, was an ocean away. Mr. Greenway had offered some solace, but the matter of death loomed for him here in Philadelphia where he was now presumably at home. What home is there, he asked himself, without affection, without family? He was left to try to manage with his own wits.

His thoughts tossed about like a frigate sailing through a storm at sea. Worse, going forward in his life, there was to be no one to issue approval or disapproval of his thoughts, of his actions, of his deeds. He, young Robert Morris, no longer Junior, was now very much on his own—completely so. How was he to manage, to set his life's course? He was to be his own master. No one else was present in his life! His mind told him again, repeating over and over, that he was, suddenly, the one to determine his own values, the one and only one to set the course for his life, manage the path for his future. Conflicting emotions of weakness and strength confronted him, clouding his mind, challenging him to face his future, keep his face into the wind and not crumble, not defer, not allow himself to descend into the depths of discouragement.

After today, after now, in his future, he asked himself, where would be the guiding shout from the crow's nest above or from a harbormaster's bond fire on shore, sending messages and offering directions as to the course on which to steer his life?

Robert jumped down and briskly walked among the rows of tobacco bales. He began to instruct himself as to how he would endeavor to shape his future—on his own, by himself with his own thoughts, his own efforts, his own intelligence, his personal honor, yes, all the while trying to emulate the good traits of his dear but now deceased father. His rage against his father was waning and now turning to admiration and a growing desire to best his father's life and successes, and of course, hopefully to live longer.

Later, maybe minutes, maybe even hours, looking back at Captain Smythe's letter, Robert remembered there was still more writing. He read again:

"Robert, I have in my possession your father's last will and testament, as that morning after his dream, he entrusted it to me. 'Just in case,' your father said as he laughed, albeit a little fearfully. Here are the details. I will send the signed and witnessed document to you in a few days, once it is recorded in the courthouse here in Oxford: you, Sir, even at your young age, you are to inherit your father's estate, which consists of some 2,500 British pound sterling. He gives you instructions to provide for raising your two half-sisters in Bristol until age18, and caring for your half-brother Thomas back in Liverpool."

Again, Robert was overcome with surprise, this time about his own sudden wealth. So much! The total was large, yet he knew from his exposure to the Greenway firm's accounting records that there were much larger fortunes being made by clever men, ambitious men, those men who took the big risks of ocean commerce connecting continents to continents, countries to kingdoms. Robert realized, perhaps for the first time, or perhaps he had sensed it all along, first in the fantasy of youth, but now in the seriousness of manhood, that he had always yearned to accumulate his own share of the big picture. His inheritance from his father was enough to get him in the game. Nevertheless there were the responsibilities of providing for his half-siblings, saddling him, and he still so young—an apprentice in his quest for his own fortune. He asked himself if he was up to the task, a task that earlier today he had never considered to be facing him.

Now this list of challenges was looming, overwhelming him. His half-family. And what of Nanna? Did he not need to add her name to his list of responsibilities, all in the family? Well, yes, his father had been addressing these responsibilities, had he not? Now it was his duty. Robert brought himself to accept the fact that he had inherited money along with the self-assigned duties that he believed with all his heart accompanied wealth.

Looking again at the epistle clutched in his hand, Robert realized that on the backside of the folded paper, Captain Smythe's letter contained even more writing. He summoned the courage to focus back to the document. With apprehension, he slowly read:

"Further, Robert, I am duty bound to tell you that my lovely daughter, Sally, is with child. From her liaison with you the night you arrived in Oxford, she tells me, Mr. Morris, Sir, that her baby is yours. Until that night she was a virgin, as I am sure you realized at the time. I believe her, as she has always been honest with me, as she has been with her dear lovely mother.

"Now, Mr. Morris, I look to you as a gentleman and man of your word to do the right and proper thing with regard to my daughter Sally and her baby."

# CHAPTER TWELVE:
## MOTHER AND THE MEN AT THE TABLE

Nervous with anxiety after reading the final paragraph of Captain Smythe's letter, Robert hastily left the Greenway warehouse and returned to Mrs. Motherhouse's tavern, hoping to seek guidance from Mother, a woman with whom, during his short residency in Philadelphia, he had from time to time conversed as he sought the comfort of what he imagined might be a mother-like personage.

"You are in a pickle," Mother reacted after Robert told her of the letter and then about Sally. "You men!" she blurted in a gender-condemning bias. "None of you can keep that thing of yours corralled in your trousers!" Her laugh continued, edging Robert's emotions toward despair. As she looked about at the patrons in her establishment and surveyed the various activities taking place, Mother said to Robert, her tone, he thought, now more instructional, "Can you guess how many men in here will get it off tonight? No, nor can I, but I will wager it will be at least half. Look at my comely barmaids and consider the amount of alcohol in their patrons' bodies, the sexual drive buzzing in their heads. The image of intercourse is consuming their minds—not commerce, not thoughts of revolution against the British, and surely not..." she laughed heartedly... "church doctrine and dogma."

Robert asked, "What do you think is in their hearts?"

Mother laughed derisively. "Silly boy. Tell me truthfully, did you have your heart engaged when you impregnated this pretty filly of yours down there in Oxford?"

Robert reflected while Mother waited skeptically and impatiently for his reply. "Yes, I did," he soon advised Mother. "It was my body, my word, my own self being expressed in recognition of her beauty, myself taking her into my heart. In the act, which was my first, I felt the deepest affection for her—her beauty and her person."

"What about the other two? They came later, right? What were your thoughts with them in your night's sexual series?"

Robert appeared stumped. He tried, "Well, none really. But Sally was—"

"—Different, you are telling me?" Mother chuckled. "In my ledger book, all sex is the same."

"You have had more experience than I."

"Had is the right tense. I am through with sex. No more men for me at this point in my life. I oversee my tavern, and make money doing it. That is my nest, my substitute for sex, and it provides me with my own version of the ultimate body expression."

Yearning for female guidance, Robert waited a moment and then queried the older woman, "But in my situation, Mother, what do you think I should do about Captain Smythe writing to me and telling me about Sally being in a family way?"

"Do? My Son, the doing is now hers to do."

"Yes," Robert agreed. "I know that. But there is more to the doing than just the doing. What should I do about the situation? Just because she is with child, my child, does not automatically mean I want to, or should I marry the girl, as lovely as she is?"

"Was on that night," Mother corrected. "Face it, Robert, yours was a one-time event. How many one night episodes are in the immediate memory of my patrons' minds when they leave my tavern, or when they move farther into the back of my cave where curtains can be drawn to shut out the gossips?"

Robert was surprised with her comments. Slowly he replied, "I do not know."

"Nor do I. Nor do I care."

"But I do care, Mother. I care about Sally. About the baby. Our baby, my baby."

Mother looked intently at Robert. "Then you must ask another male, a gentleman like Mr. Charles Willing. He is sitting over there." She gestured at a table occupied by a bevy of well-dressed gentlemen who seemed to be focusing their conversational attention on Mr. Willing. Looking at their faces, Robert surmised they were hoping he would address them with his words of wisdom."

"No, not him!" Robert pleaded. "Not here. Not now! Mr. Greenway says I may soon apprentice with him and his firm. Tonight he might judge me as not being worthy—"

"—Of him and his firm? Or maybe of you not being worthy of yourself?"

"Yes, you are describing my angst."

He felt her grip. Firm in her grasp, Mother led Robert to the far table, saying as they went, "Mr. Charles Willing is the smartest man in Philadelphia—twice elected mayor."

With Mother nudging him onward, Robert confirmed that Mr. Willing clearly had the attention of the men at his table. He watched as one stood to toast him. The toast having been voiced, on cue of the raised tankard, the men all rose in unison, heisting their mugs and loudly expressing their admiration and their well wishes, shouting in unison, "To our revered host, Mr. Charles Willing."

Graciously the Philadelphia icon acknowledged their respect. They each downed their elixirs and were soon again seated. By now Mother, with Robert in tow, was standing beside the distinguished Mr. Charles Willing.

Seeing her, the man who was twice mayor rose and politely kissed her on her cheek. He said softly, "Mother dear, how nice to see you looking so beautiful this evening." He glanced at Robert. "And who is your young man?"

The men, noticing Mr. Willing's attention, stopped their cross-table chatter and focused with curiosity upon Mother and her young male charge, awaiting her introduction.

Gathering his nerve, Robert spoke up. "Mr. Willing, Sir, I am Robert Morris, Junior, from Liverpool. These past weeks and months I have been learning the merchant tobacco trade as an apprentice in Mr. Greenway's firm."

In the accepted gentlemanly manner, Mr. Willing extended his hand, and the two males, their different ages not a barrier, shook hands with firm masculine strength.

Several men nodded. One announced, "Yes, young Robert, I do know your father. Cunliffe and Sons, is it not? Liverpool and Oxford, Maryland. Tell me, how is your father these days?"

Mother inserted softly and with lament, "I am afraid, Sirs, Senior is dead. Victim of a tragic accident in Oxford harbor."

Stunned for only a moment, Charles Willing patted Robert on the shoulder. "I am truly sorry to hear of this sad news, Robert."

Robert nodded his acknowledgement of the older man's compassion. Show no tears, he told himself and tried not to.

Slowly, as if a custom under such circumstances, the men at the table each rose to offer a toast to the honor and the memory of Robert Morris, Senior.

"Ben, you knew him well, did you not?" Charles Willing asked an older man wearing eyeglasses.

Mother whispered in Robert's ear, "Benjamin Franklin."

Ben nodded and suggested. "Yes, I did. And I now offer a second toast to this boy's father, a man whom I have known well, a man of his word. He was a valued member serving on the board of my American Philosophical Society."

Again tankards were hoisted. A barmaid rushed to hand a special glass, brimming with foaming beer suds, to young Robert and another for Mother. In the ceremony to the deceased, the men and Mother raised their glasses and drank ceremoniously.

With everyone again seated, room at the table being made for Robert, while Mother stood, Charles Willing addressed the young man, "Tell me, Robert, what will you do now?" The men at the table focused their attention as they awaited Robert's answer, that is, Robert guessed, were he up to speaking his mind to them.

Hesitatingly he began, "Ah, Mr. Willing, Sir, no longer having a father to consult, Mother here wants me to ask your advice about a…well, I guess it is a problem, Sir." He added, "But one of rather broad interest to all men…" and he looked around the table at the array of gentlemen. He added, "Possibly my question may have meaning in each of our lives."

"Sounds like the boy is talking sex," Ben ventured to a medley of chuckles.

"Well, Sirs," Robert began and hesitated.

Mother encouraged, "Go on, Robert. Pose your question, tell these gentlemen of your moral dilemma."

Starting to address Mr. Charles Willing, Robert quickly turned his attention to the men. "I need to ask you all a serious question."

"Yes?" several urged the young man on.

Summoning his courage, Robert continued, "If a man fathers a child with a woman who is not his wife, and she and he are not married to someone else, what is or what are his obligations to her and to the baby? I mean, what behavioral code applies here in Pennsylvania, and is such a matter regarded any differently here in the Colonies than in Liverpool?"

One gentleman ventured, "It depends on who the girl is, whether she is young enough to still be her father's property...."

"But how is her ownership status to be determined?" Robert asked.

Another spoke. "Remember, women are not citizens here in the Colonies. And only men who own significant property can vote. You see, women do not count, that is, of course, except for their beauty, their babes and, on rare occasion, their financial standing and social status when one of us marries one of them.

Mother spat on the floor. "We women are going to change all that!"

Hoots from the men.

"She is my age," Robert said. "Her father is a ship's captain." Having said that, he searched the men's faces for hints of advice that might be forthcoming.

Charles Willing offered, "If you marry her, then you will be tied down. At your young age, your career could be constrained with your daily responsibilities to her and to the child." The opinion leader thought for a moment, then asked, "Does this girl have a home, a mother to look after her?"

Robert nodded. "Yes, she does."

Looking around the table and then back at Robert, Ben Franklin said, "We all, being loyal subjects of His Majesty, George III, may find it helpful to look to the ethics of royalty for guidance in important matters, such as we are discussing here."

Robert saw rather restrained nods from everyone. He heard subdued murmurs of agreement.

Likely sensing their mood, Mr. Franklin allowed, "While the status of that royal monarch may somehow change, the principle I feel will not, so let me, at my more advanced age, express myself accordingly: "Master Morris, what I would do, were I in your shoes, and now that I presume you have funds from your father's inheritance—"

"—I do, Mr. Franklin."

"Then I would advise you to write to this girl's father and assure him, on the strength of your personal word, that you will provide for the expenses with the baby's birth and further, should the babe live, you will provide for his or her upbringing and education, in the event the child, even a daughter, should desire some level of formal schooling or tutoring."

Charles Willing, looking pleased with Ben's advice, put his hand on Robert's shoulder once again and said, "Yes, if you do that, Robert, if you follow Mr. Franklin's advice, then I will want you to start your apprenticeship with me at Willing & Son."

"Thank you, Sir," Robert said. His voice conveyed his gratefulness. Then he asked, "Son?"

"Yes. May I introduce my son, Thomas Willing IV?" He gestured to the far end of the table where a young man, who Robert assumed was close to his own age, stood and nodded. He did not smile but, with purpose in his gait, Thomas strode up to Robert, and the two young men firmly shook hands. Thomas said, "Welcome, young Sir. Our firm is located at Carpenter's Wharf, center on the docks, where you will henceforth be most welcome."

Robert wondered if he was really feeling Thomas' sincerity, or was he simply hoping it was there? He pondered the question while another round of raised tankards was called for. Toasts to the firm of Willing and Son, but then, to his surprise, as their glasses thrust upward, Charles and Thomas, in unison, appended to add the name of Robert Morris. No "junior." Their toast that included him, he now knew, meant his future, and he vowed to make the most of what might lie ahead. For sure, he felt Thomas' look of support connoted a coming camaraderie between the two young men.

## CHAPTER THIRTEEN:
## WILLING & SON

Welcomed as an apprentice at Willing & Son, Robert's learning curve about trans-Atlantic trade continued to rise. Stimulated by both the father and son, the firm's intellectual atmosphere inspired Robert to work even harder. As time went by, he felt comfortable, being encouraged by them to express his observations and ideas. And he had many of each. Ennobled, as he learned more intricacies of the business, Robert regularly asserted himself.

He became familiar with each ship's cargo, as well as writing the manifests, which were often, but not always, detailing bales of tobacco. With cotton and sugarcane soon added to the cargo lists, Robert was entrusted to oversee the dockside stevedores, slaves, and free blacks as they loaded the ships. He was precise in tallying and verifying each cargo and obtaining the ship captain's confirming signature. He also became adept at preparing the detailed documentation for customs inspectors in the port city of each ship's overseas destination.

He soon asked himself how far could he go in discussing with Charles and Thomas the broader reaching questions that kept gnawing at him? Could he participate in the firm's planning? And its decision making? After all, Charles and Thomas each lived in stately brick homes, while he was ensconced in his tiny cubicle in the back of the warehouse—a social imbalance in a city in which status mattered in human relations.

In the City Tavern, he came in contact with the barmaid named Betsey, as that night she was the one who brought him his cider and dinner. Later that evening, their conversation developed into more personal matters as hints of a closer intimacy arose. He shared with her his association with Willing & Son. He was pleased with her interest, as it enhanced his self-esteem. His renewed confidence, given her support as they talked, led him to pose one particular concern he had been mulling over—a matter important to the firm, yet one he believed was not being addressed.

He realized he was scowling, for Betsey asked, "What's troubling you, Mr. Morris?"

"The risk," he said simply. "My firm is taking more risk than it should."

He felt she was showing interest, so he explained, "If you lose a dinner order on your way from the kitchen to a table, either someone hijacks it from your hands, or maybe you stumble and fall and spill the food on the floor—it is lost to the dogs and cats, right? What would you do?"

"Go back to the kitchen and get another tankard or dinner."

"But let's say you have had to pay the kitchen for the order before the cook will allow you to take it away."

Betsey puzzled for a moment and said, "I'd be out them coins."

"Exactly. Unless your fellow barmaids had united and set up an insurance fund to reimburse you for such a loss."

"Guess so."

"Same with ocean commerce. Our firm needs to get together with other shippers and set up an insurance fund to cover our possible losses at sea, from hijackings by pirates, to storms, and shipwrecks."

Betsey nodded. "Yes, but...."

Morris went on, "And then there is the question of our being paid for the cargo once it is delivered to the buyer in that foreign port. You see, Bets, we need to know how we are going to be paid before the ship leaves the wharf."

"I gets paid by the customer before I goes off to the kitchen."

"But suppose he says he'll pay you sometime later."

"Then I don't puts in his order."

"But that is your job. I mean, you have to trust the patron."

Betsey laughed. "Silly man you is."

"Maybe that is not a convincing example for you."

She nodded.

He said, "You see, Willing & Son cannot be expected to dispatch a ship to the other side of the ocean in the hope that someday payment might arrive on some returning ship. Payment might never arrive back in Philadelphia. The returning ship might encounter a storm and be lost at sea. It might be boarded by pirates from the Caribbean or Algeria in North Africa. The ship's cargo could be confiscated along with the ship and its crew, the pirate thieves demanding a raucous ransom. Failure to pay could spell death for all who had sailed."

"I'm beginning to see what you is talking about."

"That is what I must talk to Charles and Thomas about. I think I know how to mitigate these risks."

*      *      *

From his apprenticeship with Mr. Cunliffe, Robert had come to learn that in England there were companies that did insure voyages, but he had heard of none in the Colonies. Soon he had mustered the courage to broach the matter to the father-son partners.

"What steps might we pursue," Robert queried the partners, "to insure ourselves against the loss of a ship and its cargo?" He recited stories he had heard on the docks concerning the dire risks of ocean-going commerce: describing sudden violent storms, then vividly talking about a mutiny of the crew, in which the ship was commandeered and sailed into an alien port, its valuable cargo sold on the open market, each member of the crew pocketing their share from sale of the stolen loot.

That evening the two Willings and Morris went to the City Tavern. Savoring his cider, with a go-to-it wink from Betsey, Robert suggested to the partners, "We pride ourselves on being a creative firm, and now that there are three of us, let me pose this idea: if we were to pool some of our resources with other merchant shipping firms here in Philadelphia, we could form a reservoir of funds to reimburse any of us in the event of a catastrophic loss."

"Insurance, yes!" Charles raised his glass to toast the idea and said, "Ahead of sailing, each shipper could contribute a set amount to this fund. If there is a loss, the fund would compensate the shipper from this pool."

Robert realized the hurdles as Thomas asked, "How many of our competitors, if any, will buy into the idea?"

Charles said, "Several will do so because they are familiar with the risks and, in the past have suffered losses. They know that in England the cost of insurance for us here in the Colonies is prohibitive. Here, we would set the premiums without the English raking in money off the top."

Robert agreed, "Living in this New World, and doing business here is as undefined and uncharted as the western lands. Look at what my father did in Maryland in establishing a system of grading the tobacco leaves—saved time in putting the bales together and made the quality of the cargo consistent for English buyers. The result was the English buyers paying a higher price and creating more profit for the shipper."

Charles and Thomas nodded. Robert went on, "Sirs, I volunteer to write up a plan and take it to the other firms quayside here and sign up as many as I can."

Charles calculated and said, "We will put up 1,000 pounds to get started."

Offering a toast, Robert said, "I believe our firm needs to explore new inventive concepts if we are to flourish in this frontier environment."

"Other ideas?" The inquisitive tone of the question asked by Thomas triggered Robert to say, "Yes, capital."

Thomas urged, "Go on."

Robert said, "If, as it is rumored, you will receive an appointment to the Indian Affairs Board—there are nine members, I believe—then once a member, you could persuade them to raise private capital by selling bonds that, say, could pay the going Colonial interest rate of 6 percent. The proceeds from the bonds could be used to finance our merchant trade—ours and others, especially those who sign up for the insurance pool—by offering backing for bank loans from London. For, as each of us knows, there is no bank here in the Colonies."

Thomas nodded. With enthusiasm, he said, "Indeed, I have been asked by the Continental Congress to serve on the Indian Affairs Board, and now with your new idea inspiring me, I will accept the appointment." He laughed, adding, "It is a another capital idea, Robert, to establish a bank in Philadelphia. I don't see how we can have a country or even a colony without a bank." He asked, "Where have the British been in helping Colonial merchants with their trade? I know from my studies abroad that merchants in Italy—Venice,

Rome, and Florence—had commercial banks more than 350 years ago. I read that there were more than 70 banks in Florence. Some say the Medici Bank financed the Renaissance." He asked, "Where have King George and his Parliament, and the banks they control and influence, been in helping us develop commerce in our Colonies?"

Charles pounded the table with his fist. "It is in the interests of the moneyed class in England to keep finance locked up. They do not want to allow wealth to creep out of their grasp into the hands of Colonials."

Thomas said, "Yes, even back in the financial chaos of the 1400's in Italy, France, and England, the Swiss in Geneva came up with what they called the Golden Mark, a coin backed by gold. It was used across Europe to pay for merchant transactions. We need something like that here in the New World."

Charles added, "Thomas. Your education is showing! The Brits are keeping all wealth locked into vaults on their little island for their own benefit."

Robert said, "Is not that another reason for our Colony to seek its independence? If we set up our own bank, we can keep the profits from financing at home, and not allow those profits to further enrich the nobility in England."

Thoughtful "yeses" were expressed. "Those profits must fall into our collective pockets," Charles added, rubbing his hands together.

In the silence that followed, Robert sensed pride in his ability to be part of this father-son partnership. As time passed, he continued to participate in the conversations about both political and business issues. There was growing dissatisfaction with the English King and his Parliament, especially surrounding the British Navy and their blockade, which was adversely affecting ocean commerce. And Robert worried about the future and his role in the Colonies.

# CHAPTER FOURTEEN:
# DEFYING PIRATES, MORRIS MOVES UP

Months later, Robert was assigned by Charles and Thomas Willing to sail with the captain of The Little Delaware bound for the Caribbean island of St. Thomas.

With his hard work and participatory attitude during this time, he had been moved up to junior partner. Perhaps the pace with which ocean-going commerce was advancing in the fourth quarter of the 18th century prodded him onward. Or maybe it was the partners' need for someone they could implicitly trust. Or simply luck. Some contemporaries thought it was the confidence he exhibited and the trust he effused among the Philadelphia merchant class.

Typical of the sloops loading at dockside, The Little Delaware's cargo consisted mostly of tobacco, which on this particular journey was supplemented with a secret strongbox containing, as Robert soon learned, a cache of banknotes earmarked for a Caribbean shipper in payment for a cargo of sought-after Jamaica rum.

After they had cast off, The Little Delaware's captain revealed that this was his first voyage in command. Pleadingly, the captain sought Robert's navigational assistance. He tried to help though he had limited knowledge of Caribbean waters. Together, they poured over the charts and decided upon the course. Two days out, having sailed down Chesapeake Bay, aided by favorable winds from the northwest, they broke out into the vast Atlantic.

On the fourth day, with neither the captain nor Robert adept at navigating a secure course, The Little Delaware was confronted by a multi-mast pirate frigate, its frightening Jolly Roger blowing ominously in the breeze. The renegade vessel fired a canon shot across The Little Delaware's bow and quickly came alongside. Its trained crew threw a boarding plank across the gap between the ships. Before Robert, the captain, or the small crew could defend themselves, a band of awesome pirates charged across the plank and took control of The Little Delaware.

Two days later, the pirate ship, with its prize in tow, sailed into a port on a Caribbean island, the identity of which neither Robert nor the captain knew, except for a French flag flying from the harbor's flagpole. After docking, The Little Delaware was boarded by two French soldiers, with whom the pirates appeared to be on friendly terms. Promptly Robert and the captain were taken off the ship and soon found themselves locked in a cell in a quayside harbor jail. Ransom, or so Robert speculated, was what the pirates were after.

The Little Delaware's crew were nowhere in sight, the captain suggesting they may have thrown in their lot with the pirates, or else, having delivered the strongbox and the cargo of tobacco into the pirates' hands, had been hanged, their bodies now lost in the offshore Caribbean waters.

Fearing a similar fate, as they had not been approached by their jailor asking for names and contacts from whom to seek ransom, and denied the opportunity to contact a French harbor official, Robert told the captain they must make their escape as soon as possible. Reluctantly the captain agreed, then changed his mind. Instead, he offered to divert the lone jail guard with a ruse, allowing Robert to make his break for freedom.

They waited a day so that the jailors would think them resigned to their captivity. In the interim, their treatment at the end of the many lashes from the jailor's whip was harsh and painful. Their food was limited, and their confinement threatened to be mentally and physically debilitating.

At the conclusion of the fourth day, as night fell and the island darkness engulfed the harbor, the black bearded jailer opened a fresh cask of Jamaica rum, and in a show of presumed friendship, offered to share the elixir with Robert and the captain. The captain readily joined the guard in the libation, while Robert barely sipped. Later into the night, having not let up in his enjoyment of the rum, the intoxicated jailer slumped from his guard post, sliding down onto the jail's stone floor. There he lay in a stupor, his body propped awkwardly against the cell door.

They waited, observing the now-snoring guard. Convinced he was out cold, Robert stretched his arm through the bars. After trying several times twisting and turning his arm, he was finally able to get his fingers on the chain of keys and pull it back through the bars. Extracting the brass cell key from the jailer's belt, he quickly let himself and the captain out of the jail into the freedom of the dark night. The captain, fairly well inebriated, stumbled after Robert who, moving at a more rapid pace, soon left the captain behind.

Robert ran as fast as he could along the quayside. Seeing a flickering light up ahead, he realized it was from a lantern on a ship anchored farther along the dock. Robert urged himself onward and was soon at the ship's gunwale. Peering aboard, he saw the Watch and called out, asking when the ship was sailing. Being told they were leaving on the high tide, Robert hurtled the gunwale. Aboard, he asked to speak to the captain, who, as the Watch pointed, was on deck. Looking up, in the dim light against the stars, Robert made out the captain strolling back and forth and glancing from time to time up into the sky, admiring the stars shining from above on this peaceful cloudless night.

Robert moved rapidly up to the captain and introduced himself as a merchant trader from Philadelphia who had been apprehended by pirates, but had escaped the harbor prison. The captain seemed friendly, congratulating Robert on his escape. In their ensuing conversation, Robert learned that the captain was a man named Roland Clividen, who was originally from Liverpool. Under the magical starlight, amid sips of rum, the two Liverpudlians found much about which they could converse.

Invited into the captain's quarters to share his ale and food, a less hungry Robert soon inquired, "What cargo have you loaded on board, Sir?"

Captain Clividen referred to his manifest and reported, "Gunpowder from France, flour also, and several crates of china from Holland, you know, the blue and white Delft tiles and dishes."

"Gunpowder!"

"Yes. We are calling at Hispaniola—there is slave unrest there and a slave revolt is feared."

"So I have heard." Robert asked, "If the gunpowder is for the slaves, who is paying for it?"

Captain Clividen consulted his documents. "A partnership of Dutch merchants in Amsterdam. As I am sure you are aware, the

Dutch want to assure their full independence from Spain. Given their sympathy with others who are revolting from oppressive powers, these open-minded benefactors are backing any group who dreams of freedom. In this case, it is the slaves on French Hispaniola."

Robert mused, "Slaves revolting...."

"Frightening, is it not?"

Robert agreed. "I have heard of the Stono Rebellion, was it not so called?"

Captain Clividen unfurled a map and pointed to Charleston, South Carolina. "Yes, as I recall, it was Portuguese-speaking slaves from the African Kingdom of Kongo back around 1739."

"The result was not good for anyone."

The captain nodded. "Both slaves and owners were killed—a lot of each. It is said that some slaves escaped to freedom in Spanish Florida. But their rebellion did influence the South Carolina Assembly to pass a law protecting slaves from harsh treatment, but of course not emancipating them, that's for sure."

"Same result is surely in line for this nascent rebellion for which you have the gunpowder, would you not say?"

Captain Clividen shrugged his shoulders. "Maybe. Anyway, the Dutch are paying me in florin coin to deliver the gunpowder to a secret hideaway in a remote port in case the slaves do rise up, which they say they are likely to do once the French troops leave, which, I hear, is expected to happen soon."

Robert reflected. "My partners own five slaves. I do not own any as yet. I have not given much thought to a slave revolt. If it were to happen where I come from...well, there would be panic in the streets."

"Tell me, Mr. Morris, what do you really think of such a slave revolt?"

Robert acknowledged that he had not thought much about the slavery question, only that on occasion slaves were a ship's cargo, and cargo meant profit.

Captain Clividen mused, "I wonder what is in the mind of the slaves we load on board in that port in Africa and deliver either to one of these Caribbean islands, or to Savannah, or one of the ports farther north."

"Did you ever ask a slave? Or one of the plantation owners, or his overseer who bought the Negros in the slave market? The overseers can be cruel, so I have heard listening to tavern talk."

Captain Clividen replied, "Slaves don't speak our language, well, maybe some do speak a little French, or possibly some Portuguese. It depends on where in Africa they come from, and which tribal chief sold them to one of the European buyers." Downing more ale, the captain added, "All I know is that the unfortunate lot are confined for weeks down in the dank hold of a slave ship. God, it must be awful for them. How do they endure? You and I would not last in such circumstances. You know, if I were one of them—heaven forbid—I would try, once on land, to escape. I would try to organize others to unite and stage a revolt. That is why, Sir, I am in sympathy with the Dutch group." He paused. "Still, word is that God did not imbue this slave lot with the skills to organize and lead others. Rarely on their own have they tried to rally the troops, as the English would say. Except, of course for that time in Charleston. Now there may be this revolutionary attempt on Hispaniola."

Robert downed his ale and directed a different question, "After Hispaniola, to what port are the flour and Dutch china going?"

Captain Clividen's expression showed surprise. "Why do you ask? Is it that you want to come along?"

"More than that," Robert's mind charged forward. He was quick to propose, "I want to buy your entire cargo."

Surprised, the captain exclaimed, "But it is already paid for."

"Not at the higher prices I can get in Philadelphia."

The captain stared quizzically at Robert.

Robert's tone was conspiratorial, yet strategized to entice the captain. "I shall make it worth your while, Captain Clividen. So that you can still honor your commitment to the Dutch merchants."

"But what about my promise to supply the slaves in their possible revolt in Hispaniola?"

At that, Robert puzzled about the Negro slave dissidents on that large island, but only briefly, then explained, "Gunpowder is sorely in demand in the Colonies. We have no factories with the capability to make gunpowder in any quantity for our flint-loaded rifles. In addition, flour is in short supply and, as such, quite dear. Moreover, wealthy plantation owners in Virginia and Carolina, along with our merchant friends in Pennsylvania, crave the blue and white Dutch china to be set out on their dinner tables to impress their important guests with their cultural acumen. These buyers will pay any price to exhibit such social prestige to society."

The Captain waited, his thick eyebrows raised, mulling over and then anticipating his new role, or so Robert deduced as he commented further, "As to the slave cause, Captain, I say we call in at that remote port on Hispaniola, unload a third of the gunpowder for the revolutionaries to stockpile, then sail for Philadelphia. I will see to it that you get a nice commission for your cooperation once my trading house of Willing and Son sells all the cargo on board."

The captain, so Robert discerned in his body language and facial expressions, was becoming entranced with the proposed scheme. Robert sweetened the pot with, "And then, Captain Clividen, my firm will buy your ship and agree to hire you to captain future merchant voyages."

Captain Clividen was silent, surveying Robert. "How do I know if I can I trust you, Mr. Morris?"

His gaze intent, Robert said, "You have my word, which I give with honest sincerity."

His gaze locked on Robert, Captain Clividen no longer hesitated. He said with avowal, "With that assurance, I will indeed trust you, Sir."

With gusto, Robert thrust his tankard upward, as did the captain, in a deal-making toast.

High tide nigh, the two new sailing chums, their refilled tankards in hand, went on deck to supervise the casting off. Toasting again their newly-crafted deal, the two watched the port disappear, now lost in the dim horizon as the warm gentle night breeze allowed the ship to sail off across the Caribbean, its newly charted course guided by the array of stars shining down on them from the heavens.

*    *    *

Back in Philadelphia, Charles Willing and Thomas waxed ecstatic about Robert having gained his release from the Caribbean jail. They were even more excited about Robert having acquired the sloop's cargo as they anticipated the profits for which he was the architect and which the firm promptly realized.

Together with the partners, Robert entered the City Tavern feeling proud of his successful escapade. To his surprise, Charles Willing rose for a toast as Thomas proclaimed, "Tonight I stand to salute young Robert Morris—the newest partner in our firm—henceforth to be known as Willing & Morris!"

"Hip, hip, hooray!" came the duo exclamation from father and son. Eagerly Robert joined in the second round of celebration as the tavern's clientele stood to toast and join the loud hoorays.

# CHAPTER FIFTEEN:
## SHIP FEVER AND THE FUTURE

L ate one night, Thomas Willing burst open the wooden door that cordoned off Robert Morris' modest in-town living quarters, which also served as his office tucked away in the rear of the firm's quayside warehouse.

Working intently at his green felt-covered table, Robert looked up in alarm at the interruption. What sound dare break the supreme silence of a man contemplating and then making entries in his leather-bound ledger book? Other than the delicate scratch of a quill pen entering one number after the other, except in his calculating mind, silence prevailed. That is, until now. With dismay dominating his voice, Thomas blurted, "Charles—my dear father—has just died!"

Robert jumped to his feet, exclaiming, "Thomas, what are you saying?"

His voice dripping with emotion, Thomas said, "Charles contracted that dread ship fever. Yesterday...just yesterday. He became ill." He repeated with incredulity, "That was just yesterday. And now he is...." Thomas' voice choked. Silence conveyed his grief.

Stunned, Robert reflected, "The fever has been spreading—comes ashore from arriving ships. I remember during my long crossing how the frigate became so filthy. It gets so bad that the disease spreads. Then, at dockside, the plague-like sickness is carried on to land. Healthy people in town catch it. Ship fever can kill." Robert stopped short, aware of his insensitive summary. Apologetically he said, "I am sorry, Thomas. The disease is vicious. Our population is being decimated." He reflected, "How could your father contract it? He is...was...so young and healthy."

Thomas shook his head. "The disease knows no logic. It is not compassionate or respectful of its victim's age or position in society."

Robert nodded. "There was no warning? Just this evening?"

"I have come from his bedside. The sickness can consume a person rapidly, as it did with my dear father."

From his own experience with his father's death, Robert said, "Death is so unwelcome, always, and so difficult to understand, always."

Silence pervaded the room as the two young men, standing in stunned states of mind, searched for some semblance of solution to life's ultimate mystery.

In the numbness of the moment, Robert's thoughts began to survey his own future, a future without the revered Charles Willing. Puzzling as to what course might be ahead for the partnership and for himself, Robert realized how much he had come to treasure his bond with father Charles and son Thomas. His relationship had grown stronger over time and was now, he felt, even more solid. With Charles' passing, the bond between himself and Thomas had become a necessary kinship, more so at this moment than earlier that same day.

Observing Robert's reflective demeanor, Thomas firmly placed his hands on Robert's shoulders. Eyes sparkling with conviction, the young man spoke with authority. "Robert, now this day, with the death of my father, it is you and I, the two of us together. Forthwith, we are to be equal partners running the firm."

Softly Robert repeated, "The two of us?" Recalling their different social status, he said, "But, Thomas, you are the one with the formal education. Your esteemed family made sure you went to Watts Academy, which is, so I hear, the finest preparatory school in England. It is you who have been welcomed into the exclusive Inner Temple of the Inns of Court in London. Those appointments are for men of the times who are at the pinnacle of the English legal esteem. I have been told that the Inns are considered 'the third university after Oxford and Cambridge.' Some say it has been that way since the Magna Carta."

"Yes, that is the English custom. So, it was natural that here in Philadelphia I was selected to be a justice on the Court of Common Pleas."

"What a splendid blue-blooded English heritage you bring to the people of Philadelphia!" Robert went on, "As such, you are experienced in the English practice of concealing your emotions, expressing them in drink and in song instead, but never revealing your personal feelings." Robert paused. "Tell me, honestly, do not your credentials allow you to feel superior, for instance, above me in social status? Given your attributes, Thomas, how can you and I be equal in anything, let alone partners in business?" Robert watched his partner's facial expression. "Thomas, I do not really know how you feel, deep down, about our business relationship."

In the momentary silence, Robert reflected that during their business dealings, Thomas seldom laughed. In fact others were known to observe that each of them, in the seriousness of their business dealings, appeared intense, exuding a no-nonsense demeanor. To their fellow Colonists, it had become apparent that business matters held priority in their minds and their actions.

Thomas smiled, his father's death not quelling his response to Robert's concerns. "Acceptance in the New World, Robert, is measured by a man's ideas, by a man's work ethic, a man's determination to get ahead, his desire to conquer the unknown, whether it be this vast unexplored land or the many business opportunities it offers." Thomas looked intently at Robert. "The past is the past. It is behind us, along with outdated and restraining cultural practices of the Old World. Now is the now, the present, our present, in which you and I need to look forward to our respective futures."

"If I hear your correctly, Thomas, you are saying that it makes no difference that I do not have comparable education or social credentials, and that I do not have the connections in which your prominent family basks throughout the Colonies?"

"That is exactly what I am saying. Let us leave Old England behind. That is what almost every Colonist who has come here is doing. It is exactly that motivation that the ruling class back in England—to which I would still belong had I not come here—does not understand."

"So, the fact that I am only twenty-three, and you are three years my senior and..." He looked up into Thomas' face... "and an inch taller makes no difference?" Robert's fist aimed playfully into his new partner's soft merino wool coat.

Feigning defense by moving a step backward, Thomas was quick to retort, "All well and good, but to me and to most people these social positions in the community make no difference between you and me in this partnership of ours."

"Not to belabor the point, Thomas, do you not believe that when someone of prominence, someone with your poise, for example, advances an idea or advocates a plan, they are respectfully listened to? Their words, spoken in the cultured dialect of upper class England, enjoy more credence than if, say, one of the lesser people in town, such as myself, advances the same or similar idea or plan, and speaks, as I believe I do in the dialect of Colonial newness, perhaps refined a bit, or so I would hope, from the language of the docks of Liverpool."

Thomas shook his head negatively. "Robert, it is you who has the extraordinary imagination, the gift of creativity, that conceptual understanding of finance that is needed in our firm and that, so I predict, is sorely needed by America if we are to realize and prosper, given the God-given destiny inherent in this new land. Robert, your prestige among the Colonists is recognized. You are right up there in admiration with Alexander Hamilton, even our beloved Ben Franklin."

To himself, Robert thought, "No wonder 'Old Square Toes,' as he is affectionately known around town, gets elected to public office. He could convince anyone about any subject, given the magic of his vocal charisma."

Thomas said, "Think about Alexander Hamilton. He is a little guy, barely five feet, so I wager. Truth be told, he is an immigrant from the miserable little island of Nevis, with dubious family roots. Some say he is not even sure who his father is. To all those presumed negatives, I say rubbish!"

Robert suggested, "If this were England, you would judge him by tried-and-true Old Europe standards. Hamilton would get nowhere in that structured society. He would never become, as he has here, an integral part in a new vision of finance. As do we, he advocates a national bank, a national treasury, and for the people to have a say as to who is at the helm of government and how a country is to be governed."

Thomas said, "And do not forget, you and I want to maximize our fortunes."

Robert smiled in agreement. "Hamilton advocates individual freedom, which I interpret to mean the freedom to accumulate wealth—the freedom to determine personal destinies. Is not that what we are talking about? Ours is a philosophy of individualism, not of mass pluralism, in which everyone's participation and reward are equal."

The two reflected silently, Thomas seeming to focus on his late father's ideals. "Individualism...it is our credo. It is to be you and me. Against the world, if you want to look at it that way. We are to be equal commercial partners. It is incumbent upon us to legalize our pact. This firm is to be as much your success as mine. My father, who admired you greatly, would want it to be so—you and me, together in the firm of Willing & Morris."

His attention switching to his own future, Robert smiled acceptance. In a tone of sincerity he said, "Thomas, I solemnly promise to do my best for the firm."

"Our firm, Robert!" Thomas appended, underscoring the word our. "In the course of conducting our partnership's mercantile business, we will do our best for the Colonies. And for our American Revolution. Each is in our own best interest."

"That is, if revolution is indeed the only option open to us."

# CHAPTER SIXTEEN

## Mary White – "Molly"

*"In lovely White's most pleasing form,*
*"What various graces meet!*
  *"How blest with every striking charm!*
  *"How languishingly sweet!"*

*—Excerpted from an 1877*
*family eulogy written by an heir*

Babes are beautiful, and so was "Molly," exceptionally so. From her birth in 1749 and ongoing. Not the first or the last of siblings born to Maryland landowner, Colonel Thomas White and his wife Esther, she came to be affectionately known as "Molly" when, at age 20 she and Robert Morris, age 35, were married.

*        *        *

## Her Mother's Guidance

Mary White had grown up in comfort in a socially important Colonial home of style, to become regarded as outstanding among the young women who could be seen and admired at the social engagements attended by British officers, Colonial merchants, religious figures, attorneys, and other influential people.

While still a toddler, mother Esther began to educate her in the social graces. It must always be that her dresses were elegant, of the latest style from England, her manners practiced, her language cultured in the Philadelphia intonations in order to rid her conversations of any possibly acquired backwoods dialects. "After all," her mother explained to her blooming coming-of-age daughter, "a Philadelphia woman today will be judged by her manner of speech and by any number of strict social standards."

Mary's older brother, William, was a respected elder in the Anglican Church, Britain's official religion that, in these revolutionary times, was becoming known in the Colonies as the American Episcopal Church. Despite the English church's efforts to establish an Anglican Bishopric in Philadelphia, the attempt foundering as the Colonial churches' financial and doctrinaire support from the mother country eroded in direct proportion to the rising rumors of revolution, which, so William came to suggest, was yet another reason to seek independence from England and its religious dominance.

Apart from Esther's counsel on a woman's role in the Colony, brother William took on the assignment of overseeing Mary's upbringing, contending to their parents that it was his responsibility as her educated older brother, beyond theirs as parents, to enhance his sister's education. Inasmuch as there were no schools for young women in the Colonies, William instructed Mary in writing and skills that he deemed important, enabling her to stand out from most of the young women of the day who remained uneducated. Her brother's tutelage instilled in Mary a basic literary understanding of the fiction and non-fiction writings of the day, plus the classics of the past, and of course, the deep-rooted elements of the White family's Colonial Episcopal religion.

On the verge of her debut into Philadelphia society, seated at her writing desk, her blonde locks flowing over her shoulders in a cascade of comeliness, Mary took up her quill pen and dipped it into her reservoir of black ink. This was the day for her, and she was ready to transcribe her mother's guiding words, which were to be laced with propriety and were now duly forthcoming. She readied her sheet of rare parchment, given to her by her mother, who had noted, "The British keep paper making in England, depriving us of mills." She had then asserted, "That is another reason for our independence—so that with it we can go through the laborious, but important, process of manufacturing our own parchment."

This morning, in attentive response to her mother's words, Mary wrote:

"Dress properly at every social occasion where you will be noticed and where you may meet people of importance in our society. Your outfit must always represent the latest style.

"Dance and music. You must know the correct steps that are in vogue. You must have a melodic feel for the music and know the titles, as well as the pace of each piece.

"Your learned manners must be apparent to all. As your husband's wife, you must conform to the accepted way of hosting guests in your home, whether in the parlor or at the dinner table."

"Or in my bridal bedroom?" Mary wanted to ask, but refrained, as her mother was going on with: "Language. Express yourself in the manner of the gentry, the cultured ways of the best people of society, whether from England or here in the Colony. Most importantly, eschew slang. Do not allow yourself to pick up crude frontier dialects or local Indian sayings.

"Grace must be evidenced in your actions, not conceit, not confrontation, only gracious sweetness. Yet do not disdain from speaking your mind if and when a special occasion arises wherein you would be untrue to yourself and to your beliefs by refraining from contributing your thoughts to the conversation.

"You need to learn needlepoint, and remember the beauty of your womanly person. Regularly, you must apply rouge and makeup, but not in excess. Humility and beauty go hand in hand.

"Entertainment in the parlor and during dinner. Always encourage others to speak by posing your well-composed questions to them in your sweet and sincere voice. Guests are present to express themselves, so encourage them to make known their bravado. Do not interfere in what they are saying, so that you, as the gracious hostess, carry out your role. But if they should ask personal questions about you, reply to them gracefully and quickly, before shifting the conversation back to them and asking about one or more of their accomplishments. Follow up by inquiring about their thoughts on what, to them on the particular occasion, are pressing matters of importance to them and to the other guests, and yes, to the Colonies.

"Your personal belongings, the things with which you surround yourself in your home, when you marry, in what will be your husband's home, must be of the finest craftsmanship, the best cloth, and the most appropriate to enhance your husband's image and reputation."

Finished writing on her stationery, Mary thanked her mother and asked, "But, Mother, when and where will I meet this handsome man, this mystery male, who may possibly become my husband?"

"Soon, My Dear. Brother William has someone dashing in mind. He has met him through the Church." The mother added with emphasis, "You do realize, Mary, your dear brother is to be appointed America's first Episcopal Bishop."

"That is nice for William," Mary politely commented. "But, Mother, who is this man my brother wants me to meet. He must be important if William knows him. Is he a suitor? What do you think, Mother?" From her mother's knowing smile, Mary's hope for matrimony rose.

"You may have seen him at service on Sundays when our family was seated in our private box at the front of the sanctuary."

Mary admitted, "I do observe the men, hoping something might develop with one of the most eligible among them. Please, Mother, tell me his name?"

Her mother smiled. "His name is Robert Morris. He is a wealthy merchant, a trader in goods, an owner of ships—"

"—Robert Morris!"

In unconstrained excitement, the daughter dropped her quill pen and threw her arms around her mother in a filial embrace.

# CHAPTER SEVENTEEN:
# COURTSHIP AND MARRIAGE

The blossoming array of Colonial flowers in the garden outside St. Peter's Episcopal Church contrasted with the pure stark white of the waist-high wood panels delineating the private boxes for Philadelphia's prominent worshipers in the sanctuary's interior. The White Family's box, so labeled for their exclusive occupancy, its location closest to the Christian cross behind and above the pulpit, affirmed the family's importance in the ranks of society.

At this Sunday's service, as was usual, Robert Morris found a seat toward the rear in those pews designated for yet unmarried men. Apart from feeling obliged to participate in the dutiful dogma of the service, he had come with one objective in mind: to see once again and this time talk in a more serious vein with Mary White. As luck would have it, he had entered the chapel at the same time as the members of the White Family. Passing beneath the stately entry arch, he had tipped his tri-cornered hat to bid a good morning to her. He smiled warmly. Mary returned his smile with alluring feminine tact. In fact, to his delight, they shook hands, she gently, he firmly. Appropriately, he had also shaken hands with her brother William, the two exchanging firm and sincere greetings. Yes, Robert vowed, this was to be the day, the Big Day for him.

William's sermon came after the singing of the hymns—and with each hymn he could detect her lilting voice floating his way like a seductive message. He could hear it even amidst the singing congregation, in the same way it had reached his ears on those many previous Sundays during the last year since he had become interested in Mary. And then, this morning, so he recalled, had come those welcome Sunday dinner invitations to their home. But not, he regretted, an invitation to sit with the family in their church's private box.

In his sermon, William, the newly appointed Bishop of the Colonial Episcopal Church, called upon the parishioners, along with every citizen in Philadelphia, to converse with each other, especially man and wife, but also, he said, should the governed and the governing converse. Not to forget that the Colonials and the British should talk to each other, as well. He concluded with, "Through our expressing ourselves and listening to others, will we exchange ideas and better come to know and understand each other."

After the benediction, eloquently delivered by William, the congregation filed outside into the warm Sunday air. Moving adroitly in the crowd, Robert gently touched Mary's elbow and suggested they talk in the garden. There, to his embarrassment, with beads of sweat forming on his brow, he whispered to her, "I have something important I wish to discuss with you, Miss White."

Amidst the flowering and fragrant garden, she whispered back, "Oh, Robert, please call me Mary."

Under the sweet apple blossoms overhead, Robert said, "Mary...and I can't help it, but I want to call you "Molly...."

She laughed. "I like that better," she said. Her quiet laugh further excited him.

Robert could not take his eyes off her lips. He leaned closer, she not moving away. Albeit briefly, their lips met. Then again, their bodies now closer, now lingering, looking into each other's eyes, they stood together, there in the church garden in the warmth of the Philadelphia spring.

Still close to Mary, Robert, his voice at first faltering, then steadying into male strength, gazed into her brown eyes and said sincerely, or so he hoped, "Molly White, I would like it very much— that is, I will be the happiest man in the Colony, if you will consent to be my wife."

Molly White, looking into his blue eyes, said with equal sincerity, "Yes, I will, Robert Morris, I will be equally happy to be your loving wife."

Robert kissed Molly, and she him. Moments later, she said, "You must ask my father for his consent."

A tender kiss later, he said, "I have done so, and Mr. White gave me his permission to ask you here this morning."

*       *       *

As the attractive and gracious young wife of a man who was rapidly joining the exclusive group of wealthy Colonial merchants, Molly Morris became a role model for Colonial women in every social, ethnic, and religious group.

In addition to the commitment to her marriage and eventually to their seven children, Molly exhibited a contagious female strength that helped fuel the breadth of the manifesto of American continental destiny. Or so Robert, in her praise, often told his business associates, who, in their elite male circles, came to acknowledge Molly's social importance.

Not long after the wedding, over tea, brother William said, "Sister, it is being whispered about that you have become the wealthiest woman in all of the Colonies."

Molly replied, "But how is such trivial information relevant to our Colony and our American Revolution?"

"After church service, when members of my congregation gather, it is the time and place where significant information is exchanged. It is also important to both you and Robert, for the defining personal trait of wealth adds to the esteem to which you each are held in our Philadelphia social circles. In other words—"

"—What does my supposed wealth have to do with matters that, I am sure, are much more important."

"Such as?"

Molly replied quickly, "The status of our Colony, the talk of independence—those are the really important matters, are they not?"

"Yes, and you fit into them."

"But how?"

"It is your husband's reputation. His word. His honor. For he must raise money, and on occasion pledge his own credit to buy supplies and gunpowder for our brave fighting soldiers."

"Yet, I do not understand, William. I have heard Robert say that few merchants will accept paper script."

"I predict that one day that script will be valuable—worth real money."

"But not now. Robert tells me that in Philadelphia alone there are so many different types of engraved paper notes circulating in the merchant trade that many times he does not know whom to pay with which kind of note. He says some merchants demand only silver or gold. Yet he says hard coin is not easy to come by."

"The church accepts everything," William said, smiling. "Anything deemed to be coin of the realm: especially British pounds, but even French livres, Dutch florins, Spanish reales, and even the paper currencies of several of the Colonies, though each can fluctuate in value from one day to the next." William went on, "Then there are bills of exchange, promissory notes drawn by merchants or even by a factor—drawn against a distant creditor, usually across the Atlantic. You can see how complex trade is."

"Then how do you measure this wealth concept you ascribe to me? In what form of this so-called money is this presumed wealth of mine being calculated?"

"Here in the New World there are no banks, as in London, Liverpool, or Paris. Without commercial banks, merchants rely on loans from distant trading houses. As Robert says, it can take up to 90 days—often as long as a year—for a merchant or a factor to receive payment."

"How then does he manage?"

"Your husband leverages."

Bewildered, Mary asked, "How does that work? I mean, he has to make a lot of money, does he not, to maintain our lifestyle?"

"And to help support the Church." William smiled and went on, "In using leverage, Robert borrows funds today based on monies due him in the future, monies that will likely not be paid for months, but for which the parties involved have excellent reputations for paying. Leverage and reputation go hand in hand."

Mary poured them each a second cup of her tea from India.

William sipped and said, "In the final analysis, I say wealth today lies in assets such as land, one's beautiful personal possessions, a stately house like yours and the finely crafted furniture plus the paintings—oil portraits on canvas by Elouis or Peale, good wine and spirits, tailored dresses, and especially your handsome carriage and the horses."

"Slaves, too?" Molly asked.

William's slow nod revealed reluctaance. "Only two," he said softly.

Mary said, "Well, if people want to talk about me, maybe spread rumors, I cannot control them. Instead, I wish they would talk about how to help Robert pay the troops, buy the supplies and pay for all the vital guns and ammunition General Washington needs for our military men."

William looked worried. "Yes, you are right." Changing the subject, he said, "Mary, I am so proud of you. Your marriage to Robert has worked out splendidly. Here we are, the two of us enjoying tea in The Hills, your splendid country estate overlooking the capital city of the Colonies."

Mary looked at the portrait-in-progress of Robert Morris she had commissioned Elouis to paint and proudly smiled.

# CHAPTER EIGHTEEN:
# THE MERCENARY MAJOR MEETS MORRIS

Major Wilhelm von Lowenstein had been advised by Dr. von Hogarth that Robert Morris would be expecting him at an exact time on a day certain at the center point of Philadelphia revolutionary life, the City Tavern. Arriving and removing his greatcoat, which covered his military dress uniform for protection from possibly hostile crowds while walking the Philadelphia streets, the Major made certain his uniform displayed its salad of military ribbons garnished with his collection of Hessian campaign medals. He asked the barmaid, Betsey, to hasten him away to a secluded table upstairs in order to assure privacy for what he hoped would be an intimate meeting replete with revealing conversation, per orders from his far-away Landgraf. He waited impatiently for the arrival of his target—the American Revolutionary leader.

The Major seemed unable to help himself as, in his trained military manner, he acted confrontationally after Betsey's introduction. Not waiting for the disengagement from the obligatory male handshake and disdaining the niceties of gentlemanly conversation, he plunged right in, challenging the Revolutionary. "Mr. Morris, Sir, please tell me why you dare remonstrate against your sovereign king, your God-ordained ruler?" Not waiting for a reply, he fired a second volley. "You do believe in God, don't you? And in His right to rule by selecting rulers for His people?" The buttons on the Major's Hessian uniform vibrated with vehemence as, still standing, he clicked his heels together in military manner, signifying his readiness for combat and willingness to address any situation presented, be it physical or verbal.

Yet, internally, his doctor's mind battled his verbiage, negatively critiquing his outbursts. His trained medical mind advised, "You are not going to get into Morris' mind with this tack of questioning. Instead, you will be the target in his retaliatory anger's line of sight."

Startled at the Major's confrontational opening, Morris concluded the Major was egging him on in order to evince a range of illegal reactions. He feared that, in his tirade, the military man was trying to trick him into firing back in language the Major, and/or the British, could some day hold against him. It could be that he wanted to give the British evidence at what would turn out to be his sham trial for treason, or for when the Major returned to Hesse-Kassel to prove to his fellow military men the mental incompetence of a Revolutionary, or perhaps he wanted to justify the many mercenaries in their mission helping the British wipe out what, from their perspective, was the Colonies' rebellion against royalty and, looking through the traditional European lens, a heretical act against God Himself.

The Major, appearing unable to vary from his conversational maneuver, despite his own mental warnings, waited for Morris' reply, anticipation evident in his back and forth body sway, his raised eyebrows and his nervously twitching upper lip. As if anticipating Morris' words, he appeared ready and willing to fire off yet another verbal round.

Instead, the Major's inner voice prevailed, and he delivered a friendlier message in a more cordial tone. "Sir, it is my pleasure to meet you. I hope to elicit your views in depth, as the two of us come to know one another."

Given the cue, Morris replied, "Major von Lowenstein, Sir, in respect to you carrying a pass signed by my friend and colleague, General George Washington, it is my pleasure to welcome you to Philadelphia." He motioned for the Major to sit. Now, across the table, the Major surveyed the Revolutionary as Betsey served two tankards brimming with the cider of the house. She said, "Gentlemen, as a woman concerned for the people of Pennsylvania, I hopes you will begin with a toast, not to war but to peace."

The Major was startled. Morris winked at Betsey. The two men promptly followed her wish, toasting each other and then peace.

Morris asserted, "If, as you say, Sir, God is the deity ruling the high seas of American commerce, then He, along with his chosen English King have got it all wrong. We good Colonial people simply wish to be allowed to lead our lives in peace, pursuing the New World's economic opportunities, while adhering to our societal duties as his majesty's loyal citizens."

"Citizens! Not subjects?" Between his teeth the Major exhaled a whistling sound, a German scorn understood in Hesse-Kassel as a rebuke of someone's statement.

Ignoring the rebuke, Morris went on, "I ask you, Major, to bear in mind that King George III has declined to heed each written and reverently transmitted remonstrance. Nor does he respond other than with more military force, including another shipload of your mercenary countrymen. While some in Parliament do argue on behalf of our cause, the majority in that elected body has voted to impose tariffs, taxes, and regulations that crimp our commerce. Further they authorized the Royal Navy to blockade our ports and board our ships. Moreover, the King continues to tell the world we are in revolt. But, Sir, I can advise you that we are not."

To his surprise, Morris saw the Major taking notes on a folio sheet with a quill pen, which he had extracted from his jacket in company with a small container of ink. Not hesitating, Morris went on, "Please tell me, Major, how else we here in the Colonies might act in advocating our position and protecting our interests other than what we have so far done?"

The Major was quick to retort, "Remember, Sir, your milita fired on British troops at Lexington and Concord, killing many."

Morris interjected, "But it is not clear, Sir, who fired the first shot heard 'round the world on that landmark day."

Ignoring the remark, the Major said, "Then came your Continental Congress. And you recruited farmers to bear arms and fight the lawful soldiers of the British Army. You appointed officers in a newly formed militia and voted one among you as the general in charge. You fired on British ships and, disguised as Indians, boarded their East India Company frigate in Boston Harbor and tossed the tea. Is that not a revolution, Sir? Such are clearly not acts of fealty to your rightful ruler."

To Morris' surprise, the Major stopped talking. He raised his tankard, "Skoal." As a surprised Morris slowly raised his glass, the military man said, "I salute you, Sir." He waited. "My dear Mr. Morris, I have come here to look into what is in your mind, Sir. I want to know what goes on up there..." he pointed to his own head… "that compels you to carry out these bellicose acts. Please explain to me your thinking. More, Sir, please tell me your thoughts about events that have taken place?"

"Why?"

"I must learn and try to understand what is in your mind."

In changing shades of dismay and disbelief, Morris stared at the Major. After a moment, he said, "You and I, Sir, do not agree on divine prerogative and, I suspect, on the scope of our Colonial rights."

"Forget these disagreements, Sir. I have not come all this way to debate you. Instead, I want to know what is really, deep down, in your mind. I want to learn about your passions of the soul, as Descartes described it, what has come to be called emotions."

Their glasses met in an ephemeral moment, a clink of male connection being expressed. The Major said, "That is my assigned mission, my orders from my Landgraf, as well as my Hessian general in Trenton." He tipped his tankard, drank, and said, "By the way, or perhaps you are already aware that your sovereign, King George III, is my Prince's nephew."

"All in the family," Morris chuckled derisively at the genealogical links connecting the many rulers who, apparently by God's grace, were in charge of world governance.

The Major countered, "But, Sir, you must acknowledge that our royal system—the entire world's, in fact—is orderly. Every subject knows who is next in line to be in charge of a country or a principality. The rules of bloodline ascension to power, as ordained by the Almighty, are accepted by everyone from peasant to nobility. An ordinary person can be about their business, their farm, their shop, their profession without having to worry about who is going to be their leader, today or tomorrow."

"Until palace intrigue casts doubts, and some dissident relative emerges and connives for the crown."

"And is usually sent to the Tower, or—"

"—Murdered."

The Major smiled. "Even so, tell me, Sir, is there not a marked advantage of this well established world-wide system of governance that protects one's property over your proposed free-for-all, untried anarchical approach? I mean, the aftermath of your revolution, assuming it is successful, exudes uncertainty, anxiety, fear, and I do not know what else. Our established system means peaceful transition, with wonderful parades, pomp, ceremony, marching bands, while yours is replete with angst, gunfire and death."

"And freedom."

"But, I ask you, Sir, is there really that much difference? In the Old World, we have our nobles, our ruler's trusted advisors, and our property class with its vested interests in the wellbeing of all the people, as well as those nobles in charge of society. Do you not, Sir, have the same arrangement with your revolution? The landed gentry are behind it, and you have chosen a new ruler, a general to whom the nobles extend their loyalty. Now come clean, Sir. What are the differences? I want to know what goes on in your mind that allows you to defy the tried and true customs of centuries?"

Morris did not want to reveal his thoughts. One refrained from showing emotions if one remained true to the image of male steadfastness. Rather than sitting stoically, he said, "Look at it this way, Major, simply by being here and being free, one's 'property' includes one's self. The result is that all people have property— simply for being people, being alive, and being themselves. As such, people are entitled to a say in their governance."

The Major said, "I have observed in your society that the families in charge of affairs—for example, your partner, Thomas Willing, and his relatives have married into other families, as royalty do in Europe. In Philadelphia, they and a finite number of close-knit families own most every business, most every good piece of property, and make up the elders in each of their places of worship. They are the Colonial equivalent of nobles at court, the moneyed class, are they not, Sir?"

A nod from Morris encouraged the Major to go on; yet Morris observed the Major's inner self seemed to be raising caution. He heard the military man say, "But I am doing all the talking. My assignment is to encourage you to talk more deeply. Now, Sir, I am wondering if the structure of society might be irrelevant. After all, this place—this Philadelphia, these Colonies—well, we're in the "New World." In a sincere tone, he added, "Please tell me what you, the Revolutionary, are thinking. That is, if you will be so kind, Sir."

Quickly came Morris' reply: "I think that to your comparisons, there are no answers, for what is taking place here is on the cutting edge of a new mix of society. Ideas that have never before been tried, or even thought of anywhere else on Earth, are in the air here, floating on the breezes of time, activating the minds and hearts of men and women who are basking in fresh thoughts. The outcome, as you suggest, remains as unknown as next week's weather."

"But I want to know whence have come these new ideas?"

"Necessity. Necessity is the mother of new ideas, new explorations by free men. Necessity, because a king and his Parliament have become, and remain, intransient to any correction to their doings, unwilling to undo their judgmental mistakes, unaware of our Colonial society needing redress from ignorance on their part. You see, Sir, that is the trouble with your old established system— there is no available path for correction, other than armed revolution. Here, our Revolution, if that is what you must call it, is not fully developed. Although, I must say it appears to me to be imminent and irreversible. You ask what I think. Some sort of new system is inevitable, given the political, economic and even religious constraints in which we are trapped."

"And your feelings?"

"Mine?" Morris questioned. "Mine have nothing to do with the politics of the Europe I left behind years ago."

"On what, then, do your feelings focus?"

"Feelings?" Morris' impatience with the conversation was growing. He acknowledged that the Major was searching for some explanation of the Revolution, that is, if there really was one. Yet wanting to be gentlemanly, he said, "My focus, Sir, in my mind, is on what I am going to do to take commercial advantage of this seminal situation. Perhaps in preparing a porridge of patriotism, I will help the boil along."

The Major came right back with, "And how do you feel about helping things along?"

"If my fellow men entrust me with assignments to bring in supplies and raise funds to help finance this Colonial endeavor, then I feel as if I am needed. And I do know how to perform the merchant and financial tasks for our cause. I can tell you, Sir, that I feel good about that."

"So, you feel peer acceptance is important over and above a royal top-down acknowledgement—"

"—There is no more top-down as you put it, Sir, for there is no longer a 'top' to look down upon us. Other than God himself. Here in the Colonies, we are forming our own 'top.' If in your culture, you are accustomed to bowing to an age-old so-called 'top,' then you will be uncomfortable remaining in this place once independence is achieved. And I believe it will come sooner or later. When that event occurs, and if you are still clinging to your outdated principles, not willing to march to the fife and drum tune, you will be obliged to return to Germany or move north to Quebec, or south to Spanish Florida. As a Loyalist, you will have become an outcast."

The Major considered Morris' statement and asked, "But who will decide the form of this new government, Sir? Will it not be the landed families—those to whom we would refer as the king's nobles?"

"Yes, of course. They are the ones with the most at stake. It is their properties, their families, their reputations, their wealth, and their standings in the communities."

Their verbal exchange grew silent and the two men sat in silence, sipping the cider, considering what the other had said in response to their remarks. Eventually they rose, shaking hands. The Major clicked his heels. "We must continue our discussion, Sir."

They agreed to meet again, Revolution or not, war or not. And they parted.

# CHAPTER NINETEEN:
# MRS. G

Mrs. Horatio Gates summoned Betsey to her trestle table in the City Tavern. Discreetly she thrust a small leather pouch into the barmaid's hand.

Feeling the coins inside, Betsey said, "Thank you, Ma'am. But what—"

"—I want you to bring that Robert Morris over here and introduce him to me. And then—"

"—Yes?"

"—After tonight, I want you to report to me what he says and what he tells you. Whenever I come into this place, I will expect a full report."

Betsey felt the elegantly clad Mrs. G was demeaning what had become her learned role of getting to know the male patrons—her practice of earning a livelihood. Nevertheless, again fingering the coins, she nodded her agreement.

"Now bring him here!"

Across the large room, as Betsey approached, Morris seemed to be arguing with a man she would label as an "ordinary." She heard him tell the man in a reassuring tone, "You will be paid for your furniture shipment to Martinique when I get paid, but not before. Your craftsmanship is excellent, and our firm has dealt with the buyer before. Their word is good, and so is mine."

The man downed his foaming ale, smiled, and stood. The two men shook. "If I have your word, Mr. Morris—"

"—You do, Sir."

After the man nodded, smiled, bowed slightly and wiped the suds from his mouth and had left, Betsey approached Morris and said,

"That lady over there…" she gestured toward Mrs. G… "wants me to introduce you to her."

Morris looked in the direction and saw an elegantly attired and beautiful woman. Her Negro slave was standing nearby in the shadows. "Who is she, Betsey?"

"Her name is Mrs. G."

He held down her arm as she started to point. Picking up his tankard, he said, "I'll go see her in a moment."

"Now!" Betsey insisted. "Robert, she's some general's wife. She's a very important woman." An agitated Betsey added, "She told me to get you right now!"

Nodding at Betsey, Morris strode over to her table. He bowed slightly and accepted her white-gloved hand in his. Their eyes met. Hands and eyes lingered.

# CHAPTER TWENTY:
# THE STAMP ACT, MORRIS,
# HUGHES, AND FRANKLIN

Benjamin Franklin was trying his best to override the outburst arising against complying with the new Stamp Act passed by Parliament. Agitated, the crowd in the City Tavern had become aware that the cargo of engraved stamps was to arrive on the schooner, Royal Charlotte, which that afternoon had been sighted sailing up the Delaware. The revered elder statesman urged calm to the protests swelling up throughout the tavern. Speaking loudly, yet in a reassuring voice, Franklin advised everyone that the Crown was justified in imposing this ubiquitously applied stamp tax upon the commerce of the Colonists. "It is lawful and right for them to do this," he decreed to the recalcitrant patrons.

When Ben spoke everyone was compelled by respect for the man to listen and usually accept his words of wisdom. "Parliament," Ben went on, "needs to raise money to help recover and today pay for expenses of its army during the French and Indian Wars. The Crown is burdened with the additional costs of quartering its troops in the Colonies for our protection and also—"

Surprisingly to Ben, impatient mutterings growled and quickly grew louder, interrupting his defense of Parliament's Stamp Act.

"—But, Ben, Sir, the soldiers of the British Army have been eating our food and commandeering our living quarters, all against our will."

"—And trying to bed our daughters."

"—Yes, and their officers remain oblivious to our demands for redress from this new tax—these damned stamps."

"—And now we must buy these stamps and paste them on every newspaper, every legal document, every commercial transaction, every book—"

"—And probably on every barmaid...."

Male guffaws reverberated around the drinking establishment. Yet, to Robert Morris observing, the hoots were derisive, not humorous.

"Gentlemen!" Ben called out, his command slowly returning the room to a reluctant silence. "We must respect the authority of the Crown to tax its subjects and support its army and navy—"

"—But, Mr. Franklin, Sir, your friend John Hughes is to receive these stamps when the Royal Charlotte docks. You persuaded the Crown to appoint him to this lucrative distribution position, did you not, Sir?"

Ben nodded. "Yes, I did, Sir."

"Hughes gets a commission for selling each and every stamp, does he not?"

Robert Morris started to explain, "That is the practice in such matters." But he, too, was interrupted.

"—Hughes is going to make each of us buy the stamps and affix them on every document every day."

"—We can't afford to buy the stamps. The law is confiscatory!"

"—I say Hughes is a traitor to our Colony."

"—Yes, let us all march to his house and convince him to burn the crates containing the sheets of stamps once they are trundled off the ship."

"—Or else make him dump the crates into the Delaware like unwanted tea."

"—Yes, and if that fails, then I say we refuse to buy any stamps from Hughes."

"—Or from anyone."

"—And if we are forced to buy them by the British Army, we will refuse to affix them to any document."

"—But let us act first. I say we find and arrest Hughes."

"—I will get the Sheriff!"

"—No time for that. Follow me, men!" cried out a self-assigned leader.

Robert Morris, with alarm, whispered to Benjamin Franklin, "Sir, we had better get this lot under some sort of control or there is going to be bloodshed, maybe even a killing on this night, so I fear."

Franklin nodded agreement and replied, "My dear Robert, there may be violence this night despite our efforts. To my regret, I have just heard that word is spreading across the Colonies. The mass objections are beyond anything I ever dreamed of." Ben appeared dejected. "I assured the Crown that such as this would never happen. And now it has."

Morris said, "I have heard that even British merchants are opposed. For them back in England, as for us here, the stamps will raise the cost of doing business and eat into profits. It is royal interference in our right to conduct commerce."

"Robert, it has now become obvious that I did not think this matter through."

"You, Sir, are not a merchant. I will allow you such a misunderstanding."

Franklin queried, "Must every law and every decision be written from the merchant's point of view?"

"No, Sir, indeed not, as you yourself are proving on both ides of the Atlantic. But as for me, I am a merchant and a man of finance. As such, in my accounting ledgers, legal tender trumps most other considerations."

With vigor, Franklin waved his cane around. With Morris standing by his side, Ben's action and Morris' support proved effective as the crowd's boisterousness bogged down. Calm begat action as Ben said, "Gentlemen, come with me now. With our numbers, we will march to Hughes' house and reason with him. Perhaps, or so I hope, given our steadfast opposition, we will persuade him to delay implementing the law, pending our appeal to Parliament to revoke it."

Reacting to Ben, the crowd began once more to call out with protestations and proposed actions.

"—Tar and feather him first," shouted one. "That way, we will delay the implementation of this onerous Stamp Act."

"—Yes, march him around town so everyone who is against him and the tax can be counted. He'll soon see the magnitude of the merchant opposition."

One man proposed a toast, added to by others and accompanied by unruly shouts sounding like "tar" and then "feather."

"No, no!" Franklin shouted. "Hughes is an honorable man. He will do what he deems best, both for himself and for the Colonies. Trust me, gentlemen."

"—Well, maybe he will and maybe he won't, so let us first

threaten the tar and feather—that way he will come to his senses and do what is best for all of us."

"—And if he does not, well, then bring a bucket of tar and some sticks to start a fire." Commandeering the first barmaid he could find, the man demanded she summon a tavern slave. When the barmaid complied and the slave arrived, the same man, joined by others, issued instructions for the Negro to fetch a pot, a large wad of tar and sticks for a fire, plus bags of feathers.

Morris wanted to intervene, calm the crowd, but by now the night had taken on its own character. His admonishments were drowned out by what by now he feared was an unruly mob.

The ugly punishment of tar and feathers having been arranged, by a mass of voices, the Negro was ordered to follow the men in their march and to carry his bucket and packages. In the ensuing melee, almost in unison, the men upended their tankards and downed what remained of their grog. Fortified, they secured their pistols in their knickers. Then, marching shoulder to shoulder out the door of the City Tavern and into the early evening dimness, the rowdy crowd set off north on Second Street searching for the candlelight shining from Hughes' house. Franklin and Morris led the way.

Not far away, Hughes' three-story brick house loomed like a fortress. Several street-level lighted windows welcomed the crowd with the tease of flickering candlelight. From the crowd, the shouts began.

"Drag him out here!"

"Where is that slave with the tar?"

"What is the Negro's name?"

"'Junior', I think."

"Hey, Junior!"

Repeated summons, but no answer.

One man commented, "Damn those free blacks. Junior must have run away and hid in their secret enclave. I hear it is in a riverbank cave along the Schuylkill."

"Never mind. We will tell Hughes the slave is standing behind us in the dark, waiting to act."

"With black skin, Hughes cannot see him and will never know he may have run off."

In the forefront, Ben Franklin pounded repeatedly on Hughes' entry door with the brass tip of his cane. The door cracked a sliver.

Warily Hughes peered out. Seeing Franklin who had positioned himself at the head of the crowd, Hughes called out in what Morris took as a tone of innocence. "Ben, what is going on? Who are all these men?"

Franklin spoke loudly, "We have come to implore you to wait before you impose the new law and distribute the stamps."

Hughes responded, as if automatically, "You know I cannot do that, Sir. I am empowered—I mean, you secured this appointment for me. The Stamp Act is the law of the land and must be implemented as soon as possible after the Royal Charlotte docks and the stamps are off-loaded."

"But, Mr. Hughes, there is much opposition." Ben gestured at the crowd. "You see all these men here. They are merchants. Every one of them is violently opposed to the law. It is going to tax them dearly. In hindsight, I was too hasty in supporting the act. I now believe the act is a mistake—a grievous error on Parliament's part."

Robert Morris jumped in, shouting at Hughes, "As a merchant, I, too, Sir, am opposed. I implore you to heed the plea of those of us who are in business."

Shouts from the men, as they supported Morris. "Drag him out here!"

Franklin waved his cane, urging quiet. He then addressed Hughes, "Sir, the men gathered here want you to assure us that you will burn the crates of stamps. Or else they propose to tar and feather you right here, right now and march you through the streets."

In a muffled voice, one man quietly asked, "Where is that damned Negro?"

"Nowhere in sight," came the whispered response.

Hughes shut his door. Quickly the candles inside were snuffed. But just as quickly several rocks hit one window allowing the last of the candle smoke to escape. Just as quickly, a man in the crowd lunged against the window, bending the framing muntins and the panes inward, forming a distorted pattern.

From the interior a pistol shot rang out, the pellet whistling over the crowd. In an automatically choreographed movement, the men recoiled backward.

"Next time, I will surely shoot to kill," Hughes bellowed through the broken glass.

Franklin called out, "My good Mr. Hughes, please heed the

demands of the men of Philadelphia and of all Pennsylvania, which is your royally assigned territory for distribution. Do not force the stamps upon us until we—I, and others, have had the opportunity to solicit Parliament for repeal of what I now realize is a most unpopular and oppressive act, both in England and here in the Colonies."

Hughes protested, "What about the commissions I am due to earn from selling the stamps?"

Franklin spoke loudly so all in the crowd could hear. "There are times, Sir, when personal gain must be subordinated to the good of the people. To me, this evening is one of those times. You, Sir, are being asked to make such a sacrifice."

Standing in silence in his open doorway, Hughes seemed to Robert to be thinking the matter over. The crowd, now silent, watched and waited. Hughes looked at Franklin and at Morris, their stern stares seeming to unnerve him. Finally, he nodded and announced to the crowd that he would comply by waiting a reasonable amount of time for the appeal to be submitted to Parliament.

Ben said loudly, "That is good enough for me, if I have your word, Sir."

They all saw Hughes nod in the affirmative.

Cheers rose as the crowd heeded the call from one among them to march forthwith to the nearest drinking establishment to celebrate.

## CHAPTER TWENTY-ONE:
## FEARS OF THE BRITISH

The next meeting of Robert Morris and Mrs. G was arranged by Arnold, her slave, delivering a note to Morris two hours ahead of the appointed time. Then, at precisely noon, her carriage arrived at his warehouse. In their conversation as Arnold drove them to quayside, Morris deduced Mrs. G would be enjoying trying to tease out of him a response to her questions during their time together snuggled inside her luxury carriage.

With a mischievous glint in her eyes, her questions did ensue. "Given your risk-taking position in Colonial society, Robert Dear, what do you fear the most? Is it fear about your life? Or is it fear about commerce? Or is it fear about the Revolution? Perhaps it is the fear of British troops invading and occupying Philadelphia, searching you out and arresting you...to be followed by a quick sham trial and their promptly hanging you from the nearest oak tree? Or is it the savages on some moonless night coming into town from out there on the frontier and mercilessly scalping you? Or would it be the harsh winter with snow banks and ever-present pointed icicles dropping down from off the edge of an overhead eve and slicing into your big head and splashing blood all over your cute sandy curls?" The persistent questioner tittered teasingly as she pressed her finely clad body against the personage of Robert Morris.

Easing away from her ever so slightly, perhaps reluctantly on the velvet seat, Morris thoughtfully sipped from his tankard of cider he had taken from the tavern when Arnold had fetched him for this afternoon's outing. He marveled at how quickly the general's wife had made efforts to pursue their new friendship. The intimacy of a carriage ride, with curtains drawn, assuring their privacy, had at first intrigued him. Yet he was unsure of her motive. To her question, he replied, "Mrs. G, you and your general husband are old friends with the British, so I believe you would intercede on my behalf at the last moment and not allow them to hang me, that is, when and if they do occupy our city and take me prisoner. Would you not do so...rescue me, that is, as I cringed there on the gallows?"

"Only if you are today and continue to be nice to me."

"I am nice to everyone. I do not want to offend—"

"—You are offending your King with your merchant ships supporting the Colonial rebels!" Mrs. G's tone startled Morris. "With every trade you make in your factoring business, with every ship that completes its journey, you are offending the Crown." As emphatic as she stated her case, her voice grew softer and she smiled warmly at him. "Robert, you are English, born in Britain; you are a bloody bloke." She chuckled knowingly, he thought, as she mocked his revolutionary role with her imitated Cockney accent. "I have learned a lot about you, Mr. American Rebel."

Morris clapped his hands together in mock applause. He admonished, "But you do not know anything about my flotilla of ships, to where they are sailing today, or where they are going off to tomorrow, or next month, or whence they have come, nor do you know the cargoes any of them are carrying, outbound or inbound."

Mrs. G held up her index finger and said, "You mean the gunpowder from France you have purchased with your own money for the Colonial militia—"

"—Yes, purchased with my own money, mind you, inasmuch as the Continental Congress has no money." Morris was emphatic. "Moreover, I am taking the risk of my ships being captured by the British Navy."

Mrs. G smiled. "The rest of the details, be assured, Robert, I will find out sooner or later."

"And tell—"

"—The Brits, you bet."

"And they will—"

"—Next time intercept one or more of your ships on the high seas, confiscate your cargo, imprison your captains and, without me there to stop them, hang the ship's crew—in short, I am telling you that the all-powerful British Navy will cut short this silly bound-to-fail Revolution of yours."

Momentarily angered, Morris held his tongue. They sat in silence as Mrs. G's Negro drove the fancy carriage along the cobblestone streets. Robert finally acknowledged, "Yes, Mrs. G, it is not a secret. I am supplying the patriots. It is common knowledge. So what is behind your bringing up the matter now with your harangue of my supposed role in the Revolution?"

She nodded in a petite gesture. Her English designer hat flounced in exclamation as, so it seemed to him, her whole person vibrated with intrigue.

Admiring her body's language, Robert verbally explored, "So, tell me, my pretty lady of prominence, how can you rationalize being a spy for the British, as you rather claim to be...or, really, are you? To me, I think it is a game with you. As a general's wife—and I mean the head Colonial general in this Colony—you enjoy your free passage to rove throughout Philadelphia and, should you wish, explore drinking establishments where you may, yielding to your fancy of the moment, elicit intelligence information from those men who you think are important in social and revolutionary circles. Just by your presence, your dress, your hat, your makeup, your looks, you can attract any man's attention and easily engage him in what might first appear as flippant conversation and then steer the talk to more serious and revealing conversation that may produce what you believe to be vital information that you can then siphon off to your contact with the British—is not that your method?"

She held a white-gloved finger to his lips and smiled sensually. "You have disproved your own statement. You see, I tried with you a moment ago, seeking seriousness, and you dodged and still have not answered my question...ah...my clever and mentally strong Mr. Robert Morris."

He said, "You insist on knowing what I fear most?"

"Yes," she purred. "Tell me."

"Well, Mrs. Gage—"

"—Please, do not say my name out loud. People in Philadelphia—the lowlies—are known to walk alongside a carriage as elegant as mine, hoping to overhear tidbits, start rumors. With the curtains drawn, we never know who is alongside. So, you and I must have an unwritten agreement for secrecy and observe it always."

"Yes, of course, if you so desire. A real man in these Colonies keeps a bond he has entered into. That moral code is inbred in me."

Almost as if a boy reciting for a teacher, or maybe really reciting lessons from his late father, Morris continued, perhaps repeating in learned rote, yet his tone came across as earnest, "Here in the Colonies personal trust is the real king, for trust in the King in London is waning." His clenched fist hit his open palm with mock emphasis. "Trust and one's reputation for keeping one's word, and one's promises in financial matters are beacons lighting the path, sooner or later, for our new America to go forward on its destined course to power and greatness."

"Come off these high and mighty romanticized statements," Mrs. G implored, to his discomfort. "You sound as if you have memorized a mission statement. Tell me, Mr. Merchant, at the end of the day, do you not yearn to become rich and, after that, to become even more wealthy?"

"Richer," he whispered, accenting the second syllable while smiling at her. "As you are well aware, the money-making opportunities here in the New World are phenomenal! This virgin land stretches to the horizon. Ocean commerce is open to us, even across the Pacific to China."

"China?" she exclaimed. "It is on the other side of the world. Your ships have to sail either around Africa or around Cape Horn. Be realistic, Robert Dear, China is too far away for you or any merchant in the Colonies."

"But while it is a great distance away, China is in my plans for a year or so hence. In my vision, I will be the first American merchant to send cargo ships there. The opportunity for a trade windfall is fantastic. That is, for those of us who play the lead in opening up that vast untapped marketplace."

"And if your ships do make it back to Philadelphia, what will you do with your profits? Buy another luxurious carriage to drive around town and back and forth to your Hill House? Perhaps buy another slave or two at the auction on Second Street to drive the carriage? The carriage you have now is…well, so luxuriously appointed…I mean, how can you improve upon it? And the Negro you own is so proper and, well, smart…why…he is like a manservant. What is his name?"

"Johannes. And he is a free black."

As the coach jerked forward, Mrs. G gestured toward her Negro. "My husband bought Arnold a few months ago at the slave auction on Second Street. Horatio boasts to his fellow militia officers that he got a 'real good price'. Named after Benedict, my husband's other favorite Colonial general, that is, after himself, of course."

Morris whispered back, "Why not Benedict?"

She answered, continuing her discreet tone, "Too long. You know these Africans are not that bright, especially with long words." She chuckled as if everyone in the world surely agreed with her. "But I have discovered that our Arnold is brighter than most, the Negroes, I mean. Yes, I do agree with my husband that we got a good buy. Do you know how much slaves are going for these days, what with prices for everything going up here in the Colonies? I mean, you must know...."

"Occasionally my firm does import Negroes from the Caribbean. They are a commodity, like tobacco and rum."

"Yesterday your Johannes gave me a ride back to the outskirts of town where our militia is encamped. Your coachman riding on the back of the carriage was most polite. He is white. But your Negro was so attentive. I felt like a queen."

"Queens are soon to be out of fashion, Mrs. G, if not so already. But, in a different interpretation, you, My Dear, are a royal queen of a more personal sort."

Mrs. G laughed wickedly. "You are a devil." As she spoke, her gloved hand traced the silk interior of the coach.

Noticing her action, pride in his voice, Robert said, "We now have a coach maker here from Germany—no longer must we import the frames, springs and wheels from England. We also have a merchant from one of those Northern Italian cities crafting velvet interiors. I know. I am importing the fabrics he ships from Belgium—the same marketplace those famous tapestries come from."

To him, her smile seemed to betray her admiration. Her voice challenging, she said, "Perhaps with more riches, you might acquire another expensive horse for when you ride around town calling in at the various drinking establishments?" She paused, her voice lowering, more tender he sensed, "So, tell me, Mr. Rich Colonist, in the end, I mean the final end, will you take bundles of bonds, bank notes and coin with you on that day when you ascend into the sacred heaven that hovers in eternal promise above this fertile New World of yours?"

Robert shook his head. "No, Mrs. G, I intend for my wealth, my bank notes, my properties, and my possessions to go to my Molly and our children for their perpetual care and well-being."

"Spoken like a devoted husband. Wish I had such a man."

"You do, Mrs.—"

"—Shh," she shushed.

"I think you are not a British spy. Instead, I am coming to believe you are a member of your General's thought police monitoring the merchants."

Mrs. G said, "Be that as it may, Robert, it is high time you answered my question."

Robert reflected.

Mrs. G said, "I will tell you what my friend, the honorable Edward Bancroft, told me when I posed the same query."

Morris frowned. "He is rumored to be a spy for the British, or so Silas Deane confided to me."

Mrs. G waited.

He looked into her blue eyes and said, "All right, Mrs. G, I will tell you what in these revolutionary times I fear the most."

She looked at him, showing patience.

"I fear my hard-earned wealth being lost, disappearing, evaporating, and me being left poor, destitute, maybe even starving, certainly forgotten, unable to pay my debts, unable to retain my valuable honor, eventually languishing, even rotting in the Prune Street Debtor's Prison."

"Your money all gone," she said softly, almost, so he perceived, as if she were echoing his fears. Then with a hint of a twitter, she said, "Along with your cute little curly head dangling in the hangman's noose?"

Robert Morris rubbed his neck. "No, Mrs. G, I do not fear for my head, but for my family. Wealth is the entry ticket to this vast New World. Wealth is also the passport to pleasurable living. In this land of opportunity, we merchants want to be free from Old England's domination—those restrictive laws and their confiscatory taxation—so that here in America we can accumulate as much wealth as possible."

"On behalf of not only yourself but also the Revolution?"

Robert Morris' nod was delivered most assuredly. He added, "Yes, if such wealth is not assembled this year, then next, or for sure the year after that."

# CHAPTER TWENTY-TWO:
## REFLECTIONS ON THE BEGINNING

In the evening light of a springtime full moon, two young men walked the cobblestones along Second Street toward the City Tavern. Greeting Thomas Willing and Robert Morris at the entry, Betsey led them up the stairs to a private room. Smiling sweetly and, yes, seductively, she brought each his personal tankard of cider.

"A private room?" Thomas asked Betsey.

"Safer for you mens. All them Loyalists is throwing a party tonight. The whole lot of 'em booked the great room."

"How many?" Robert Morris asked.

"Mor'n I woulda thought."

"They're toasting someone or something?" Thomas asked.

She nodded. "The King's cousin, some duke...his birthday."

Morris said, "It is an excuse to bolster their fading cause."

"Anyways," she said, "best to keep your voices down." As she turned to leave, she added, "Mum's the word that you two gentlemen are here."

Thomas went to peer over the railing. He returned to say, "Maybe a hundred in their wigs and finery."

Reflecting, Morris said, "How could there be so many men still loyal to the Crown?"

"Property," Thomas said. "They want to protect their property— land, slaves, possessions. They fear it all being taken away, confiscated if the Revolution succeeds. Meanwhile, they want to preserve their social status. They feel protected if they continue to be loyal, hoping the King and his Hessian mercenaries will put down the Revolution."

Robert asked, "Loyalty...but not for ideological reasons?"

"To some of my English friends, property and class are trump cards. It is that way in England, and, I might add, so it is with the desire to protect their possessions in Ireland. Following the English tradition, Colonists hope for similar assurances that property here will also be so protected."

The two sat in silence. Then, alternating toasts, Thomas Willing IV and Robert Morris rose and hoisted their tankards. Robert said, "To the future." After sips, Thomas proposed, "To our future and to our firm's future." Robert concluded with, "To the future of America."

Betsey brought their dinners and stood by.

Motivated by their forward-looking pronouncements, the two men reflected. Thomas began. "It is apparent to me that the Colonial break away has been England's doing. The conflict we face is their fault, not ours."

"It started with the British Revenue Acts."

Thomas nodded.

"King George and his ministers told us the government needed money. And they saw us as a taxing source, enabling them to pay for running and expanding the British Empire."

Thomas agreed. "We had no say in the matter, no representatives in Parliament. But suppose, Robert, that I had somehow been elected to Parliament instead of following in the footsteps of my dear father and been elected mayor of Philadelphia? It might have been a different story."

"As eloquent in your public speeches as you are, Thomas, are you saying you single handedly could have swayed the British Empire? Even had you enjoyed the support of other MPs from the Colonies, say Benjamin Franklin, or even Patrick Henry. Would our commercial and political dilemma be any better?"

"It is moot. There never was an election for a Colonial representative to sail off across the ocean and sit amongst the gentlemen in Parliament. An opportunity to talk was never offered. It was probably never even thought of by the King. My friends in London have written that whenever an MP with any sympathy to us rose to speak, he was shouted down."

Robert said, "Then came the Stamp Act. Even our friend Benjamin Franklin spoke in favor of the act. In arranging for his colleague John Hughes to be appointed by Parliament to collect the money, Ben admitted he thought it a justified law and a legitimate tax."

"You know, I must say at first I thought Ben was right. Like him, many of us wanted peace, wanted tranquility with the Mother Country. What was so wrong about that point of view?"

Morris suggested, "Nothing. What was wrong was that no one on either side of the Atlantic thought about the other's position or motivation. There was no opportunity for conversation. What if the King, or more likely, a mixed delegation of nobles and merchants, or better yet, a contingent from Parliament had come here, met with us, seen and felt the commercial and political opportunities—would such a trip or trips have changed things? I mean, you would understand the benefits of an elected official seeing firsthand a troubling situation—how such an experience might influence your viewpoint."

Thomas nodded. "Many of the ruling class did go to India and to other parts of the world where the British had Colonies and commercial influence."

"Their Generals were here during the French and Indian Wars and the battle for Quebec. Surely having seen the Colonies up close they must have become infused, as we are, with the aura of this virgin continent."

"Most generals do as they are ordered. They are not good at understanding the people. For by the time the battles began, the Colonists had become adversaries. They had shot at their troops and killed many at Lexington and Concord."

Betsey spoke up. "But, Robert, what's in a general's mind? The Hessian Major keeps asking me these sorts of questions. Does a general issue orders and then observe in a callous manner the killing, or does he feels anything for the soldiers on the other side of the battlefield, or the women and children unlucky enough to get caught in the flying bullets and cannon balls?"

"What I cannot understand," Thomas said, reflecting, "is what was in the hearts and minds of the royal rulers? Given the divine guidance they are supposed to receive from Heaven, should not they be concerned about the well-being of their subjects?"

"Including the women and children." Betsey's tone was emphatic. "So much for the Almighty's role."

Thomas said, "Unless we consider God to be on our side, guiding us, rooting for our Revolution and directing our path to independence. Is not God always on the side of good."

"Define good," Robert challenged.

"Good is what we, you and I and like-minded associates here in the Colonies advocate and pray for, is it not? But, Robert, is it not the same good that the British advocate? So where is truth? On which side of the Atlantic does truth call home port?"

"The truth, Thomas, lies in our hearts." Morris added, "And maybe in our minds, as the Hessian Major insists on suggesting."

"Yeah, he does that," Betsey said.

"Heart or mind?" Robert asked. "Is what is in the heart the same as in the mind?"

Thomas said, "Perhaps your Major is right-on."

"Anyway, Thomas, in many respects the American Revolution has already taken place. Coming up soon, if you and I and the other delegates vote for the Declaration, we will simply be confirming a fait accompli."

Interrupting, from the great room below a loud toast lifted toward them. "God Save the King!"

Taking a swig of cider, Morris left their private room. He leaned over the railing and shouted down, "Gentlemen, I offer a toast to us all! To truth, the truth of America, the future truth of whether or not we will have our own a nation."

Down below, Robert saw patrons standing and looking up at him. Barmaids quieted. The City Tavern tensed. Robert knew most of the Loyalists. They knew him. With some he regularly engaged in commercial transactions. He read the fear of the future in their faces and watched their hesitancy to join in his toast.

Coming to his side was Thomas, who the Loyalists quickly recognized as one of their own—a member of their comfortable ruling class. As Thomas raised his tankard, some below followed his gesture. Moments later they were grudgingly joined by more Loyalists. Silence, then clinks ensued among the American Colonists, below and above, gathered this evening in the City Tavern.

*       *       *

On the canvas of time—the sketchpad of world history—remained a revolutionary picture not yet painted, now only roughly outlined.

\*       \*       \*

Before she left for the kitchen, Morris asked Betsey about her two young boys, explaining to Thomas that Luke and Mark had left with their father to venture into the wilds of The Westward, hoping to carve a farm out of the wilderness and make their living.

"I tried to travel there, but the fear of the frontier overcame me."

"As you reported to me," Robert said. "Any word since? Did they receive the letter you wrote?

She reached out and grasped Robert's hand. He felt the dampness of a tear dropping onto his hand. Haltingly she told them, "A Delaware—a tribal matriarch—came to see me here a few days ago. She told me she had heard somehow, and I don't know how, except by way of her Indians, that the squaw was still living with my husband and the boys. The squaw, Robin something or other, wanted me—mother to mother—to know my boys were well and not sick with the pox or fever. They were working hard to clear the land and plant crops. The matriarch left as quickly as she came."

Thomas said, "You, Betsey, with your children and the British King with his colonies, have something in common."

Betsey dried her tears with her apron and looked at him questioningly.

"You are each losing your offspring." Kissing her on the cheek, Robert said, "Hopefully for a better life ahead."

# CHAPTER TWENTY-THREE:
## AN ALTERNATIVE

S oon thereafter at quayside, while monitoring one of their firm's three-mast frigates being loaded with tobacco bales and other cargo, Thomas Willing IV asked his business partner, "Do you think we have a choice? Is there any other course open to us as merchants, other than to join in the Revolution?"

Robert Morris said, "There is one alternative."

Eyebrows raised, Thomas asked, "And it is?"

Putting aside the ship's manifest, Robert said, "The Loyalists in Philadelphia, and indeed the other Colonies, harbor hopes—perhaps blind hopes, or maybe it is simply their faith and comfort in the status quo. They believe in the endurance and strength of the British Empire, its King, his ministers, and its Parliamentary system of governance. They believe that the King and a majority of those in Parliament will come to their senses and acknowledge America's role in the New World. They believe the Colonies, remaining under British rule rather than testing  the chaos of independence, will benefit financially and politically now and into the future."

Thomas pressed, "Could such developments come to pass?"

"Some days, I suppose I do so hope," Robert admitted. "Maybe it is a lingering desire. It is so logical, practical, and comforting to preserve the past and continue on with it." He mused. "Perhaps political consistency would be in everyone's interest."

"But back in London," Thomas countered, "I do not think the British will ever come around to such a position. Look at what happened when our distinguished John Jay presented his carefully drafted Olive Branch Petition to Parliament. That earnest effort, which was signed by so many men in the Colonies, was a bona fide attempt to promote peace and reconciliation."

"Indeed it was, yet Jay's carefully worded petition was ignored…not even seriously considered by those few in Parliament who took time to read it. The Brits had a reasonable solution handed to them on a sterling silver platter and ignored it. They chose to continue the problem rather than explore a solution. Yet, in spite of his rebuff, Jay told me he continues to harbor hope for some sort of peacemaking gesture from the Crown. But I doubt his daydream will ever see reality."

"Our distinguished Huguenot, though he is married to New Jersey Governor Livingston's charming daughter Sarah—"

"—Is ignoring her advice—"

"—But I do not understand, with the likelihood of English solders' lives being lost, land owners' property confiscated if the Revolution succeeds, English merchant commerce boycotted, why does not their government come to its senses?"

Robert suggested, "Might—military, social, and commercial— does not automatically engender a country's mental acumen."

Thomas agreed, "The English are not like our William Penn Quakers who eschew violence. The empire's financial equation requires Brits to colonize their acquired lands, milk the raw materials, and sell back at huge profits to the locals the goods crafted by workers in towns all across their little island."

"The British Empire," Robert reflected. "What did Shakespeare so lovingly call it? 'This blessed plot, this land, this realm, this England.' But in so ruling the waves and the lands, Britannia does provide those of us who want to make our fortunes in commerce with golden opportunities."

"But consider the adverse effect on our business from the laws Parliament has passed."

Robert nodded. "The Currency Act has affected our ability to raise capital and make money."

"That was back in 1764." Thomas said, "Go even farther to the Townshend Acts that discriminated against the Colonies."

"The English thought we Colonists were not equals, that we were a lesser rank of humans, not slaves, but down the line on the importance scale."

Thomas nodded. "I say the die has been cast for Revolution, at least from our partnership's point of view."

"We are so far from London that no other solution is realistic."

"So, where does all this talk of independence leave us in the firm of Willing & Morris? If the Revolution gives birth to a country managed by forward-looking men who are well intentioned, well informed, imaginative, and who can create a sound economy, that will spell freedom and financial independence for us."

Robert suggested, "We will need a national bank, a currency, and a Congress that will legislate supportive laws. And our Congress must collect taxes in order to support the new federal government. Can we bring it about, Thomas? Or should we stand apart from the mounting popular feelings, sit back and continue our commerce and pursue our profits?"

Thomas observed, "Mr. Jefferson shared with me a draft of the Declaration that he and others have put together, isolated for days as they were in that old house on Sixth Street. They list our grievances against the Monarch—a long list actually, very long. He sets forth everything we are confronting in our pursuit of life, liberty, and happiness. Jefferson asserts our inalienable rights."

"A radical document indeed."

"Stirring a hornet's nest."

Robert said, "I do have my fears signing Jefferson's Declaration of Independence."

"Richard Henry Lee plans to introduce the resolution in Congress."

Robert reflected, "Yes, we each, in our souls, have that decision to wrestle with. Do we as elected members, sign?" Mulling over the dilemma, he commented, "Thomas, this breakaway climate is being engineered by men. Where are the women?"

"Where does your Molly stand?"

"Molly is with me, urges me onward, supports me in whatever course I decide. Is not that the way it is in our Colonial society? The men are taming the horizon stretching west, while the women are bearing children to populate the new lands—children who will grow up to clear the land and lay out the farms, as well as plat the cities that are sure to follow."

"Anne supports me. She says that men are the gender to decide important matters. I notice that the men—at least some—listen to their women. They heed their thoughts and feelings and often take their advice respectfully."

Storm clouds began to blow in, and soon they felt the rain. The two young partners left the dockside for the warehouse to survey cargos to be loaded on the next arriving ship. Robert picked up a sheet of paper detailing a waiting cargo. "These goods will sail off to Europe in either event."

Thomas looked intently at Robert. "As to the Declaration of Independence, will you sign it? And will I sign?"

"Right now, I do not know what I will do, but I believe that in the story of the New World, the result—at least some time not far away—will be the formation of a new nation. That act is inevitable."

Thomas said, "I continue to ponder the question of legitimacy. If we sign, then we are saying we will form—elect—a body of men to make the same decisions, enact similar laws that Parliament has passed. All along we have been saying they have no legal authority to do so. So, who does have the authority? Who is there on Earth who will acknowledge the legitimacy of this new group of Colonial men who are poised to take legislative action for the new country? None of these men—you and I, or Benjamin Franklin, or George Washington, or Alexander Hamilton, or John Adams, or John Jay, or Thomas Paine, or Thomas Jefferson, or any Colonial personages have been elected or even appointed by virtue of a divine decree from heaven, as supposedly has been King George III. If he no longer counts as a ruler, then who or what group does?"

Both young men grew silent, their thoughts churning. Finally Thomas said, "But now we have a war, a war that is being fought and will likely expand, as more British troops and Hessian mercenaries arrive and more of our Colonials volunteer to join the Continental Army under Washington."

Robert said, "This nascent Revolution of ours will make its own laws. It is unlike a peaceful society, which has laws of conduct that are steady through time. In a revolution, what I fear the most is that unwritten codes of conduct will be subject to violent change as the winds of public opinion shift. In the aftermath, there might come a counter-revolution, which would allow the previous group of Loyalists to rally their forces and return matters to conditions that could be worse than before the Revolution."

Thomas said, "It is up to those of us who are leaders in the Colonies to make sure we build a solid structure for our new government and assure that it passes laws fair to every citizen."

"Add a solid plan for how the new nation is to be financed—a plan recognized by investors here and in the Old World."

Thomas returned to the issues troubling him. "Unfortunately, you and I have no time to ponder and debate a philosophy of government, or how it might be financed."

Robert said, "We have precious time to acquire gunpowder, forge cannon, and hope for good generalship. And be certain that we have adequate money to pay for all of it. And that, my partner, is where you and I must perform." He added thoughtfully, "Revolution is a stage upon which many men are required to play, hopefully most being destined to survive."

# CHAPTER TWENTY-FOUR:
# ROBERT VISITS HIS DAUGHTER POLLY

Johannes, Robert Morris's free black carriage driver, who told those who asked that he had come to Philadelphia from the islands off the Carolina coast, drove the four horses south toward Oxford, Maryland. The journey required two days of stomach-churning travel on dusty and rutted roads, some little better than forest trails. At dusk, halfway to their destination, they stopped at the Silent Frog, a roadside tavern astride the crude pike. Robert booked a room and ordered his dinner, while Johannes wrapped himself in a blanket and slept inside the carriage after being given scraps of meat from the kitchen and caring for the horses with the aid of the tavern's stable boy.

At dinner in the tavern's smallish room, Robert listened to the conversations. Introducing himself, he asked the loudest speaker to expand on his strongly stated political positions, noting that he was "a gentleman of the South."

Carter Calhoun said, "Mr. Morris, Sir, if the British Parliament outlaws slavery, they will bankrupt us plantation owners. Our wealth is in our land, of course, but our land cannot be productive without our slaves."

"Hearing your argument, Mr. Calhoun, Sir, I conclude you must be an advocate for independence for all the Colonies?"

"Absolutely," Calhoun replied as he banged the tabletop with his clenched fist. "To us, it is a simple a matter of business. Our South Carolina Colony must become independent of England so that we can make our own laws. That way we can retain our institution of slavery. It is our lifeblood, don't y'all see that?" Several companion planters sitting at the table dutifully and emotionally toasted slavery.

Morris deferred and said, "You have singled out your colony. What about other colonies and the unity of our 13?"

Calhoun replied, "Trouble with that argument, Mr. Morris, is that your northern Colonies are not really slave states. But all the Colonies need to stick together in support of slavery, otherwise we will not be united, but rather divided over the slavery issue. That division would threaten Colonial unity and weaken our effort for independence. In fact, we fear there is a growing movement for manumission in New England and especially among your Quakers in Pennsylvania."

Another planter said, "Or so we hear from men who have travelled there and read Ben Franklin's Gazette."

Robert said, "Quakers do not own slaves."

"Do you?"

Robert shook his head negatively. "My driver is a free black, speaks Gullah."

"Yet as a merchant, do you not trade in the Negro." Calhoun's was a statement, not a question.

Robert nodded. "Sometimes slaves are cargo on our ships."

"Ahh, then slavery is also a source of income for you merchants."

"True."

"Then, Sir, we are in agreement."

All the Southern gentlemen at the table stood, raising their glasses and toasted: "To the institution of slavery."

*     *     *

Perplexed at the questions slavery raised, both the human and the commercial, Robert retired, bidding a goodnight to Calhoun and his fellow slave owners.

On the morrow Morris thought about seeing his daughter. Years had passed, and she would have grown in stature and beauty. Though later in life he had fathered seven babes with Molly, Polly was his first—and Molly would never know. He had been at Sally's side when Polly was born. He had kissed the newborn, promising her mother that he would provide for the babe's education, such as it was for girls in the Colonies at that time. Poise, household matters, sewing, sometimes food preparation, canning, gardening, too, even flower arrangement, sometime drawing. Some girls were known to even study French, Latin, and he had heard about a tutor in Greek.

Back then he had wanted the best for Polly. After he and Molly were married, it was the same for their seven children—the best. When Molly had suggested that their eldest two boys were ready to be sent abroad to study—in Germany at Leipzig, he was all for it. But this night, alas, he acknowledged he had never thought about such a plan for daughter Polly.

The next day, Johannes drove the carriage up to a modest house in Oxford. And there she was—no there they were, waiting for him—mother and daughter, Sally and Polly. Each was elegantly dressed in the fashion of the times, probably so Morris guessed, brought by Sally's father, Captain Smythe, on his frigate returning from France. Now a grown young woman, Polly stood as tall, no, even taller than her mother. She was equally as beautiful, no, even prettier.

As Johannes reined in the horses and pulled on the brake lever, Morris jumped from the carriage. There were hugs all around. With his linen handkerchief he gently wiped away the tears of joy from Sally's eyes, leaving his own to glisten in the sunlight. He laughed at the joy in Polly's demeanor as she encircled herself in his outstretched receiving arms.

With Sally, that first night, their frolic together had been love and affection in the coming of age episode for each of them. Yes, love! Attraction—one to the other. Love; of course, he could not know for sure if the affection was equal in her mind. But, this day, with her outward display toward him, with Polly's ebullience, these long years since, he knew it was love, then, that night, as it was now for her, and for sure for him. And the now was the now, and he knew it to be brief, the now soon to fade into the past, and the future to move to the present and promptly consume him in its demanding monetary and political embrace when, too soon, he was to return north.

For sure, through the months and years ahead he knew he would continue to provide for Polly, yes. For what Sally was to do with her life had been left to her to determine. Perhaps she had already done so, as he surveyed her house—either her father's house, a ship's captain, or a husband's; he hoped for her sake, with another's love for her, that he, whoever he was, was a good and caring husband.

With his Molly, their marriage had been the right thing to do—a marriage destined to work in Philadelphia, gaining the support of her prominent family, enjoying the prestige of the endorsement from the church in Pennsylvania, along with her brother William, now head of the new and growing Episcopal Colonial faith.

With Sally, for him and for her that night it had been too soon, an affair too young, a time unlearned, a pleasure fleeting, yet lasting in his mind—forever, he thought, he knew, as he kissed her again the same tender, yet aggressive way he had that first night off the ship in Oxford. Her beauty then and her beauty now consumed his mind. Fleetingly he puzzled over his own values in life. Money. Fortune. His compulsion to seek both. Of those values, desire for Sally, both back then and now this day in Oxford overwhelmed him. Yes, he knew then, and he knew now, the affection of another for a person was life's biggest reward. To him, the cognizance of such affection continued to propel his drive for money and fortune.

Polly held up a doll from the days of her childhood, sharing it with her father. A black doll. A slave doll. Dutifully he kissed the doll as she placed it to his lips, eliciting for it, and also for her, a show of fatherly affection for all the years he had missed during her growing up. They talked and she told him of her youth, and of reading his letters to Sally—his words, she told him as Sally nodded her agreement, gave her, no, gave both mother and daughter, she told him, the sense of ongoing love.

Later, when Johannes advised it was time to leave, Morris lamented their parting, yet, buoyed with gladness from the visit, began to re-charge himself to return to the challenges of ocean commerce, and the anticipation of further business victories. His good-bye wave, in unison with theirs, launched him onward into his future.

# CHAPTER TWENTY-FIVE:
# MORRIS AND THE MAJOR TALK MORE

This time, Dr. Hogarth had arranged for them to meet in Morris' warehouse office. Major von Lowenstein was not in his Hessian uniform for, as he expressed, he harbored fear of physical reprisal from roving bands of Revolutionaries should he walk in his uniform along the streets and the bustling wharf. There, as well, the stevedores could be antagonistic, or so he had been warned. Popular animosity was rising as word spread about Hessian mercenaries reinforcing the British redcoats.

Morris welcomed the Major. "Your proper European attire blends well among our German population."

"Yes, I am regarded as a merchant. No one guesses my military mission."

Morris showed the Major through the warehouse bulging with bales of New World tobacco, cotton, and sugar cane awaiting shipment afar to where Old World processing would prepare the crops for consumer consumption. Promptly the Major ventured his query. "Mr. Morris, Sir, allow me to ask you a personal question."

"A personal question is most unusual in my affairs. We seldom get beyond business dialogue and hard-nail negotiations. But what is it you want to know, Sir?"

The Major said, "I have been ordered to find out how you regard this American Revolution. Not the bravado Thomas Paine writes, or the thoughtful pen of John Adams, or the recognized rhetoric of Patrick Henry, or what might be called the studious outlook of Benjamin Franklin. Rather, Sir, what is your personal assessment?"

"Your curiosity is a surprise, that is, coming from a mercenary."

"Our officer class is educated, Sir. For me, the University of

Leipzig—three years. As a result of education and medical training, and with my Landgraf's encouragement, I have become challenged to explore new horizons." He added, "I refer to mental horizons."

"Alas, Major, I lack formal education—that I regret. I have had no time or opportunity to seek a college. In the Colonies, we do not yet enjoy an institution such as you have attended in Germany." He perked up. "But that educational deficit will be dealt with for the benefit of young people if my vision for our new nation comes to pass. Education may be another reason for independence. You see, the British have kept education to themselves, confined it to their little island, allowing only a select few of their overseas subjects to pursue such enlightening goals. They do not wish advanced education for distant subjects, fearing such learning might somehow develop into threats that might undo their rule."

Examining a tobacco leaf, the Major said, "If I understand you, you believe you have a significant role to play in this Revolution and, assuming its success, in your vision for its aftermath."

"Yes. That is what I feel in my heart and in my gut."

"Then tell me why your role is so significant for the changes you see coming to this New World."

Edged by the Major's question, Morris shot back, "My part is important! Each of our roles is significant." He worried he was betraying the English custom of concealing emotions, keeping a stiff upper lip regardless of circumstances. He cautioned himself that he could be making a mistake by not following the age-old close-to-the-chest custom with this inquisitive doctor/soldier.

"But Sir, what if there was no significance…no importance to the matters you are advocating?"

"What?" Morris' question rang with antagonism laced with confusion. He could not curtail his annoyance. "No significance indeed!"

The Major persisted. "Please answer my question, Sir."

Morris stumbled back with, "Everyone knows—"

"—In that case, you will have no difficulty sharing your thoughts."

"I never have trouble expressing myself in writing or verbally."

The Major smiled. "I am waiting." His tone edged more aggressively. "Sir, please tell me your thoughts, that is, if you can, or if you dare."

They strolled on amidst the bales. Troubled, Morris took out his pipe, inserting a crumpled-up tobacco leaf and ceremoniously lit the pipe. Ensuing smoke engulfed the two. Morris mused, "Major, you have asked a stupid question."

The Major chuckled. "Then, Sir, a stupid question, if such it is, is readily answered."

Morris puffed repeatedly and said, "If there were no significance in what I am doing and in my ideas—my visions—for the future of the Colonies, then I would be staring into a vast void, looking into a nothingness, living with an absence of motivation, oblivious to the forces around us that are playing the game of history."

"If that is the scenario, how would you confront this possible absence of significance? How do you feel about this emptiness you call a 'void'?"

Morris' mind seemed to circle, harmonic rings of smoke rising from his pipe. All he could manage was, "You do explore, Sir."

"Your mind is my mission."

"The heart is my mind."

"Are you telling me you are speaking from the heart?"

"Well, yes, of course, Major. Is not that the source within each of us from which one expresses themself?"

"My orders from my Landgraf are to find out."

"And if you had no such orders?"

"Touché, Mr. Morris." The Major allowed a little laugh. "But, Sir, I do have such orders, and I am obliged, curious, and determined to understand what transpires in your masterful mind." Having hopped atop a tobacco bale, the Major was looking directly into Morris' eyes. "Let me ask you this, Sir, why don't you—I mean, you have sufficient money, so I presume, to do what you wish with your life. Why do you not simply enjoy life—go to your country estate, embrace your wife, play games with your admiring children, who, I imagine, miss their time with you, enjoy the birds singing and the deer bounding, watch the river traffic, attend the church of your choice—I assume, you have made your choice of religions—in other words, yield your life to the magical moments at hand, while being mindful of life as it churns around you, enjoying the contours and the collages of the world as it turns and turns."

"Become an observer to the events around me, you mean?"

"Yes, you could be an onlooker to life and to history unfolding around you." The Major shot off an accusation that later he wished he had not: "Otherwise, are you not, Sir, just another fanatic, obsessed with yourself and clinging to wild-eyed monetary and political notions and, yes, ambitions?"

Morris seemed to meditate while the Major waited. Ignoring the Major's cutting barb, the merchant ventured, "Sir, under such circumstances, I would not be loyal to my colleagues, the men and women of Pennsylvania, indeed all the Colonies, who have an idea long germinating in their hearts that calls for us to join together and form a new nation and, in the process, permit us to enhance our personal fortunes."

"Money, is it, then?"

Morris nodded. "Yes, that is true. But given our situation, I see the world changing. We in the Colonies are players on the world stage," He waited to assess the Major's facial expressions and body language. Detecting interest there, Morris went on, "Do you not agree that once on stage—as we are here—one is called upon to speak their lines, act their role, gesture to those who look on, participate actively in the plot? If the play's storyline has been written by a Higher Authority, Major, the events taking place in the New World are part of a divine drama."

"Driven by destiny? Is that what you are thinking? But how can you know?"

Morris was quick to reply. "I cannot know the answer, and the uncertainty of not knowing a possible heavenly answer is the dilemma I confront as I make my way across the Colonial stage. You see, in this life of mine, I believe I am beholden to some playwright somewhere to perform as my role has been cast and to do so as directed by my conscience and my loyalty to fellow Colonists."

"And women? Tell me, Sir, does your wife share this dedication of yours?"

Again, Morris appeared confused. "Why do you ask such a question?"

"I simply ask it."

Morris searched his thoughts. He asked, "Do I know the answer? Of course, I know because she does."

The Negro Johannes came running in and announced in his Gullah-accented English, "Suh, that artist man is here—wants you to dress formal like and again take up your flattering pose."

Morris replied, "Johannes, do you want to be in my portrait by standing behind me?"

The Negro laughed and shook his head. "Suh, we—my kind—will always be in the rear of the picture." He added, "That is, if we are to be seen at all. Suh. Portraits are for you important people, not the likes of my people."

Morris said to the Major, "You must excuse me. I am to sit once more so that, hopefully, Mr. Elouis will finish."

The Major pressed, "But are you happy in this role you have chosen?"

Morris said, "I believe the role has chosen me."

# CHAPTER TWENTY-SIX:
# HAYM SOLOMON

A well-dressed yet frail and gaunt man, short with a noticeable forward bent, approached the official Clerk of Philadelphia in his cluttered office in the temporary State House.

Greeting him, the Clerk advised, "Mr. Solomon, much as I admire your efforts at helping Robert Morris in his efforts to pay the bills of the militia, and your position as agent to the French consul here, as well as your role as paymaster for our friendly French troops, I am legally bound by the action of the Continental Congress and the Religious Test Laws to advise you that you cannot hold an official office in our new country, even though you enjoy the endorsement and support of the esteemed Mr. Morris and a host of other founding fathers."

In the strongest voice he could muster, Solomon said, "It pains me—your decision!" Mellowing, he added, "I realize you are following the law as you understand it. But Congress does not appreciate the many deeds for which I am responsible, nor do they understand the magnitude of the funds I have personally raised from foreign governments on behalf of the Revolution, nor are they willing to recognize the patriotism of my chosen people, both in Europe and the Americas."

"Oh, but Congress does so very much acknowledge you, Mr. Solomon. I mean, in my opinion, you have been and still are a vital player in the cause of the American Revolution."

Solomon replied, "I do not care about official titles. I am doing what needs to be done for the future of our Western Civilization. But tell me, and tell me in your own words, please, why I am to be deprived of an official title that would connote formal recognition."

The Clerk hesitated, as if consulting his conscience, or so Solomon presumed. "Well, Sir, the denial is not specifically because you are an immigrant. I mean everyone knows you came from Portugal."

Haym Solomon corrected, "I am originally from Poland. I came to America via Portugal."

"Another immigrant!" the clerk said, his comment a tad derogatory.

"We are all immigrants here, Sir," Haym declared, adding in a didactic tone, "Except for the Lenape, the Delawares."

The clerk thought for a moment and smiled. "Yes, you are right, Sir. After all, Mr. Morris, Mr. Jay, and Mr. Hamilton are immigrants."

Solomon nodded, averring, "Does not my time spent confined in that British prison in New York mean anything? You see the state of my poor health—the result of several years languishing in that dank place, almost starving and without adequate medical attention."

"You managed to escape."

Solomon smiled. "Twice, actually."

"You were recaptured once."

"And sent back to that awful prison"

Hoping to put a different slant on their conversation, the Clerk asked, "Tell me, Sir, how do you regard the British, that is, thinking about your imprisonment?"

"They can be as cruel as any New World savage. Or they can, on occasion, act with civility. In my case, I do blame them for their mistreatment. It was inhuman—the torture I was forced to endure...."

The clerk wanted to explore further. He looked at Solomon, expecting, hoping for more detail, perhaps precise and lurid descriptions of his prison confinement.

Solomon remained silent.

The clerk waited. Finally, feeling at liberty to explain matters to the patriot in front of him, he said, "Mr. Solomon, you asked me why I cannot officially recognize your role in the Revolution. So, I will tell you. You do not qualify for official position in the Colonial government because you, Sir, are a Jew."

Not hesitating, Haym shot back, "Yes, I am a Jew. More specifically Ashkenazi. Let me ask you, Mr. Clerk, have you ever looked at the official seal proposed for our new country?"

The Clerk shifted, his body language revealing unease.

"It is in the shape of the Star of David—a six pointed star, right?"

The clerk studied the seal on his official stamp. Astonished, he nodded.

The two men faced off, each seeming to explore the other's soul.

Unease evident, the Clerk absently twirled his quill pen, then slowly commented, "Mr. Solomon, Sir, I did read in the last issue of Mr. Franklin's Gazette that your friend Robert Morris has sponsored legislation to repeal the Religious Test Laws. I believe he has done so out of his admiration and respect for you, Sir, Mr. Solomon."

Haym nodded. "Robert told me that in the petition, he says that I, personally, was responsible for financing the American Revolution. Of course, that is a gross over statement—partly true perhaps—but only in conjunction with his efforts, along with those of his business partner, Thomas Willing."

"Patriots all," the Clerk declared as if in his official capacity he was bestowing a medal of honor on each member in the cadre of Founding Fathers.

Haym wished he were in a tavern so he could propose a toast to the Clerk. Instead he announced proudly, "The hoped-for repeal of that anti-Semitic law will coincide with the construction of our temple—the first to be built in Pennsylvania."

"Oh, yes," the Clerk acknowledged, adding knowingly, gesturing, "Over there on Cherry Alley between Third and Fourth Streets. It will join the existing houses of worship of Philadelphia."

# CHAPTER TWENTY-SEVEN:
# THE OTHER ROBERT MORRIS

"Suh," the stranger entering the Willing & Morris warehouse addressed Robert Morris. "Y'all'uns run this here shippin' warehouse?" He bowed slightly, extending his arm, initiating a businessman's handshake.

"Yes, Sir," Morris replied, their hands grasping.

"I am Alonzo Cotton," the Stranger announced with dignity. "My esteemed colleague from South Carolina, Henry Laurens, dispatched me to Philadelphia to call upon you, since y'all have been elected members of the Continental Congress."

Morris nodded, waiting.

"You see, Suh, I am a plantation owner. Mr. Laurens and I have the largest landholdings north of the Oconee River, and on this side—that is, south of North Carolina." He went on, "I been fixin' to come up here for weeks, but finally, after that last straw happenin', I carried myself by ship and carriage all this way to see you—took more'n a week. And not without untoward events, let me tell you."

Morris motioned to a wingback chair, inviting Cotton to sit. "Tell me, Sir, what was this 'last straw'?"

"Well, Suh, my Charleston factor had two ships for carrying our cargo of tobacco to England. A few weeks ago, I got word one ship had disappeared, sunk, probably, or else captured by one of them Algerian pirate ships—we don't know, other than the ship and its cargo are lost. Mind you, and without payment for its cargo of valuable sugar cane."

Morris poured Calhoun a cider and sipped one himself, waiting.

Cotton continued, "One day our Charleston factor boarded a ship and fled back to England. He left without paying the money he owed us. After that, we…I want to trust only somebody of esteemed stature, and you, Suh, enjoy such a reputation." Cotton downed his cider, looked inquisitively at Morris and asked, "Mr. Morris, Suh, say, are you the barrister who defended Lord Baltimore. I mean that barrister's name was Robert Morris."

Morris laughed.

Cotton asked, "What do you find humorous? Is Lord Baltimore not revered? I mean, you Colonists here have named one of your towns after him. In that regard, anyone associated with him would certainly be well thought of."

"I am not so sure of that."

"What do you mean?"

"Sir, I am not *that* Robert Morris." Even more emphatically, Morris stated, "I am the American Robert Morris. Anyway, that other Robert Morris defended Lord Baltimore in a trial. One of my sea captains related the story."

The stranger exclaimed, "But why was a British Lord on trial?"

"He was accused of rape. Even Lords cannot do that."

"But his barrister—I mean, that's not you?"

Morris smiled and shook his head.

"Well then, Suh, can you tell me what was the outcome of the trial? I mean, the English do not place Lords in irons and shut them off in jails, do they, ever?"

"I do not know, but the other Robert Morris got the Lord acquitted."

"End of story?"

"Not exactly."

"How so?"

Morris reported, "Well, my devilish namesake then ran off with Lord Baltimore's 12-year old daughter."

"You mean to tell me?"

"Yes, my namesake eloped with the Lord's ever-so-young child."

## CHAPTER TWENTY-EIGHT:
## MISSISSIPPI ORANGES

The City Tavern never slept, for patrons marched in and flowed out pretty much 'round the clock, keeping the bevy of barmaids bouncing between the kitchen, the bar and the patrons and, in certain situations, pursuing a more intimate enterprise.

This night, quite late, Robert Morris sat alone sipping cider when Betsey came to him and whispered, "See that man over there?" She gestured with her eyes across the now sparsely occupied room.

He searched and nodded absently.

"He wants to sell a lot of land. He's looking for a buyer here in Philadelphia, where he says rich men likes you live. He told me that groves of oranges will grow nicely on this land of his. He also says oranges, if eaten by sailors on ocean voyages, will prevent scurvy. I think he is some sort of crackpot, but anyways I told him I'd introduce him to you."

Always on the lookout for moneymaking opportunities, Morris asked Betsey, "How large is his parcel? And do slaves go with his land?"

Betsey replied, "Ask him yourself, Robert Dear? Here he comes now." She made the introduction, brought two tankards of ale and left.

"Angus Trueblood," the stranger announced, holding out his hand, indicating the shaking ritual. "Scotland is my home...er...was my home."

The man's faded red neckpiece entwining the top of his soiled white blouse did not measure up to the more genuine red of his hair. To Robert, he was a seller in need—rather urgently—of a buyer for his land. "What, Sir, may I do for you this night?"

"You are, Sir, a wealthy merchant, and I want to tell you about my land." Before Robert could reply, Angus added, "You see, I'm a gambler, and—"

"—You bet on the wrong horse," Robert interrupted. "From what I have heard, you may have been at the races in Williamsburg." Robert visualized the gamble of betting on horses with mounts riding them down that straight quarter-mile racecourse. "Colorful and exciting, I would say from what I have heard, but gambling is not for me. I am not a man to bet on blind luck."

Angus sheepishly replied, "No, Sir, it was a cock fight."

"An even less attractive bet." Robert recalled the one he had witnessed in Oxford his first night ashore in the New World. "Yes, I have watched two roosters go after each other."

Angus downed his ale with one tilt of his arm, smacking his lips and burping loudly.

With impatience Robert said, "Betsey tells me you have a plantation in Mississippi?"

Angus nodded, his hopeful attention focused on the financier.

Morris said, "My friends say the Georgia Colony owns what some are calling Mississippi, its Colonial borders stretching all the way west to touch the banks of the Great River."

"The Mississippi River," Angus said with a wide smile. "That is where my land lies—in that lush tropical climate where oranges will grow nicely."

Morris displayed his interest. "How much land are you offering?"

"My plantation consists of 4,000 hectares on the eastern bank of the Great River."

"Slaves included?"

"A hundred, plus the overseer, an assistant enforcer, a log cabin, and several buildings used as slave quarters. He is overseeing the slaves planting more orange trees. That was the case weeks ago when I left to make my way here to Philadelphia via horseback, boat, and carriage."

Robert asked, "How much for it all—land, orange trees, slaves, buildings, and you must have a boat dock on the Great River from which to ship the oranges?"

"Yes, Sir. I told the overseer to construct a dock." He looked longingly at Morris. "But it depends on how you pay. I mean, I prefer sterling for my price of 500 English pounds."

Robert laughed. "So would everybody prefer English pound sterling. But paper notes are coin of the realm, given the constraints of the Currency Act. The English are depriving us of hard currency. Both real money and credit are scarce, and, as I am sure you know, there is no bank in the Colonies to make loans or advance credit."

"You do have bank notes, though, do you not, for sure, I mean?"

"No, for the reasons I have explained."

"How then would you pay me for my valuable orange grove land?"

Robert sipped his ale and said, "Promissory notes based on my good credit and my reputation for honoring my debts."

Cotton acted impressed. "Earning interest?"

Robert nodded. "Six per cent. Due in, say, 10 years."

"Payable in what form of money?"

"Continentals."

"Are they worth a continental?"

"You can discount the continentals—officially issued, as you know, by the Second Continental Congress—and receive some amount of payment in bank notes, if you can find an investor who will buy some of the continentals."

"At a discount," Angus mused, his eyes showing his growing understanding of the outcome of his proposed transaction. He concluded, saying softly, "I guess that's better for me than debtor's prison or for a gun pointed at my head by one of my creditors."

Robert Morris smiled his agreement.

Angus nodded, slowly accepting the deal.

Robert took out his leather folio and counted out the right number of continentals.

*       *       *

The next morning, Robert announced to Thomas Willing, "We have bought an orange grove in Mississippi."

At first, Thomas was skeptical. But thinking about the news, he expressed excitement. "It will be our look into the future for crops out there in The Westward." The two partners shook hands and, after Robert mentioned that oranges might be a cure for the scourge of scurvy, the two headed to the nearest tavern to toast oranges as a perceived bonanza.

Over tankards of ale, after his toast of praise to partner Robert, Thomas queried, "How do you feel, having made this clever purchase?"

"Every investment in America has to be, by definition, a good one. You...we cannot go wrong betting all the money and credit we can on this new land of ours."

Thomas held up his hand. "Not all investments are destined to turn out as hoped. Take Baron Henry Stiegel, for example. You bought his house in Manheim for a pittance after his attempt at establishing an iron and glassworks factory failed. He was forced to sell his house at a fraction of what he spent to build it."

"The baron allowed his passion to overrule his business judgment."

"Are not we making a similar mistake in this land purchase—a new and untried passion for oranges?"

Robert paused to reflect. "You could be right, Thomas, but we are smarter than our baron friend, are we not? Our combined pockets are deeper, are they not?"

Thomas nodded. He rose to hoist his tankard. "Here's to our being smarter than the next Colonial capitalist."

Morris mused, "Those other fortune seekers have been attracted to the Colonies from England, Scotland, and Europe, God bless them, for in their greed, their zeal, their ignorance, and their stumbling, they have set up opportunities for the rest of us to avail— we who, I believe, are smarter, more determined, and more dedicated to our goals."

"And what are your goals, Robert? Can you define them? Beyond money, I mean, can you tell me what lies on the far side of that rugged mountain range that stands in the path of earning your fortune? I refer to that distant—and maybe not so distant—horizon that is to be either Revolution from or reconciliation with England."

Robert Morris seemed to be trying to come out from a closet of circumspection. Intent on his choice of words, he enunciated each carefully. "I sense that you and I, and many others in Philadelphia, are players on a stage on which no performance has previously taken place. The final script has not been written—only drafts circulated to certain actors in order to elicit their reactions. Nor will the players have time, or stage direction from any source to rehearse their roles.

The playwright, if he is a God somewhere, or if he is fictional, some amorphous image, may himself be undecided as to the lines to write, let alone choosing which player to speak them and what plot will prevail."

Thomas wanted to ask how important it was for Robert—and, yes, even for himself, to receive praise from the Philadelphia community. Of course, he himself had been recipient of votes to be elected mayor, and to sit on the court, but votes were votes, and maybe that was because no one wanted to vote for any opponent, seeing him as the least worrisome of all the candidates. "Is it more important that we receive praise from our fellow men than to make money and build our fortunes?"

Robert was quick to reply, "Not significant, in my opinion, because men seldom praise other men, unless it is in their own interest to do so, such as enhancing their own business profits or improving their personal standing in the community. In the competition for the favors of women, enhancing another man's image competitively erodes their own standing. Certainly it does seem wiser, in the presence of women, to tear down another man verbally than to extol his virtues." He added, "Women are attracted to male power and enhance their own prestige when they align with a man deemed powerful and influential."

Being married with a family, all events having been properly positioned in English social circles, and now in the Colony, Thomas recognized his own emerging feelings of becoming a bit uncomfortable in this conversation. All of a sudden, so it seemed, he was confronting a conflict—or was it a male clash of goals?— between himself and his business partner—their divergent backgrounds: his formal education versus Robert's lack thereof, his higher social standing compared to, yes, a man born out of wedlock. Yet Robert, because of his business successes and newfound wealth, was moving—no, had moved into the elite of Colonial America, overcoming social obstacles. With his recognized patriotism plus his financial and business skills, Robert was comfortably sharing the spotlight with himself and others, ranging from Thomas Paine to Benjamin Franklin. Thomas managed, "Is that how you see your marriage with Molly, or rather how you think she sees it?"

Robert smiled, but did not respond, only tugging at his blue silk neck cloth, a nervous gesture he performed when he was focusing on the question at hand.

Thomas waited with anticipation to hear Robert's thoughts. He sensed that Robert's mind was moving into some distant place, as the junior partner in the firm of Willing & Morris began to speak, suggesting to Thomas, "I feel that what actions we—all of us in Philadelphia and the other Colonies—do take on this Colonial stage, in the months and years ahead, will configure the future values of the Western world as we know it, if not set guiding values for the entire planet."

## CHAPTER TWENTY-NINE:
## MRS. G AND ROBERT MORRIS

At noontime, the bronze clapper on the town clock close to the docks on First Street, gonged 12 times as Mrs. G arrived at the Willing & Morris warehouse, having been driven by her Negro slave Arnold in her elegant carriage pulled by four handsome well-groomed horses. The carriage's cream color, accentuated with its thin lines of gold trim, exuded the elegance commensurate with her social position. With a wave of her white-gloved hand, she dispatched her slave, whom she curtly addressed as "you," to climb down from his driver's seat and enter the warehouse. "Get him out here," she instructed, her voice as lilting as the cool breeze, yet characteristically firm, befitting a woman esteemed in Philadelphia society.

Bursting open the door and entering the vast warehouse, the Negro called out in his loudest voice, "Mr. Morris, Suh!" Arnold waited only a moment before adding, "Y'all's presence, Suh, is required."

Looking up from his desk, annoyed at the interruption, Morris recognized the Negro. The financier closed his ledger book, locked it amidst others in his secret place and followed Arnold. Outside, he smiled at the woman he recognized through the carriage window. The curtain was drawn back with her gloved hand revealing her well-powdered face. Robert bowed ceremoniously, exaggerating his movement while needling her in what he felt would be a moment of displeasure, all the while enhancing his amusement.

Opening the carriage window enough so her voice could be directed toward him in no uncertain terms, Mrs. G commanded, leaving no chance for declination, "Climb in, Mister Master Merchant." Morris complied. Arnold assumed the reins. Within the intimate velvety coach, Mrs. G, so he sensed, was deliberately seated toward the middle, forcing him to snuggle next to her stylish overflowing flowery and fashionable skirts.

She pointed toward the front of the carriage and said, "I'm teaching Arnold to read and write. My General has instructed him to carry a paper on which he notes the places where he drives me so that Horatio will get a report on my outings." She seemed to Morris to be reflective. "You know, husbands don't trust their wives these days, especially here where there are so many handsome men such as yourself."

Morris chuckled his reply. "I do not think of myself as handsome."

"Oh, Robert Dear...."

"Why do you dare spend time with me?"

"My General wants to know more about you."

Morris wondered why and asked but got no answer only silence, other than a few minutes of niceties about the weather, the people they passed, and the ships at dock. Growing impatient with the dockside drive, Morris pressed, his voice firm, almost commanding, "You have a purpose in summoning me, of that I feel certain." He smiled. He saw that her eyes were focusing on his dimple. "What are you wanting to find out from me, my dear Mrs. G?"

"I love it, Robert, when you get agitated because that cute dimple in your left cheek comes into view."

Embarrassment swelled within.

Avoiding social pleasantries, she said, "My husband wants to know, if and when the British do occupy Philadelphia, which he says they likely will do soon, will you and your partner, Thomas Willing, remain here in town, or will you flee with the Continental Congress to the hinterlands, say to that place in the west called Lancaster or south to Baltimore?"

"To you, any place other than our Quaker City represents the end of the world."

"Of course," she said in mock agreement. "Those outback places are rife with savage Indians and vagabond thieves, not to mention the throngs of penniless Colonial riff-raff moving west into the hinterland seeking opportunities. Not my type, any of them." She paused, touching his silk sleeve ever so gently with her gloved hand. "Answer my question, Robert Dear, about your leaving town."

"So that you can tell the British?"

"Silly boy, my husband is a Colonial general. Why would I tell the British?"

"Perhaps for hard coin—so rare and sought after these days."

With disbelief in her tone, and looking at him with mock interest, she posited, "Do you think I am a spy for King George's boys?" Her laugh seemed to him to discount the charge, but he was not convinced. "And their General Howe, as well?"

"What should I think?"

"That I am a loyal subject of my King." She giggled into silence.

The carriage passed several ships being loaded with tobacco bales. He pointed. "My ships, those that are not on the high seas."

Mrs. G said, "Do not your ships return from France with gunpowder for the militia fighting in my husband's regiment?"

Morris' fingers traced her gloved hand. He looked into her blue eyes, lingering there in thoughts as to her physical desirability, trying with difficulty to control his growing desire to possess her.

The carriage stopped in front of a tavern. Swishing a corner of the curtain aside, Robert saw a woman come hurrying out, her hand outstretched. He couldn't see further as to what transpired, but he did notice, as she returned to the tavern, that she was nervously tucking a paper into her bodice.

Looking at his hostess, he said, "To answer your question—and I know you know the answer—that being the three-cornered trade scheme. Gunpowder is a sure moneymaker for us merchant shippers, unless the British patrols disrupt the voyages by boarding the ships, either sinking or adding them to their fleet, but for sure confiscating the cargos."

"You are indeed engaged in a risky business, Mr. Leading Merchant Man of Philadelphia."

"But with lucrative rewards for ships that navigate through the Royal Navy's blockades."

Her voice turning didactic, she warned, "But if your Revolution fails, you will lose your flotilla of dear little sailing ships."

"And my head if I throw in with the Revolution and it fails, with the British prevailing."

Her voice changed into what he felt was a more intimate tone as she snuggled closer and said, "That is, unless instead, you allow me to arrange for your expression of overdue loyalty to your King." She reminded, "You are a British subject. Follow my advice and your safety and wellbeing will be assured. A quiet, respected life in England will be in store for you and your family—guaranteed by royal decree."

"To which each of us is automatically entitled as British subjects."

"As my husband so says."

The carriage passed more anchored ships tied to their respective wharfs, either being loaded or unloaded by husky dockworkers. Gesturing at a frigate with colors flying, she asked, "Also yours?"

Morris nodded and pointed to another. "Both bound for Liverpool with prize cargos of rum and tobacco. The Captains and I have profitable journeys planned."

Her voice turning almost motherly, a tone with which she seldom felt comfortable, as Morris had come to sense, she exclaimed, "Robert, you could climb on board one of those ships tonight. You could go home to England." Hinting promise, she added, "Allow me to intercede with Governor Penn on your behalf, arrange a return to your homeland. For you and your dear family, the return would be a joyful reunion with your siblings, your grandmother and your heritage."

Slowly, nostalgia overcame him. "Yes, Liverpool," he pined, his voice almost inaudible. He thought lovingly of returning, of again walking amidst the bustling wharfs, and then conversing with dear Nanna. But he reminded himself that Nanna had passed away. The letter from Evelyn, his half-sister, had arrived that morning. Riding along with Mrs. G in the carriage in thought, Robert knew he must share the news with his half-brother TM, and he must do so this day.

After Arnold steered the carriage back into the narrow grid pattern of the cobblestone streets of Philadelphia, Mrs. G and Robert Morris rode in silence, the only sounds coming from the clickety clack of the wooden wheels hitting the uneven surfaces of the smoothed-by-years-of-traffic river rocks.

Finally, Mrs. G suggested, "You see, Robert, it would be so easy for you. Don't you want to go back to your roots, revisit England, enjoy the comfortable life you have earned, live in peace with the world and with yourself, and do the same for your family?"

Robert shook his head. "No, Mrs. G, such is not the case in my situation. Let me remind you about Hernan Cortes, who, you will recall, was the Spanish Conquistadore who invaded Mexico and conquered it for Spain from the Aztec Empire. It was not all that many years ago, as my partner, Thomas Willing IV, tells me from his having read the Florentine Codex. It was less than 100 years prior to the first British attempt to set up colonies in Maine and Virginia."

Mrs. G looked at Morris, her control of the conversation having been lost to a history tale. Reluctantly she managed, "Do remind me, Robert."

Arnold had stopped the carriage back at the Morris warehouse. Robert moved to climb down from the carriage, but turned and confided to Mrs. G, "There are times when we cannot go back. You see, with the Spanish galleons at anchor at Vera Cruz in Mexico, Cortes issued orders to his men to burn the ships. They protested, of course, saying the ships were their only way home to Spain, to their families, and to safety from the frightening Aztec warriors. Nevertheless, Cortez told his soldiers, 'We cannot and we will not go back. We have come to Mexico to stay, to conquer, and to rule.' He added, 'And to go for gold and silver.' That incentive inspired his men with promises of wealth. You know the rest, Mrs. G."

She slowly replied, "They burned the ships. And so, almost all of Central and South America with its riches came under Spanish control. Yes, Robert, your hero Cortez changed the world forever."

"So, I say to you, Mrs. G, for me and for my family, there is no going back to England, or for others to Scotland, or Germany, or Holland, or wherever. For the American Revolution, or what may come in its place, or whenever it may happen, will not allow a return to British rule, to going back to being part of an old homeland thousands of miles distant. We free thinkers and Revolutionaries, if you must label us as such, are here to stay. We have figuratively burned our return ships."

# CHAPTER THIRTY:
## ROBERT MORRIS' HALF-BROTHER TM

Presuming his half brother Thomas, who Nanna and now he called TM, was working somewhere in the warehouse, Robert Morris called out, "TM where are you?" Waving a letter, he shouted, "I have a letter from our half-sister Evelyn.

As he heard footsteps approaching, Robert recalled having sent for TM a year earlier. Finally, he had arrived from Liverpool. Robert reflected that with his strict daily direction, TM had begun to learn the merchant trade, slowly, maybe too slowly, but learn he had.

TM emerged from a row of cotton bales. Showing his half-brother the letter, Robert explained, "It was entrusted to the captain of the Liverpool frigate that arrived on the early morning tide." He waited for a reply. Hearing none, he went on, "Nana, our dear grandmother has died."

TM's response lacked tenderness. His tone was confrontational, the almost jealous attitude that Robert had come to dislike in his sibling, who now discourteously remarked, "She was more your grandmother than mine. She raised you, not me."

Robert acknowledged the angst of his own childhood, "TM, you were fortunate to know your own mother." Vindictively he knifed, "Even if your mother was known around Liverpool as a boozer."

TM quickly countered, "My mother taught me to enjoy myself and my life. The ale she drank enabled her to make the most of her life, a life without a husband—without that father of ours—our dear philandering father, and also, dear brother, father to our two half-sisters."

Robert tried to ignore the truth, yet couldn't help but admonish, "In your enjoying life here in the Colony, in keeping with our good family reputation—mine especially—you must learn to exercise control. I mean, with your women and your drinking."

"Why, Robert? I enjoy the comely wenches in your taverns, and I fancy the cider, the ale, even the whiskey, and the rum when the feisty barmaids serve it to me."

Edged, Robert said, "The ladies flock to you because you are my brother. They ogle you because of my wealth, which is a reflection of my influence with Colonial leaders."

The force of TM's counter disturbed Morris even more. "You have it all wrong, half-brother. The women are attracted to me because of me. It is none of your doing, Older Brother." Reflectively he added, "But I suppose we are each wanting to be like our common father. A rake. Rich. We are trying to live up to what he would expect of us. To be like him, our dear Father—"

"—That is enough! Stop!" Robert interrupted, his rage showing, affection for his deceased father underlying his emotional outburst.

TM shot back, "But I am right. I know it. That is what drives you—you are compelled by some mysterious force to emulate our father, to best him in wealth. As for me? Only a little that way. I am more interested in the ladies. Actually, I am like my father in the sex department—a chip off the old block."

Changing his tone, Robert reminded, "TM, I sent for you to come to Philadelphia so I could offer you the opportunity to learn the merchant trade, our father's merchant trade, to apprentice with Willing & Morris."

"Thank you once again." TM was obsequious. He added in a more upbeat manner, "I am learning, and I want to learn more. Yes, and I do thank you for arranging this opportunity...older half-brother."

Silent for a moment, then changing the subject, Robert said, "Benjamin Franklin...you met him."

"Yeah, he tried to teach me how to fly a sheet of cloth up in the breeze. Said he wanted to tie a key to it in a thunderstorm. Strange old man." TM added, "Your friends are—"

"—Well, TM, listen to this. Days ago Ben told me that he had proposed to Congress that the Colonies establish a merchant representative in Paris. They have agreed to appoint someone. In deference to me, Ben and the Congress want you to be the man over there in France who will officially represent the Colonies, especially our Pennsylvania."

Surprised, TM asked, "What are you saying, Robert?" His demeanor changed to curiosity.

Robert repeated, "The position in Paris is open, TM, that is, if you want it."

TM's response mixed eagerness with suspicion. "You have chosen me to fill this position?"

"Yes, TM, because you are my brother. Moreover, Ben Franklin trusts me, along with anyone I trust. And of course I trust you. For you are my brother."

TM did not hesitate, eagerness apparent. Laughing, he allowed, "I hear those French women are tigresses on the prowl." He added, "From his experiences in the Paris social scene, your friend Ben told me as much in his many stories."

# CHAPTER THIRTY-ONE:
# WHITHER PENNSYLVANIA?

Following his return from Maryland, incredulity in his voice, Robert said to Thomas Willing, "Ben Franklin is advocating what?"

"Royal Colony status." Thomas provided Robert with the details. "Ben proposed his idea to the Assembly while you were away. They approved it and promptly dispatched him to London. As you will recall, Ben continues to hope for some sort of reconciliation with the Crown. So, Congressional document in hand, Ben left for England prepared to petition the King and/or Parliament for Royal Colony status solely for our Pennsylvania Colony."

"Ben's got it all wrong—again."

"Yes he does in my opinion. But then a day ago our newly elected Assembly quickly voted its indignation at Ben's idea of separating our Colony from the other 12. I was one of two elected members from the city, along with John Dickinson from the surrounding county. Almost unanimously the new Congress voted down the idea of seeking a separate deal with the King. In opposition to Ben's formal request to the English Parliament, we voted to remove Ben from his post as our Colony's representative to England. Almost all of us believe that for the Colonies to be most effective against Parliament and the King, we must stick together and not go it alone."

"Ben tries. He is respected. This was one of his bad ideas. But he has sailed for London."

"Carrying the 'royal colony' idea."

Robert said, "It is hard enough doing business across the ocean in these uncertain times, but if our commerce was regulated by 13 different sets of laws, we would be confronted with 13 different legal systems. Navigating through the multitude of business hurdles would render commerce infinitely more complex."

"The simpler the better. Ben does not understand the essentials of commerce and making one's fortune."

Robert sighed. "Nor do most people."

# CHAPTER THIRTY-TWO:
# BAD NEWS AND ROBERT'S OMINOUS DREAM

One evening in May, Johannes brought him a letter from Molly at Hill House informing him of the illness of young Robert III, who had become sick the day before. She wrote that in the late afternoon, two Delawares passing by Hill House, at her bidding, had stopped. Observing the child, they lit a fire and boiled water, adding herbs from their saddlebags. They wrapped young Robert in hot blankets, giving him sips of their special herbal honey from the blossoms of the sacred tupelo tree. The Delawares had promised to spend the night on the Hill House veranda so they could see to the child the following morning before moving on. Molly said she would write again on the morrow with news of young Robert's condition. "Thank the Good Lord for the cures bestowed upon we Colonists by our native people." Molly concluded with, "Your Loving Wife."

Troubled, Robert sat down to work on his ledgers. He knew he had to enter the losses from two ships lost at sea. For Robert, the postings were an admission of dual failures—defeats that negatively drained his emotions and his capital, all of which was exacerbated by Molly's letter about young Robert's illness.

News of the first disaster had reached Willing & Morris that morning, the second arrived in the afternoon. One ship was sunk in a storm off Bermuda, the other boarded by the British Navy, its cargo of tobacco and sugar cane confiscated, the fate of the captain and the crew remaining unknown. Insurance, so Robert Morris calculated, promised to cover a fair amount of the lost cargos, but only about half of each ship's stated value. The ship boarded was a frigate, the one lost was a frail snow torn asunder in an unexpected gale coming from out of nowhere and smashing the ship on nearby rocks. Some of the crew had scrambled ashore, according to the rudimentary information conveyed to Robert by the captain of an arriving frigate that had luckily managed to pass through the edge of the storm and pick up a few surviving sailors.

Worrying, he slowly downed a tankard of prized Jamaica rum. Before long he fell into a deep and troubling sleep. His head fell back to ever-so-comfortably rest upon the goose down pillow across the back of his leather wingback chair.

Soon followed a succession of dream scenes with him standing tall on the deck of a frigate sailing into a dark and ominous storm. In his sleep-induced state, it was a frighteningly vivid, yet a weirdly abstract picture. With all his powerless sleepy might, he tried in vain to steer the ship's course away from the approaching storm. Its wind blown message cast him into a helplessness wherein his vessel and he along with it, would be devoured in a watery end. Asleep in the chair, he struggled to steer his ship clear of the imminent danger as he tossed from side to side, the storm threat replaying over and over.

Some time later, in an inexplicable change of dreams, a fuzzy picture formed. In this new dream he was on the firm footing of land viewing a crudely drawn map of the vast Westward lands of North America. He felt relief that the crenellated mountainous horizon had replaced the mountainous whitecaps of an endless ocean. The map's territories, as seen in a palette of inviting hues, beckoned his attention specifically toward the south, west, and north sections of the New York Colony.

Bags of gold coin, British sterling and some coinage unknown awaited just around the bend in the road that he now saw stretching in front of him as he tried to travel toward the known, and yet unknown, of what he was certain represented unlimited opportunity lying in wait in virgin western New York. In the map's distance he saw other American Colonies from Georgia to Pennsylvania beckoning with similar opportunities. As if a waiting mermaid, a siren luring, they each tempted him to enter their unlimited expanses— vacant lands he suddenly knew he must acquire.

Dividing these westward lands into an infinite number of parcels, he began to sell off small holdings to throngs of eager European investors. He saw them pleading to buy, either from him or from his representative, the good Silas Deane, who smiled at him as he moved from France, to Holland, and then England. His dream was making sense as he visualized the stacks of money he was surely destined to make, a fortune that would quickly grow to be larger than any man's in the New World. Smiling to himself, he watched as his wealth exceeded that of the ultra-rich King George III.

When he did awake with the rising sun, the bad news of the previous day had faded into a victorious vista enhancing his financial future. He was performing his role as patriarch of the most prominent family in the American Colonies. Robert Morris awakened as a proud and wealthy man.

## CHAPTER THIRTY-THREE:
## ROBERT AND MRS. G DISCUSS RISK

Days later, on their next carriage outing, Arnold abruptly tugged on the reins and stopped the carriage, the jolt bringing Robert back to the present moment. No longer was his mind reviewing his ongoing merchant ventures, for he realized Mrs. G was talking. He had not been listening, her mellow voice serving as background chatter to his concerns and churning doubts about half-brother TM's French mission that had been conveyed in letters from Ben Franklin and Silas Deane reporting TM's sadly blemished reputation.

With the abrupt stop of the carriage, Robert attended to Mrs. G's latest lilting comment. "Your ships could each get lost—sunk, captured, whatever—you could lose all your money, your children could become urchins wandering the streets, begging for food and ha' pennies, your dear wife would be on the streets, and even worse, with your honor and your reputation sullied, you would be confined to debtors' prison." She added ominously, "With no way out."

He replied, "Precisely the reason I am in the business I am in, Mrs. G."

"Which is?"

"To make my fortune and provide for my lovely wife and my beautiful children."

"And the many risks you take?"

"Mrs. G, I have been captured by pirates, felt myself aboard a ship that sank, and on another frigate that ran aground. I have lost money on uninsured trades where the cargos never arrived, having been captured, stolen, or lost at sea. I have lived each of these frightening risks, felt them squeeze my gut, assimilated them into my thinking, been hand-in-hand with them as their constant companion. After those disastrous experiences, why would I now run from the possibility of more repeated risks? You see, risk has become me. I live comfortably with risk."

"Men!" she voiced with a tinge of disgust.

"Women do not understand," Robert shot back.

Mrs. G laughed derisively. "That is your mistake. We understand full well," she scolded. "We are the smart ones."

"Then how would you provide—moneywise, I mean?"

She tapped the roof of the carriage twice. But the carriage did not move. He parted the curtain. A barmaid was listening to Arnold, whose Southern Negro dialect he heard through the muffling of the cushioned carriage. The barmaid, and he guessed she must be from the nearby drinking establishment, was walking away clutching a paper with inked penmanship written to its edges.

The carriage rocked as Robert realized Arnold had jumped back up into the driver's seat. He heard Arnold's command to the horses, and the carriage started up again.

Mrs. G replied to his question, "I would survive by doing what I am doing and being who I am." Sensuously she touched his cheek with her white-gloved fingertips.

"Slipping information to a Loyalist spy to transmit to the English military?"

Her feminine chuckle conveyed what to him was a warning signal. Robert wondered why on days such as this he allowed himself to be escorted around town in her carriage—perhaps a welcome diversion from the turmoil and tensions of commerce. Yet not wise on his part, for he sensed that somehow she was sneaking confidential information about him and his firm to someone somewhere. But how was he to politely decline her—she being so prominent in town and, yes, so alluring?

# CHAPTER THIRTY-FOUR:
## A DREAM OF DEBT

Bidding their good-byes to their two oldest sons, having entrusted their care and well-being on the long voyage ahead to the ship's captain, Robert and Molly watched as the receding tide floated the frigate Charlotte out into the Delaware River, where it set sail for the German port of Hamburg. Having waved off and on until the last sight of the sails, with Johannes' help, they finally boarded their carriage.

All the way to Hill House, tears flooded Molly's eyes as she lamented the departure of her two oldest sons for Leipzig. She acknowledged to Robert that there, in the university whence they were sent, they would pursue their formal and proper education. "But it will be ever so many years before we see them again," she lamented. "And the voyage is so long and fraught with danger, so I hear from those who have endured the risky crossing."

Robert soothed "The captain is our best. He has made the crossing many times. His ship is among the fastest. He can outrun almost any ship of the British blockade, as well as pirate ships from Algiers. Rest assured, Molly, he and his crew are the best."

Husband and wife soon sat down to dinner in their luxuriously appointed dining room at Hill House. Molly reflected, "General Washington was thoughtful to arrange their enrollment in the Leipzig school."

"His letter carried influence."

Throughout dinner Molly made calculations about how much time would pass for her two sons to complete their studies and return. "Germany is so far away," she lamented. "I shall write to them every day."

"Every week is more realistic," Robert suggested and briefly smiled, his merchant mind beginning to disturb him, apprising him of the dangers a risk-taking international trader in the Colonies faced: no bank, no common currency, no courts sympathetic with merchants and ready and willing to confine men who failed—either due to economic, political, or military conditions beyond their control, or maybe their own poor judgment—into debtors' prison. Was this a civilized place? Or not? The cumulative uncertainties of being on the world's frontier filled his mind. The dangers to his family, evidence his two sons traveling abroad, should there be a disaster of some sort or other, or should he make a financial mistake and suffer monetary setbacks. An array of emotions nagged at his mind, not allowing him peace, quiet, or even optimism as he eventually fell asleep next to Molly under their silk duvet atop their goose down mattress, one of their signs of wealth—niceties over and above the plight of "ordinaries" in the Colony. Those less fortunate, as the barmaid Betsey told him, slept atop straw mattress or on simple rope beds, their bodies covered with one or more scratchy Delaware Indian blankets.

In the fog of an abstract dream, he saw endless stacks of documents. Studying them, ever studying them as he slept restlessly, his dream showed him that each was marked with the nagging message advising: "Debt Due Now."

He tried to tell his mind to go beyond the dire messages. Yet an onslaught of amorphous images of personal debt engulfed him, choking him to the point that he loudly cried out for help, begging someone to save him. Alas, only Molly's sensuous feminine voice answered his desperate calls, yet her quiet, soothing message remained unheard and unheeded by his troubled mental dream state.

Eventually her sweet voice registered with him, calming his turmoil-ridden mind. Robert awoke, sweating profusely. With horror, he recalled his mind's last vision prior to awakening. It was not of his sweet Molly by his side but rather of the austere entrance to a building of granite—a prison, its locked gate thrust open, welcoming him in a macabre greeting, its grim attendant ready to close the door after he had irrevocably passed through. The smiling sheriff with a ghostly grin conveying a "your-number-is-up" message stood by his side prodding him onward toward an ominous iron gate. It was a destination to which he knew he was bound by the law of money and by decree of the court to walk toward, to enter, and to there be ensconced.

In the restfulness of Molly's sweet presence and her lovely calming voice, he forgot his dream and any message his mind might be trying to convey. And Robert Morris arose to face his day ahead.

# CHAPTER THIRTY-FIVE:
## THE WHY AND THE MEANING

Striding together in military lockstep along the planks of the Philadelphia wharf, Major von Lowenstein renewed his conversation with Robert Morris, "First off, explain to me why are you continually trying to make unlimited amounts of money to add to your accumulated wealth. Is there no end to your drive? And please explain why you are predicting a successful Revolution. Those will be our two discussion topics for our stroll today."

Morris gestured to a three-mast frigate where slaves were loading tobacco bales. "You see, Major, every time that ship completes a journey and returns with a cargo of scarce and sought-after goods from England, my firm earns a profit, assuming we get paid in sterling or negotiable bank notes."

"And if that does occur—you call it success—how does that make you feel?"

Morris looked surprised at the question. "Good," he replied, slowly adding, "Like my life is productive, like I am providing for my family—which is my duty and my God-assigned responsibility in life. I believe those are goals the Almighty intended for me to pursue here on Earth."

"How does this determination on your part compare with that of other important men in Philadelphia?"

"You will need to ask them your silly question, Major." Walking on, Morris said, "Do you mean, why do I pursue these objectives while risking my neck, my fortune, and my family's happiness?"

"Yes, this livelihood of yours sounds perilous—and, I must say, an unwise choice of endeavors, judging by the values I harbor in my structured military mind."

169

"Tell me about this military mind of yours."

The Major replied, "Discipline to orders I receive from a higher rank, usually my Landgraf. I do not have to think, to invent, or to imagine. I simply ride on the back of orders—same way my Prince does atop his white stallion when leading his birthday celebration parade through the streets of Kassel."

"Do you not wish you had the challenge of pursuing a new idea you have come up with, of conceiving something different, perhaps innovative?"

"New ideas are for risk takers such as yourself, Sir, not for us conforming military men—we follow orders and rules. We obey the existing equations of life."

"And your Landgraf's festival—has it not gone overboard?"

"Before you judge, let me describe the parade's brilliance: soldiers in their tailored dress uniforms, locally forged weapons precisely shouldered, their parade steps excellently executed. Then, in cadence with the music of the marching band, the soldiers twirl their weapons to demonstrate their dexterity. After them come the cavalry astride their magnificent prancing horses, first trotting, then briefly galloping, then walking in a show of excellent horsemanship. They are followed, to the hoorah cheers of the onlookers, by the artillery, their horses pulling bronze cannons, the trailing carts stacked with polished cannon balls. The billowing flags of our German states are hoisted prior to the dipping of flags to the Landgraf by his personal color guard—yes the pomp…"

To Robert, the Major seemed consumed by nostalgia, devoured by dogma. He saw tears running along the Major's fencing scar. "And you, Major, want to explore my mind? I think I want to examine yours. After all, a parade is a parade is a parade, nothing more or less, at least in my opinion. If you want to explore my mind, then I will tell you, in response to your so very grandiose picture, my thoughts focus on where does the money come from to stage such a parade, who pays for it—your ruling prince or his dependent people? But then that's not what we are to talk about, is it?"

"Some matters, such as royal decrees and events, are not to be questioned. But the mind? The mind and what is going on in it must be questioned."

"You are following some royal order to inquire about my thoughts, are you not?"

The Major acknowledged, "Yes…at first, that was to be my plan. But then, observing you and the other Revolutionaries—"

"—Wait a minute, Major! You are prematurely labeling me. You must know that I may not sign Thomas Jefferson's Declaration of Independence."

"Tell me, Sir, why would you not sign? I hear that many of your Colonial leaders will sign, is not that right?"

"Perhaps, but as of today, I do not know how many."

"Could you become the sole holdout?"

"Perhaps." Morris added with a chuckle, "I would be the only one not hanged after the others have been apprehended by the British and tried for treason."

"On the other hand, Sir, if you do not sign, the Declaration may go down to defeat…because of you. Blame will be upon you. You will be scorned by your contemporaries in the merchant trade."

Silently Robert contemplated such a possibility, deemed it undesirable, and remarked as such to the Major.

"Would you, Sir, want that dubious distinction to be your legacy? I mean, do not all men of power, influence, and wealth yearn to build their legacy for their heirs to covet? Do they not hope to be acknowledged in the book of history?"

"Never crossed my mind."

"What then, Sir, has crossed…does cross you mind?"

They passed a pair of sloops being loaded. Robert gestured, "Those ships and their cargo, and the resultant profits from the voyage, those are the thoughts that are going through my mind."

"Come off it, Mr. Morris, Sir, that is what I and everyone else would expect you to say. I want you to tell me whence has that insatiable drive of yours come?"

"It has been with me since I was a boy on the docks of Liverpool."

"Before you apprenticed here in…where was it?"

"Oxford in the Maryland Colony." He added, "Then here in Philadelphia."

"In both places you emulated role models?"

"Yes, but I was mostly influenced by my father." Robert paused, "And by what people said about him, especially the praising words from our beloved Colonial icon, Benjamin Franklin."

"Now we are getting somewhere."

"Where is that?"

"The history of your mind with your desire for a medley of recognition and respect from your peers."

At the gunwale of the second sloop, Morris greeted the captain and asked permission to come aboard. Automatically the captain saluted Morris and the Major. The two men climbed aboard. Weaving through tobacco bales, Robert said, "Let me portray for you what I call the money motivation."

Inside the small but opulent captain's cabin, Robert took out a sheet of beige-tinted paper. Using the captain's quill pen, he dipped the tip into an inkwell. In his practiced penmanship, he sketched out the financial details of the ship's impending voyage. He set forth the costs: the captain's pay, plus his bonus for a successful voyage, payments to the crew, investment in the cargo, the earlier cost to the shipyard to build the vessel, the insurance premiums covering the ship and the cargo, concluding with the costs of provisions for the voyage. He added the interest cost of the borrowed money that was being tied up during the normal three-month period to initiate and complete the voyage to its destination and return. He added the cost of acquiring the cargo in Europe for the ship's return—English china, textiles, stylish clothing, perhaps, and other goods in demand in the Colonies. Then he penned the revenue to be derived from the sale of the cargo in Europe.

The Major watched the numbers grow.

Entering totals, Robert drew a line and made his calculations. He pointed to the bottom of the page. "This figure, Major, is our hoped-for profit."

"A tidy sum indeed, regardless of the currency in which you have totaled."

Robert nodded. "Compensates, I say, for the perils we continuously confront as merchants. All our ships, of course, do not make the journey successfully for reasons of pirate treachery, Royal Navy, or storms on the high seas."

The Major tapped the sheet with his forefinger. "But why do you want to take on such risks?" He quickly added, "Especially here in this New World. I mean the uncertainties are clearly greater for you here than in good old England and—"

"—Forego such a profit as this?" Robert also tapped the paper.

"It is the size of the profit, not just a modest profit, that lures you?"

Robert hesitated to respond. He repeated the Major's question out loud. "No, Major, I have not thought much about it before, but now I do. My reply is that it is not the money, not the profit."

"Then what is it that is so magnetic that draws you?"

With conviction, Morris said, "It is the mental challenge to chart the ship's course, arrange the financing, as well as the lure of the profits embodied in the whole affair. And then to repeat the exercise many, many times again, each time accumulating more money." He paused, adding, "It is a game one plays, in which you set your own rules. Or perhaps it is simply my life's mission. You and I might describe it as a voyage of self, an ego expression, but one that one's own self is compelled to pursue. In other words, Major, it is out of one's control, perhaps predestined by some higher authority or power. Yet as I think more about it, I conclude the drive comes from within one's mind, one's soul, one's...." He stopped. Stumbling on, he said, "Maybe I do not really know, Major. Maybe you, listening to me, have come to know more than I, given your curiosity and your Prince's orders."

The Major surveyed Robert Morris intently for several moments, then asked, "All this—the Colonies, the continent, the Revolution— has a great historical significance for you, does it not?"

"Of course, you already asked about significance."

"But what if in your mind it had no meaning—did not register on your scale of human values."

Morris raged at the mercenary. "What! You are bloody out of your Teutonic mind!"

"Am I?"

"Yes, everyone knows that one must assign personal meaning to the things they are doing. You do. I do. Ergo, you must be balmy, my dear Major, in the service of some nutty Prince in a faraway land—a land in itself with no meaning, at least to me at this stage in my life! Talk about no meaning!"

"Sir, I assure you I am simply a curious medical person following orders and trying to learn about what goes on in your revolutionary mind. Therefore, humor me and answer my question."

"Say again."

The Major reiterated, "What if neither making money nor even your Revolution held meaning for you? I have come to believe that for many people here in the Colonies neither cause has significance or meaning—so I have observed listening to the patrons in the taverns, overhearing conversations on the streets. From my observations, the masses of men and women remain ambivalent to events, to news, to opinions as to serious discontent. They are ready and willing to be swept along, submitting to the evolution of events, helpless in the fallout from affairs far beyond their control or even the opportunity, in their own uninformed way, to exert any influence, given their lack of desire to do so. Likely the destiny or the future of North America has little meaning for the majority of your Colonial people."

"True, so I fear," Morris acknowledged, his tone downcast.

"So, Mr. Merchant Colonist, an ardent American Revolutionary, an acclaimed leader of the Colonial cause, answer my question, please, Sir."

Robert Morris' ample cheeks were turning shades of red, a colorful palette of anger and frustration beyond the natural hues brought on by overweight. He replied, "Sir, you pose questions beyond my ability to answer, for I have not thought about them prior to these moments of your inquiry. One, such as myself, who finds himself in a role of responsibility, must contemplate such matters while being true to himself."

Silence in the captain's cabin. Then Morris said, "You, Sir, are unduly obsessed with meaning." He remained silent for a moment, then shot out with, "Well, if all this—making money, building my fortune, providing for my family, helping to finance and determine the future of a continent, well, if it all had no meaning, then I would be looking out across an expanse of nothing, an infinity of uncertainty, questioning the meaning of life, the meaning of my own existence, and I would be sorely questioning the teachings of every church I know of. And finding no religion advocating such an emptiness in the human soul, I would despair."

Listening intently, the Major said, "Where then is the meaning for you, Sir?"

Morris shot back, "You know, I do not like this line of conversation."

"I'm not surprised. Our line of honest and deep verbal back and forth is new for us in the medical world, so far as I am aware."

"Never? Nowhere? Not even in Hesse-Kassel?"

"Maybe the Greeks," the Major said softly. "Socrates and those men, you know. They took a different tack." He added, "Perhaps the Chinese, or the Tibetans, but I am no authority on such philosophical matters. I am a simple soldier following military orders in asking you these important questions. I want to know what is in the mind of an American, not a Greek, not a Chinese, but an American merchant who is also a Revolutionary, ready to revolt from an established system of government—eager to discard allegiances to a powerful monarchy, perhaps the world's most powerful that has existed and been honored by millions of people for centuries, even endorsed by the Almighty, or so my Prince tells me."

"Albeit not without suffering from its own quelled revolutions."

"True enough. As an aside, I understand your partner, Thomas Willing, is a nephew of one of Oliver Cromwell's generals."

Morris chuckled, "Runs in the family perhaps, his family, I mean. Revolution or the thought of it. Are we not all Revolutionaries at heart? Seeking something better, yearning for improvements, looking to the emotional horizon for a new and brighter sunrise to take charge of our lives?"

The Major contemplated. In a pontifical voice, he said, "You know, Mr. Morris, I would summarize our little chat here aboard your frigate by saying that this movement, this Revolution of yours—"

"—Not mine, Sir, no Sir, not mine…at least not yet, maybe soon, though."

The Major went on, "This popular Revolution, then if you will, is really the revolt of the New World against the Old World, of two continents parting ways, of a new embryonic culture being hatched that cannot abide by the old culture back home. In that light, I have come to believe that this Revolution is inevitable in the story of the world, and there is no way, no Parliamentary conciliation or remedial legislation, no friendly royal decree, no oppressive military might, whether it be us mercenaries, for example, or the British Navy that is going to prevent the occurrence—oh, maybe delay it a year or two, but never prevent it from taking place. And sooner, or not very much later, it will surely be successful."

Morris agreed. "You have summed up matters, Sir. But are you not changing your mind about the New World?"

The Major smiled. "Perhaps I have listened too intently to you,

Sir."

Morris added, "If you feel we are discontent and searching for something better or even more exciting in our lives, then the real meaning is that there must be something great, so very great beyond...."

Suddenly the captain returned to his quarters, announcing, "Gentlemen, the tide. We are about to raise anchor and cast off."

Robert acknowledged the news, saying, "Major, we better get back on the firm footing of land unless we want to sail back with the captain to the Old Country and revert to its antiquated royal values."

# CHAPTER THIRTY-SIX:
## JULY 2, 1776

Apart from the thoughtfully voiced opinions, one by one so eloquently expressed by the elected Colonial delegates, Philadelphia's Independence Hall seemed in a tense, almost silent waiting mood broken only by the clerk's call of the next man on the roll, followed by the dutifully delivered answer of "present," "here," or "aye." Then that man would rise to speak. He would abstain or advocate as to the future of Philadelphia, of Pennsylvania, of the 12 other Colonies—the future of people living along the Atlantic seaboard. He might allude to the hopes and dreams of the new civilization living thereon. He might even peer into the future and predict or maybe dream about the emerging and changing nature of this distant world to which they had all come, either recently or not so recently, themselves or their parents or grandparents, all from somewhere else far away seeking a new life, their fortune, or simply adventure.

This day of debate, of speeches, of expressed opinions moved along matching the pace of a snail, for the procedure was, as everyone seemed to sense, both parliamentary and historic. Their deliberations and their vote would be a message to the world, telling of the possible change from subject to citizen, from colony to country, from rule by someone else in a system gone amuck, to one of self-determination. Today's seminal meeting had been planned for days, for weeks, for months, some even said for decades. It had been in the minds and the hearts of this group of land-owning gentlemen who had been chosen by voters—fellow male property owners—to cast the decision as to the future of 13 British Colonies touching the Atlantic—European civilization's precarious beachhead on the North

American continent. Precarious because, should the native tribes unite in a common cause, given their sheer numbers, they could drive the invaders back into the surf. Or the French might get aggressive again and attack from the north and the west, or the Spanish might swarm up from Florida and overcome.

The windows of the Hall had been closed, indeed nailed shut, the clamoring visitors from among the "ordinaries" outside thus being denied entry. The group of men inside did not want word, or rumor, or misinformation about their deliberations to leak out to the curious throngs perspiring in the mid-summer humidity. Inside, the heat of the debate merged with the combined body heat of the well-clothed delegates. The stifling atmosphere proved to be an understatement of the contested hot debate, not necessarily a precursor of the final tally in the call of the role.

The vote taking moved along at the pace of melting ice, which each man wished he had to mitigate the heat. For each delegate requested sufficient time to express his thoughts, embellished with his own depth of narration. The vote accuracy must be attested to, and when all votes had been cast and verified, the outcome must be certified by the clerk, and the final register of votes cast imprinted with his official wax seal. For posterity, for descendants, for the world, there must arise no dispute as to who voted or how they voted, so that the official disclosure of the result could not be challenged this day or any day out into the future. And, of course, the British would have their list of "most wanted" to pursue and to hang.

When their name was called, along with the Colony they represented, each delegate delivered his speech voicing for the secretary and eventually the public as to their point of view. After all, these delegates could be declaring a termination to a political and commercial tie that had lasted for almost 150 years. If approved, it would be not only a sea change of history, but also of royal allegiance, and in the process, signify the launching of a new governmental and commercial venture—its results unknown, only speculated—as to what body or bodies should be formed in order to convey law, order, happiness, and the ever so many attributes of life to the people living within its potential legal jurisdiction.

On this crucial day, in the fascination of each moment, the future became the present of human expression. It was also the now of action, or would it be inaction? The question was decision. The future had merged into the present, as the issues at hand had been on the minds and in the hearts of the delegates and the people they represented for months, if not years. The human emotions in the Hall were experiencing a new measure of time to someday perhaps become known as World Standard Time.

The moment at hand culminated the evolution of the human species' skills, its innovative minds—its ability to imagine, to conceive, to create, to envision, to sense. In this series of moments, the spiritual concept arising from a multitude of sources was rapidly rising to its intended zenith.

*    *    *

Standing amidst his contemporaries in the chamber, Robert Morris was unusually uncertain. Not like him, he thought, yet he remained unable to clarify his mind. The soon calling of his name by the clerk did not prod, did not excite, did not ignite him to the brink of decision. Instead, he stood transfixed, pondering. Was this action today too soon, too premature, too ill conceived? Worse, what would be the ramifications? Would they each of them here today, each and every one to be convicted of treason—there standing on the gallows, sacks covering their heads, concealing their angst, their tears, their laments, their wives and families weeping below, hang together following one executioner's call-out, as the Royal Fusilier Band victoriously played "God Save the King?"

Robert Morris imagined the last sight he would see, before they draped his head with that vision-killing black sack, would be his flotilla of ships anchored at the wharfs on the Philadelphia quayside. Their masts would be visible—for the final time—no longer his ships, but now confiscated by the British. At that moment, his view would forever be lost in the woven fabric of coarse blackness, the coarse cloth irritating his facial skin. He would stand along with the others, waiting for the firmness of the platform to drop from under his feet and feel the awful tug on his throat as his neck broke and life soon left his body—forever. He would hope there was something beyond, so very great beyond. Given a choice, he would rather not find out.

He visualized Molly and their seven children looking up at his trembling form—he would likely be the last one on the right—as the tears came and they called out, asking why he was to die. It would hit them hard later—their father no longer being with them. There would be no more hugs, no more fun with father in their beloved Hill House. In fact, by now the arresting British authorities would have confiscated Hill House, taken away the valuable possessions, cut down the beautiful trees for firewood and taken away the fruit from the orchards to feed the troops.

Worse ever, his dear surviving family would no longer be socially accepted, as the Loyalists would now be ruling Philadelphia. His dear family would be destitute. No one would care for them. At best, they would become wards of the city; except, in reality, they would be shunned by all and left to wander the streets in starvation. People would point at them, laugh and call them "the family of a traitor to the Crown." They would become the lowest of the castes on the English social system. Death for them would be their only relief from persecution. Even the religious organizations would dare not come to their aid, for the doctrine would be set by the renewed and now dominant Anglican Church of England, which would annex the independent American Episcopal Church, that body being cast into the hell of heretics. Molly's dear brother William would be compelled to live out a life of shame for his complicity in supporting the Morris family, her family labeled as "traitors."

*　　*　　*

As the time approached for the clerk's call for Pennsylvania delegates to vote, in indecision, John Dickinson left the meeting room along with Robert Morris. Perspiring in heat and uncertainty, the two conversed in the adjacent hallway.

Dickinson, tall, with a pointed nose suggesting forward thinking, perspiration discoloring his collar and in obvious discomfort, said, "By my tabulation, Robert, the vote will end up tied." He pondered. "What shall you and I do when the clerk gets to Pennsylvania, we being the host colony? You and I will be among the last delegates called—myself, Thomas Willing, and then your name—the last?"

"Abstain, I say," Robert replied.

"Yes, abstain," Dickinson repeated, adding, "Our abstentions will deadlock the convention, and the Declaration of Independence will be tabled." The delegate appeared relieved, turned and left Robert

Morris alone in thought.

Robert Morris was silent. Then, to his surprise, he felt a tap on his shoulder.

"Mr. Morris, Suh."

He turned to confront the black face of the Negro slave Arnold.

"How did you get in here?" Robert demanded.

"Suh, please! Mrs. G has instructed me to come and fetch you." He gestured behind. "There is a passageway to the outside. Only us slaves know the secret way."

Robert looked beyond Arnold and saw only a blank wall.

Arnold explained, "Mrs. G is outside in her carriage. Please follow me through the passageway, Suh." Whispering further, he added, "Please, Suh...my orders, it is urgent. She must speak to you, Suh."

"Not now!" Morris shot back, the heat edging up his temper.

"Suh, you must come with me to the end of the passageway, please Suh. I will beseech her to come down from the carriage and talk to you there."

Remembrances of her soft touch on his sleeve and the beauty disclosed by the sparkle of her eyes filled his mind, a welcome diversion, so he permitted himself to sense, from the heat and heaviness of the day. The financier followed the slave.

Black Arnold's white-gloved hand touched a tile in the floorboard of the wall and a small door opened, enough for the two men, even Robert with his robust body, to squeeze through. They entered a short hall leading to a small door in the rear of the building, perhaps built, Robert surmised, as a passageway for a slave from the quarters out back, where the old kitchen used to be, to bring in food or beverage for those meeting inside the hall. With Arnold's touch, the second door opened. In the daylight beyond Robert saw Mrs. G standing, waiting, beckoning. She smiled seductively, the full force of her attention and her beauty directed at him. He moved toward her.

"Robert," she began, her gloved hand reaching to grasp his, the gaze from her eyes instantly stirring his emotions. "Here is what I am offering you." She gently placed a sheet of parchment in his other hand and calmly cooed, "Read this!" She added, "My husband Horatio is a member of Parliament. What he promises, along with the British General Howe...these two members of Parliament can and will deliver as proposed."

"You husband and Howe?" Robert asked incredulously.

"Yes, neither general wants war. Neither man wants to fight. My husband, you see, back when he was bypassed in favor of Washington to be the commander in chief of the Revolutionary army, well, he has never wanted to fight, and neither does Howe—the British general has always advocated leniency toward the Colonies."

Morris read the message on the parchment: "Our dear Mr. Robert Morris, Sir, in exchange for your vote of 'no' against the Declaration of Independence, which, of course, will kill it forever, here is our offer. With your 'no vote," the Colonial revolt will end, and the 13 colonies will revert to their rightful God-given British rule. Therefore, in appreciation for your courageous 'no' vote, we offer you the following:

"*1. A monopoly covering merchant trade between the Colonies and England for Willing & Morris, to be renamed the Morris Trading Company.*
"*2. Five new frigates to be built in the Liverpool shipyards by the end of 1777, specifically for your trading firm.*
"*3. Education for each of your children at any college of their choice in England.*
"*4. A one-time payment of 50,000 English pound sterling—a sizable family fortune, we are sure you will agree for you and your heirs, the funds to be deposited into your personal account in a London bank.*
"*5. A lordship decreed by the House of Lords.*
"*6. In return, you must now return to the chamber and vote 'no' when your name is called.*"

The offer was signed: General William Howe and General Horatio Gates.

In a final tempting blaze of officialdom, each of their respective official red wax seals had been affixed to the bottom of the page.

*  *  *

Robert Morris was stunned. Looking up from the parchment, he saw Mrs. G smiling at him.

Arnold was standing by, as if at military attention, awaiting orders.

Fly the Union Jack on his ships!

Once an Englishman, always an Englishman!

Bed Mrs. G, too, probably, this very night. Yes, he could append that item verbally to the agreement and receive her consent. He knew it; he sensed it. Her eyes, her touch, her sensuous body standing, yielding before him confirmed it in his imagination. Robert felt sexually charged, imagining the intimate scene of the two of them passionately and uncontrollably making love.

But, he disciplined himself, back to the written offer. He knew he must confront it! He visualized the offer of immediate wealth. He imagined the additional fortune he could easily accrue from the exclusivity of the trading cartel. Coin and currency overwhelmed his money mind.

His father—yes, his father, even Nanna, were they still alive, yes, even now up in their heaven, would be proud of him; his life, his legacy, his place in British Colonial history would be recounted on a plaque on the new State House. Perhaps the building would be renamed "The Robert Morris Royal House." Oh, the immortality of fame. Robert Morris asked himself if every red-blooded man does not crave such a noted legacy?

Mrs. G's body language changed from patience to pondering, then to impatience and agitation. Even rigid Arnold fidgeted.

Morris realized it was time. Time coming up for his crucial vote. Action was his. He no longer hesitated. Executing an about face, he marched quickstep back into the passageway and along the short corridor. Approaching the voting chamber, he heard the clerk call out his name, "Mr. Robert Morris, duly elected delegate of the Colony of Pennsylvania, Sir, how do you cast your vote this day?"

Dickinson whispered to him, "I abstained. Willing also. The tally is tied. You, Robert, are the final delegate to vote."

In the hushed chamber, the clerk called out, "Mr. Morris, Sir, do you wish to abstain?"

From in the shadows of the hallway behind him, Morris thought he saw the image of the Hessian Major, a querulous look on his face, his right eyebrow above the fencing scar tweaked upward as if to suggest that with his curious investigative vision he was peering into his mind, demanding to know, "How do you vote, given the financially generous offer you have just received from Mrs. G on behalf of the two generals? What is going on in your mind, Sir?"

In the silence, all eyes turned toward Morris, now standing in the back of the Hall, perspiration beading on his forehead and flowing down his tailored shirt.

Morris wanted to answer the Major out loud, but did so only to himself, as if he were debating his vote. Hesitating no longer, he heard his own voice speak out loudly addressing the room. "Mr. Speaker, Delegates, Clerk of the Convention, there exists in the cosmos a force greater than personal desire that argues not for the benefit of one person or persons, but instead for the good of all the people, and for the good of future lives to come. That future will ultimately, not for me, but for the benefit of the people in the years, the decades, and the centuries to come, be more rewarding than any instantaneous—today—personal monetary gain."

Morris turned away from the shadow of the Major and called out even more loudly as he waved Mrs. G's offer in the air, then dramatically ripped it into pieces, "Robert Morris of Pennsylvania votes 'Aye' for American independence and our new country's promise of self determination."

Benjamin Franklin nodded. Thomas Jefferson smiled. "It is done," Ben said, shaking the hand of the illegitimate immigrant lad, now a man of major stature, who hailed from off the docks of Liverpool.

## CHAPTER THIRTY-SEVEN:
## BANKING ON IT

D ays later, Robert Morris called out to the diminutive and well-dressed gentleman entering the City Tavern, "Ah, Mr. Hamilton, Sir,"

"Mr. Morris," Alexander Hamilton replied, smiling. He seated himself at Morris' trestle table and looked slightly upward at his taller business associate. Hamilton said, "Bring me up to date, Sir, as to how goes our campaign to raise the necessary capital to launch our Bank of North America?"

Betsey brought cider.

"Rum for me, Betsey, please." Hamilton explained to Morris, "I have never gotten accustomed to cider. Whiskey and rum—those elixirs are what I grew up with in the Caribbean islands."

Morris smiled and said, "In England, non-alcoholic cider was our drink from childhood on. Lots of apple orchards." Morris added, "But as to the status of our bank in formation…." Waiting patiently for Betsey to return with the rum, he observed to Hamilton, "As you and I have discovered, few here understand what a bank is or what it can do for commerce."

Hamilton said, "Not surprising, since there has never been a bank for them to do business with. Consequently it is no surprise that they do not understand how a bank can enhance trade, help stock their stores with merchandise, or advance loans so they can farm new fields and plant the important crops that are so much in demand. Without a bank in our Colony to help finance increased productivity, the future will bring runaway inflation, for even now there are too few goods to supply growing consumer demand. Prices for almost everything will most assuredly continue to rise."

Morris interjected, "Few realize the money they can earn by owning stock in a bank." Looking discouraged, he advised, "I can report, Sir, that, so far, I have sold only a measly 10,000 English pounds in stock."

"Not good, Sir. We need more capital, a lot more, in any currency, if we and the new bank are going to finance our fledgling country."

Morris agreed, "Otherwise it leaves us with the only viable means: borrowing money in both France and Holland so that we can continue to purchase the necessary supplies, ammunition, wool for uniforms, and the many items available only in Europe that are needed for our militia. Worse, higher payments will raise our cost of the war."

Hamilton said, "Pity, for we will be paying big fees to foreign banks, as has always been the case in the Colonies."

Betsey came with Hamilton's rum, leaning over as she sat the glass in front of him. His sharply forged face and intense gaze followed her feminine form with delight, then focused on the glass, tilting it, and downing its contents as Betsey watched in admiration of both his body movement and his masculine drinking exhibition. "Bravo, Mr. Hamilton," she whispered, as he placed his hand on her ample thigh. She snuggled closer to the Caribbean immigrant prominent in Philadelphia parlors.

Annoyed, Morris suggested, "Time for that later, Mr. Hamilton, Sir." Downing his cider, he implored his financial cohort, "Let us, you and me, go from table to table here this evening, approaching the notable men of Philadelphia and their ladies and personally urge them to pledge to buy shares in our new Bank of North America."

Shooing Betsey away with a look of "later," Hamilton gestured toward the crowded tavern, "Yes, there are James Wilson, Benjamin Chew, Ben Franklin himself, Henry Laurens from South Carolina, John Adams, James Madison, and who knows who is ensconced upstairs."

"A full house indeed," Morris commented as the two men rose and began their salesmanship rounds.

Hamilton hesitated. "But some of the men here are Whigs. I know their argument against the bank. They will say our fledgling Congress has no authority to create such an institution, that only the English Parliament can do so, and since it has not taken such action, we must wait for that esteemed elected body to legislate such authority to our

Congress."

Preparing to move among the patrons, Morris said, "Mr. Hamilton, Sir, that is the whole argument for independence, but the Whigs do not see it. All they see is retaining and maintaining loyalty to the Crown. As a result, many among us are saying that given these Whigs' position on the matter strengthens our argument that it is time for independence and for us to cut the umbilical cord."

"Onward, then!" Hamilton proclaimed as the two men set about on their round of table talk sales pitches in their campaign to form the first ever bank in North America.

## CHAPTER THIRTY-EIGHT:
## FEAST ON A PRIZE TURTLE FROM THE
## SCHUYLKILL RIVER

One morning thereafter, Johannes, stiff and prim as always in his household servant attire, carried a huge turtle into the Willing & Morris warehouse office. "Mr. Morris, Suh, your admirer Mrs. G has had this here river fella caught on the banks of the Schuylkill delivered to us. Her slave Arnold told me that she is offering it as a tribute to your Colonial steadfastness."

Looking up from his desk and seeing the size of the giant marine animal, Thomas Willing exclaimed, "This calls for a special event."

Surveying the huge turtle, Robert Morris exclaimed, "Yes! This prize catch is larger than any before. We must stage a gala celebration—more festive than those held in past years in this town." He set about to write special invitations to each of his friends and business associates, inviting them to attend a party in a tavern on the city's edge that very evening. He urged them to bring friends and associates, for tonight's event was destined to be a lavish affair. Johannes was dispatched to deliver the invitations.

That evening, at the festive gala, the turtle having been prepared, its many parts embellishing the food offerings to the guests, music from Philadelphia's finest musicians filled the tavern. The ladies had dressed in their finest fashions. And the dancing began.

Robert Morris led the next round of dancing, but a guest soon pulled him aside and whispered. Suddenly Robert's demeanor changed. The look on his face was one of dismay turning to confusion, then anger.

Robert's change of mood became apparent as the many guests sensed something had changed and their host was deeply troubled.

The dour mood stopped the musicians in the middle of their piece. The dancers halted in mid stride. Some dared ask him what was the matter. Robert did not reply, staring instead into mystical space.

Gingerly, Major von Lowenstein approached. Quietly he queried, "Can you share with me what is in your mind right now, Sir?"

In dismay, Robert looked at the Hessian.

Patiently, the Major waited, not anticipating but curious and showing sincere worry. The room was quiet as concern pervaded.

In a subdued voice, yet loud enough for those nearby, including the Major, to hear, Robert said, "I have just been told that the man whose cannon shot the deadly wad that killed my father is one of the guests tonight at my party."

Those standing close to Robert sighed sympathy, yet no one knew what to say in comfort or even in advice. Except Benjamin Rush, who sternly advised, "Revenge is mine, saith the Lord."

Robert remained silent. The Major quietly queried, "How does his presence at your party make you feel?"

Disregarding Dr. Rush's remark, both his fists clenched, Robert replied, "Like I want to kill him right now, right here in front of all these people. My act, to be witnessed by so many people, will show the world that justice is being administered."

The Major observed, "Yours would be an extreme act, and—"

"—Yes." Morris reflected for a moment. "There would surely follow repercussions from the man's family and his shipmates, as well as the White Oaks Society of Shipwrights—they are aligned with the Quakers who are non violent, but capable of their own forms of revenge, which would likely invoke the wrath of Ben Franklin himself—and I don't want to alienate Ben—nobody does."

The Major smiled. "He seems to be untouchable?"

Nodding, Robert went on, "Then there's the Sheriff of Philadelphia, although he's mostly trying to arrest those who owe money and cannot pay."

The Major asked, "But did this man really commit a crime? Wasn't he—"

"—So it might seem to some, I suppose." Robert thought for a moment and added, "You know, as I think more, I realize he was carrying out what he understood to be orders from the ship's captain."

"Plausible, " the Major commented.

"They say he didn't know where the cannon was aimed; it was a fluke that the wad struck my father—an unfortunate happening with dire proportions."

"Will you speak to the man?"

"No, for I am not sure which man he is. Someone will have to point him out to me. Even so, I don't think I will confront him, for when I look at him face to face my temper might flair uncontrollably. Something untoward might take place." Robert added, "Also, revenge for my dear father's untimely death, as tragic as it was, is not on my agenda these days. Commerce and Revolution are. One must not allow personal emotions to obscure their mission in life."

"You have set priorities for yourself?"

"Yes, and when one does that, one must follow them. I am seeing that more clearly now, here this evening, given this circumstance that confronts me. There are times when past events must rest in the grave along with their victims."

The Major studied Robert, watching his mood evolve.

Morris returned to the party festivities he had so recently exited. The guests slowly resumed their drinks and dancing, as music once again filled the air.

Some saw a hint of admiration slowly form on the Major's face as he continued to study the party's host.

# CHAPTER THIRTY-NINE:
# THE MAJOR QUERIES MORRIS ON HIS GOALS

On a crisp fall day, with the white and red oak trees along the streetscape competing as to which species could show the most brilliant array of colorful leaves, two men in contrasting attire stood on Chestnut Street watching the construction of the State House. The Major's Old World collar and jacket made him appear stiff in comparison with the more friendly cloth collar and loose-fitting jacket of Robert Morris, although both wore their finest dress appropriate for public Philadelphia.

The Major said, "Tell me, Mr. Morris, what do you think of the progress being made on the construction of this magnificent new building? Would you say that Philadelphia, as a city, has a cause and that this building addresses that cause?"

Robert Morris nodded his agreement. "Everyone needs a cause. Cities, too."

"For me, please define 'cause'."

"Is not the definition rather obvious?"

"Then it will be easy for you to explain."

Watching the brick masons perform their craft of adding course after course to the rising walls, Morris soon said, "To me, a cause is the trumpet sounding in the morning that alerts you to address the goals you have set for yourself in life and to remind yourself to further pursue them."

"You are saying that it is the process more than it is the goal, like we are watching here with the work proceeding on this building. The workers are in the process, and the goal of completion is their objective, right?'"

"Yes, their goal is to complete the structure."

"Of course, but then after the State House is completed, the City will come up with another goal and there will ensue another process, more buildings, more streets, more docks, that is, if the City is to continue to grow, which according to you, is its ultimate goal. Yet that is a goal that may never in reality be achieved, assuming growth—population and commerce—is a never-ending development. I mean, where does growth stop? Or can it stop?"

Morris smiled. "When we run out of land."

"And, Sir, will you run out of personal causes?"

"A man can have only so many causes."

"Tell me, Sir, what are your causes? Do you have more than one? And how many causes dare you embrace at any given time?"

Morris clenched his fists. "Why do you torment me with this barrage of questions. It feels as if you are firing cannon balls at my head."

Almost whispering, the Major replied, "Because, Sir, I want to understand your thinking process."

"Why?"

"It will help me understand your Revolution."

"It is not mine alone. I am not an author, simply a player on its stage."

"Are you saying we are experiencing something that might be labeled as common knowledge?"

Morris laughed, impulsively shaking his head in a negative manner. "You, Major, have not experienced the array of opinions men here in the Colonies voice."

"I have heard a lot in the taverns, but it is difficult for me to come up with a central theme. Different groups seem to espouse different causes."

"It is so, but they are aligned in their selfish intents, perhaps seeing similar visions of the future, but not always, for there are many remaining Loyalists paying homage to the Crown and endorsing the King's royal prerogative."

"What about the women? Do they also pursue their own causes?"

Morris showed his annoyance once again. "The women?" he asked in dismay. "Of course they have their own separate causes, or so I suppose. Well, yes, I do know from what my Molly tells me."

"What do you suppose they might be?"

Morris shrugged his shoulders in a gesture of indifference. Then, seeing the Major's intense stare as if he was demanding an answer, he said, "Well, there is a list for them, as well, is there not?"

"I suppose so, but go on."

Morris recited, "Babies, children, dresses, hats, meal preparation...and, of course, cosmetics, and then the furnishings and possessions in their homes, perhaps art, although the recognized artists are back in the old country—members of the Royal Society. Thomas Willing will know their names. He added, a hint of incredulity in his tone, "Some of the artists are women, or so Thomas told me."

The Major asked, "Are there not artists here? I mean, the man who painted your portrait, Elouis...."

Robert nodded, "Oh, for sure, I guess they, too, are artists. After all, they use the same paints, canvas, all that. I have also heard they do not go out of doors to paint scenery, they paint only interior scenes."

"Are not they also creative? I mean, like you are with finance?"

"I never thought of it that way."

"Well, what do you think about what I just said?"

"You are saying that one can be creative with money, with finance?"

"Given your accomplishments, I believe you are proving it."

# CHAPTER FORTY:
## SUPERINTENDENT OF FINANCE

A New Jersey member of the Continental Congress rose to speak in objection to the power that Congress was on the verge of awarding to Robert Morris in his newly created and all-powerful position as Superintendent of Finance for the independence-seeking Colonies.

"Abraham Clark," Morris whispered to Thomas Willing, "Is a dedicated man. I admire him as quiet, yet well informed, expressive in his well thought out opinions."

"He is going to object to you having so much power."

Morris nodded and waited.

Being recognized by the Speaker, Clark rose. He straightened his well-tailored jacket, made certain his wig was properly positioned on his balding head, looked around at the other delegates, nodded at those from his native New Jersey Colony, and spoke in a slightly high-pitched voice, yet clear. His words were carefully enunciated for what he had come to realize was maximum effect: "Mr. Speaker, I recognize that for our nascent nation to act in a united way with our finances, we need a strong person to oversee matters of money. But do we realize and can we come to terms with the fact that we are assigning what I would label as 'dictatorial' powers to one man, who—there is little doubt—is eminently qualified? Yet, as Superintendent of Finance, his powers are wide ranging, powerful, and inclusive. Excessively so on all counts, I say, and with no oversight authorized on the part of this august body, or by you, Mr. Speaker."

Clark paused to let his words sink in to the members. With even more vigor, he continued, "Who among us is going to monitor this man? Who is going to oversee his actions, demand from him regular reports of the money spent for the military, for soldiers pay, for favors, and indeed there will be favors to award. Nor are we monitoring the money raised, from which Colony it comes, from which revenue source it is derived. In short, Sir, we are abdicating our duty to know from where the money is coming and where it is going. We are allowing him carte blanche. Too much power to one man, I say, Sir."

Seeing Clark sit down, the Speaker turned to Robert Morris. "What say you, Sir, to the honorable Mr. Clark's objections to the broad scope of your authority as the Superintendent of Finance? He added, "It is the one most important position in the furtherance of the cause of our 13 Colonies, that is, in my considered opinion."

Without being recognized, a delegate from a Southern colony drawled out, "You, Mr. Morris, Suh, are transcending the rights of the states to approve or disapprove expenditures. You will become a monarch like the one we are getting rid of off there in London."

Several delegates muttered, "Hear, hear." Then there was silence in the hall as each delegate waited for Morris to speak. To Morris' dismay and amidst the surprised comments expressed out loud by several delegates, Clark stood again. Without waiting for recognition, in a less diplomatic tone he pointed at Morris and bellowed, "You, Sir, cannot separate your personal merchant trade dealings and those transactions of your firm, as well as those of your partner, the honorable Mr. Thomas Willing, from those contracts authorized by you as the Superintendent of Finance. How are we in Congress to know which are your personal dealings and which are to be the country's transactions?"

A few more "hear, hears" were heard in the chamber as eyes again focused on Morris, who rose to address the Continental Congress. "Mr. Speaker, if as you say, you legislate this new position of Superintendent of Finance and desire it to function properly, you must assign full authority to the Superintendent to carry out the far-reaching duties. If you want this new country to be properly financed, to survive monetarily, and to pay as they come due the debts to our allied nations, as well as to those who with their own funds and credit are financing this Revolution, then you must, by definition, assign and award the force of office to me to perform as you are directing me to do. To proceed otherwise will amount to a mediocre performance and likely failure of the office. That, Mr. Speaker, would result in failure of the Revolution.

"The fact that I, Mr. Willing, and others, all of whose reputations you respect as honest and trustworthy, must conduct personal business transactions concurrently is, well, if I may be blunt, irrelevant! For in the course of our personal merchant dealings with foreign sources of supply and finance, we will, as a matter of convenience and expediency, perform on behalf of the Colonies."

Congress was silent, its members waiting, perhaps contemplating as Morris added, "Further, Sirs, I am unable and unwilling to take on this new responsibility for at least two months, for I am deeply engrossed in a multitude of duties, both personal and for our Revolutionary cause—in paying bills, ordering supplies, and overseeing the shipping and the receipt of goods, along with my colleague, Mr. Willing."

Several members of Congress rose to speak. Not waiting for recognition from the Speaker, the first delegate loudly called out, "You, Sir, Mr. Morris, must take over now. Time is wasting, Sir! We need your services, and we need you, not two months hence, but now!"

The second delegate nodded and, speaking loudly, called upon his fellow delegates to join him as he called out, "I move we acquiesce to Mr. Morris and approve his position and his authority, for there is not one other person anywhere in the Colonies of equal ability who merits our trust, certainly no man with Robert Morris' acumen and skill to carry out such a monumental job as Superintendent of Finance."

The Speaker called for order, for by now several were shouting. One bellowed, "Yes, we need Mr. Morris. Personally, I cannot perform the job of Superintendent of Finance, and who else is there? None of you..." he gestured around the hall..."are sufficiently knowledgeable about the complexities of ocean commerce, the foreign governments and suppliers with whom we must deal, and the manner of financing purchases with notes and paper promises—the things that Mr. Morris knows well. Who else here today...or tomorrow...or two months from now...will step forward to carry this heavy and consuming burden, and perform these responsibilities?"

Many delegates left their seats and crowded around Morris, urging him to take the reins now. Yet Abraham Clark remained with his fellow New Jersey delegates, shaking his head negatively. "We are vesting too much power in one man," he muttered over and over.

Yet several around him disagreed. One said, "Mr. Clark, do we want the job done, or do we desire a traditional description of such a job, with the chance that the assigned tasks may not be performed and the interests of the country not properly and expeditiously served?"

The Speaker repeatedly directed his gavel to hit hard on the top of his small wooden desk, but it took minutes for order to be restored and the vote to be called.

The vote to confirm his appointment, for which Thomas congratulated Robert with a vigorous handshake, was expected by most of the delegates. Afterward, Robert and Abraham Clark shook hands and walked to the City Tavern together, where they toasted each other, gaining the well wishes of a host of Revolutionaries who also hoisted their tankards.

## CHAPTER FORTY-ONE:
## MOLLY'S WARNING

Johannes reared back on the reins, bringing to a halt the four white horses pulling the carriage up to the entrance of the Willing & Morris Warehouse. Holding onto her Negro's assisting arm, Molly climbed down and immediately rushed into Robert's office and urged her husband, "Robert, we must leave Philadelphia immediately!"

Robert Morris promptly closed his ledger book and put down his quill pen. "What are you talking about, Molly?"

Molly rushed, "Anne Wiling just told me that the British Army under General Howe is on forced march to occupy Philadelphia now that General Washington's troops are bogged down containing the rest of the British Army in New York."

Jumping up from his chair, Robert lovingly extended his arms around Molly and hugged her. "Then you must take the children and flee to the country, hide away at Hill House until our militia can route the invaders."

"Not without you, Robert. You must come with us. I don't want...I mean none of us wants you to be arrested and imprisoned. It is obvious. You will not be able to raise money for the Revolution while languishing in a British prison. Congress is relying on you."

Robert's thoughts went to Haym Solomon's imprisonment in British-occupied New York. Reluctantly he nodded agreement.

"Anne says Thomas will remain here. He is practically British royalty, you know, a member of the Temple Courts and all that. She says General William Howe will treat him with respect. They know each other. And Thomas will be able to continue on with the Willing & Morris business."

Robert nodded. "And Congress will rely on me to provide funds to help finance the Revolution."

Molly went on in a nervous tone. "Anne says the members of Congress are going to Baltimore for safety. Robert, we must act fast. Time is critical!"

Complying, Robert gathered his ledger books together. "The locals who stay in town may criticize Thomas for not leaving, label him a Loyalist and call him unpatriotic to our cause."

"Anne tells me he will risk that sort of talk. So be it, he told Anne. By staying here he can placate General Howe and his officers, lull them, allow them to enjoy the taverns and barmaids of Philadelphia, if you want to look at it that way."

"I guess I do look at it that way."

"Your father and Thomas's father, were they with us today to advise the two of you, would agree."

As Johannes stood by, Robert reflected on memories of his father and of Charles Willing. Quickly he set about to hand Johannes the records he would need in exile.

## CHAPTER FORTY-TWO:
## MONEY, WHAT IS BEHIND IT?

Later, in nearby Lancaster instead of Baltimore, the Continental Congress convened out of reach of General Howe's occupying British Army.

Sequestered in his Hill House, Robert Morris read his partner Thomas Willing's latest letter: "Reputation is worth more than all the tea in the East India Company. Our bills of exchange are not being honored abroad. Our credit is being degraded by rumors spread by the British about our Colony's financial troubles. Their Tory newspaper here in Philadelphia is behind this calculated smear campaign specifically targeting our firm. Given these trying times, conducting international business has come down to a matter of trust. But with rumors spreading, fewer business people are trusting us, or at least they are questioning me to the point I must spend my days reassuring them of our firm's reputation, plus mine and yours."

Thomas went on, "I have been assured by General Howe that he laments this adverse turn of events for Willing & Morris. At the same time, I hear from my sources that he is going to pull his troops out of Philadelphia, as he fears the French will attack New York by sea, and he wants to be ready to defend that British stronghold of New Amsterdam. Another rumor has it that General Clinton will replace him, as Howe is under criticism from Parliament for his languishing in comfort in the social life of Philadelphia rather than taking military action to attack our militia."

Morris mused: Trust. Honor. One's personal reputation. The hallmarks of international trade. The guidelines for living a merchant's life. These were the codes of conduct he had learned from his tutors and his revered father. These were the merchant saints he had honored since a boy, during his internships, and from his father's brief but emphatic guidance in Oxford—the guideposts to accumulating personal wealth and providing for family. Robert asked himself if, in chaotic Revolutionary times, these values would prevail, or would there be an erosion of values into a chaos of barbaric anarchy?

To himself, Robert concluded that, while we might overthrow British rule, we could not, under any circumstances, allow the change of Colonial government to alter the codes of personal behavior. He so wrote back to his partner, concluding, "If we prevail, our political change must be accompanied by moral consistency."

## CHAPTER FORTY-THREE:
## TM THREATENS THE REVOLUTION

Having returned to Philadelphia from his Hill House exile, following the British troops leaving the city, Robert Morris watched his firm's sloop "Brandywine" sail up the Delaware River and dock at its Philadelphia wharf. He leapt on board and made straight away to the captain, asking hopefully, "At Bordeaux, Sir, did you pick up a letter from my brother Thomas?"

The captain dug into his mail pouch and sorted through the stack of correspondence. Looking at each letter in turn, scrutinizing both the sender and the recipient, he soon handed one to Morris. "Sir, to you from Silas Deane in Paris."

Clutching the letter with both hope and apprehension, Morris hurried to his warehouse office, anxious to read this third communication from Deane. It would presumably tell if TM had straightened out his life of debauchery and was fulfilling his obligation of employing the funds entrusted to him to acquire supplies for the Continental Army. Moreover, he had been instructed to pursue both social and business contacts with influential French authorities, especially their Treasury spokesman, Henri Neveau, a man whose essays setting forth his ideas on the role and responsibilities of government had inspired many Revolutionary leaders, especially Alexander Hamilton. Neveau had come to be one of the American Revolution's intellectual guiding lights, joining Baruch Spinoza from Holland, Adam Smith, who had just published his *Wealth of Nations* and, of course, Thomas Paine with his *Common Sense* pamphlet.

Morris recalled that, per his instructions and those of Benjamin Franklin, TM had been sent off and authorized to act on behalf of the Continental Congress, his authority expressed in letters from Franklin and himself. "Your brother will do well," John Jay had said in handing the official letter from Congress to Robert. "After all, TM is your brother, and your personal reputation for honesty and keeping your word will hover over his head like a heavenly halo." Jay had gone on, "We in Congress are fortunate to have such an exciting connection with the French, especially one blessed with your personal reputation, which is so well recognized."

Recalling Jay's words, Morris comforted himself as, hesitatingly and with concern, he read again and again Silas Dean's penned words.

After reciting a series of incidents describing TM's egregious behavior during Paris social events, which he had personally observed, Deane wrote, "Sir, if your brother remains in his post, we stand to quickly lose the support of the French, with the accompanying loss of their vital loan funds and their badly needed military supplies. I fear our Revolution will be doomed. I urge you to act at once to dismiss your brother from his post."

Deane appended, telling Morris that he was taking a return ship to Philadelphia "within a fortnight" in case further discussion was needed. The letter was signed, "Urgently and most sincerely, your humble servant, Silas Deane."

Robert' emotions reeled. The debacle was of his own making. Loyalty to family, support for kin—even a half-kin—and respect for his deceased father had colored his judgment. Those had been his motivations in securing for TM the position in France, in wanting to make him an integral player in the American Revolution. What had he, Robert Morris, wrought? His own reputation was at stake. His effectiveness in finance was going to be swept away by this king tide of bad news, now conveyed by Deane.

Morris took quill pen in hand and began to write to Benjamin Franklin: "My Dear Sir, as you have pointed out to me previously in your correspondence, which you based on your own observations of the scene in Paris, my half-brother, Thomas, as verified by the latest account from Silas Deane, is squandering the funds we have provided. Despite my repeated remonstrance to him, he continues to pursue his lavish and irresponsible lifestyle instead of promoting relations with the right individuals in the French government in order to secure supplies of ammunition and weapons, not to mention loans vital to our financing the Revolution.

"He is becoming the talk of the town for his excessive drinking and his wild parties with ladies of the night and others of questionable reputation. His repeated protestations claiming that he is making contacts with people of importance are refuted by Deane as being completely misrepresented. TM's demands for more money from us must be denied.

"Furthermore, I agree with you, Sir. My brother TM must be relieved of his assignment by immediate letter from Congress, to also be signed by you and by me. I will pen such a letter at once and submit it to the Speaker and to you, Sir, for signatures. I will then dispatch the letter on the first fast sloop bound for France.

"Your faithful and obedient servant...." Morris scrawled has large signature and then called Johannes. With instructions for speed, he dispatched his servant with the letter to Franklin.

He penned a second letter to his half-brother on behalf of Franklin and the Continental Congress, relieving TM of all authority to act on behalf of the American Revolution.

*     *     *

Early that evening, drinking alone in the City Tavern, Morris was consoled by Betsey. Given his mental turmoil about Deane's letter, he found it difficult to refuse her advances as Betsey's words brought him a modicum of comfort. She offered, "You tried, Robert. That is all any of us can do. We are not responsible for what others do, even if they are family."

"But, Bets—"

"—Let it pass, Robert. You've now much more important tasks to tend to."

He looked at her, query in his expression.

"Yes," she said, "just this evening I heard that General Washington is planning an important military campaign—as the particular gentleman confided to me—really important, he said it would be decisive for the war."

"Military action? What did you hear?"

Betsey said, "I can't read a map."

Morris insisted, "But what did you hear?"

"Yorktown," she said. "That British general...what's his name?

with his entire army is said to be trapped somewhere on the coast of Virginia. "Yes, Yorktown," he said. "The French fleet is blocking his escape. Washington wants to attack. But—"

"—But what, Bets."

"The troops aren't getting their back pay. Word is they're threatening to mutiny if they don't get paid. They will go home and no longer fight."

"Sailors mutiny, Bets."

"Yeah, them, too."

# CHAPTER FORTY-FOUR:
## CO-MINGLING CRITICISMS

**M**uch later that night, a worried and haggard Robert Morris sat alone in a remote and dimly lit corner of the City Tavern. As much as he loved Colonial cooking, his evening meal stared up at him barely touched.

Betsey eased close, asking, "Molly?"

"Hill House," he answered almost inaudibly, "with our five who are still here."

As if walking on eggs, Betsy tenderly stepped into the topic about which she had been worrying. "All these criticisms, Robert. I hear them. People are saying things about you. What are they talking about? Why do they say nasty things accusing you of…what do they call it? 'Co-mingling.' That's what I overheard someone say. I don't understand what he was talking about, but it sounds bad. Why, Robert Dear, do some men say things like that, demeaning you, after all you are doing for the Colonies?"

He saw her concern.

"Tell me, please."

"Bets," he tried, "I am too depressed over half-brother TM's failure in Paris to talk about my situation here."

She waited, watching him, motherly perhaps, so he thought, protective possibly. His eyes staring off into space for a while, he soon began, "But now that you bring it up, Bets, let me ask you why is it," he chose his words as he slowly continued, "that some men feel they have the right to quickly judge another man's actions when they have never walked in his shoes?"

"Who're these men?"

Shifting his gaze to look directly at her, with fire in his eyes, he told her, "Certain leaders in several of the Colonies. Men who are influential. Men who think they are judges conducting their own mock trial of my actions, my motives, and my honor in financing the Revolution."

"Why do they want to judge you? Hold you up to some undefined standard—"

"—That they themselves do not follow."

"Tell me why?"

"There is a bizarre comfort in someone delivering judgment upon another."

"Robert, I don't judge you."

He forced a smile. "Nor I you."

"Then explain to me their gripe. Maybe I can say something to them—"

"—They will laugh."

"You mean, because I am—"

"—Female? Yes."

"And women don't understand such matters?"

Robert nodded. "Regretfully so."

"Then explain to me as if I was a man."

His mood having been upgraded by Betsey's attention, Robert tried to concentrate on events past. He said, "Maybe they, like the Lees of Virginia who are social icons, see themselves as above me socially—as they would were I still in England—due to what is to them my unorthodox family situation."

"Come on, Robert, this is America. You've told me social status no longer matters."

"Would that it be so."

"It is so, so go on with your explanation."

Robert slowly nodded and said, "You see, Bets, when necessity required that my firm order supplies for the militia, we would make one of our ships ready to sail off for a port in Europe and another to the Caribbean to acquire those items. On those same ships, when they returned, we would load on board goods apart from the military supplies. If the ship maneuvered through the British Navy's blockade, then, of course, the goods—both for the Revolution, as well as for Willing & Morris—would arrive safely. I was accused of taking advantage of Congress' purchase orders and benefiting personally from co-mingling cargoes and the money involved. Similar situations occurred over several years, even after I became Superintendent of Finance."

"Did your appointment change matters?"

"It made the so-called co-mingling more egregious in their minds."

"Did anyone bring charges against you?"

"No, not yet."

"Then all this is negative talk and rumor."

Robert nodded. "Yes, but a lot of this derisive talk emanated from the Lees of Virginia and others who have always been against me. Class prejudice is a gift from the English. It lingers like winter snow, cooling the egalitarian feeling generated by the Revolution."

"These so-called higher class people are out to get you?"

"Seems so—from the beginning, but their attitude is inbred. I have deemed their actions to be not personal." Robert paused, adding, "You know, Bets, we American Revolutionaries have not agreed on everything having to do with independence, or the war. Among those who have ideologically inspired the American Revolution, there is wide disagreement as to its purpose, how it is to be carried out, and how it is to be financed. I mean, we need a bank, but a lot of the founders disagree. Not being well-informed, they fear banks."

Betsey showed confusion. "I thought—I mean, all you men—the Founding Fathers, as someone called them the other night, signed—"

"—Not everyone of us did, and some, even me, did so with reluctance—either we thought the Declaration was premature, or it was too harsh against the Crown, leaving no room for possible future compromise. Those who did not sign were afraid for their lives, their families, their fortunes, and their property. If the English caught them, they would be promptly tried by a British judge."

"Yet you, Robert, along with all those other men, did sign."

"Of course. Bets, we each affixed our signatures. I believe our collective actions were destined by some higher authority. The world, whether it knew it or not, somehow demanded we sign. That day in Independence Hall, scared as I was, some force beyond my control seemed to be moving my fingers, my quill pen tightly gripped, along its inevitable course as I signed my name onto the Declaration of Independence. Same back then when I signed the Articles of Confederation. And, I suppose, if we can ever agree on a

Constitution, I will have the same tingling feeling in my hand when I sign it.

Betsey was silent for only a moment. "Robert, what will happen to you now with these awful men who want to do you in?"

Morris began to voraciously consume his dinner as he drank vigorously of his cider. Between mouthfuls of pork and potato, he said, "Congress is going to investigate me."

"And what will you do?"

"I will, of course, cooperate with their committee. I have nothing to hide. My honor will be on trial. My honor is sacred to me. I will give them my records, the ledgers and personal papers. They can draw their own conclusions. In the end I will be vindicated, for what I have done falls within the moral rules of commerce, patriotism, and personal honor."

# CHAPTER FORTY-FIVE:
## SILAS DEANE

"Mr. Morris, Sir," the Speaker of the Continental Congress began the next afternoon as the two sat down together in a secluded corner of the City Tavern, "You are the esteemed Chairman of the Secret Committee of Commerce."

Morris nodded. "I am indeed, Mr. Speaker."

Raising his tankard in a toast to Morris, the Speaker said, "This morning in special session, we in Congress voted for you to immediately further develop our relationships with the French, and go beyond Haym Solomon's dealings with them here in the Colonies. We voted for you to drop everything and either travel yourself, or dispatch a most trusted advisor to Saint-Pierre on the Caribbean island of Martinique. Once there you are instructed to call on our friend Pierre-Augustin De Caron Beaumarchais—"

"—Morris interrupted with surprise, "Is he not the playwright who authored the libretto for the opera The Barber of Seville?"

"The same." In a lowered voice, the Speaker added, "We understand he has one million livres from the French treasury, plus a sizeable amount of Spanish coin, both of which are designated for us so we can purchase vital supplies for our militia."

"And give the soldiers in the militia some of their back pay, as well."

The Speaker nodded. "As you know, Sir, there is never enough coin to satisfy the militia. This will be a token payment, leaving most of their back pay owing."

"How well I do understand their plight," Morris said with lament, as he rose to be about his assigned task.

\*　　　\*　　　\*

Outside the tavern, Robert instructed the waiting Johannes to drive his carriage to John Dickinson's stately brick home where he knew his frequent business associate, Silas Deane, was staying. In past ventures, Robert recalled that Silas had traveled to both France and the Caribbean on behalf of the Revolution to secure military supplies, as well as to solicit funds from the treasuries of France and Spain, each country remaining anti-British.

At Dickinson's house, greeting Silas, Robert exchanged pleasantries and said, "Silas, my friend, you are authorized by me as head of the Secret Committee of Commerce to sail at once on my waiting frigate Arandel for Martinique, there to collect necessary coin waiting for us so we can buy essential supplies for our militia and, of special urgency to the Revolution itself, make token payment to our troops."

Silas asked for reassurance of his usual commission and also about how the costs of lodging and dining in Martinique were to be covered. Satisfied with the answers, Deane began to prepare for his upcoming ocean voyage, not to France this time, but instead to the Caribbean. "This will be a quick and, I can sense, an important voyage, Sir. With your fast sloop, I shall return within a fortnight."

# CHAPTER FORTY-SIX:
## YORKTOWN, MORRIS' PROMISE

It was barely weeks later when determined shouts from the mob of rowdy soldiers of the Colonial militia could be heard across Philadelphia, even before the unruly columns marched into the city. As the marauding horde drew closer, passing landmark brick houses that lined the narrow carriage-wide streets, the cacophony of their demanding voices served as an alarm for residents.

At his townhouse, a forceful knock on Robert Morris' entry door signaled a warning. Quick to respond, he opened the door to peer into the frightened face of Thomas Willing. His business partner was grasping a pistol.

Almost out of breath, Thomas rushed, "The militia is rioting tonight, this time in strength of numbers. I saw a sergeant riling them up and leading them onward. Their shouts kept repeating over and over, 'Our Pay Now!' 'Our Pay Now!' A corporal in uniform told me they have come, some from great distances, to demonstrate for their back pay. Another soldier told me they haven't been paid in months. Another told me they are refusing to go to Yorktown and fight with Washington and Lafayette unless they are paid—tonight, right here at your house, since you are the Superintendent of Finance."

Morris said, "Yes, I do sympathize with them, but I have not been able to raise the necessary money from the Colonies. I continue to write to each of their governors, as well as the 13 legislatures directly. Repeatedly I cajole, even beg—"

"—I know." Thomas pointed to his pistol, hoping his gesture would signal to Morris the urgency of retrieving his weapon. His tone of voice desperate, Willing warned, "Robert, they are coming here to force you to pay them...or else! God knows what they may do!"

Squeamishly he added, "Some have loaded buckets of tar onto a cart, along with baskets of feathers."

Morris motioned for Willing to hasten inside. From behind his partner ran up a hurried Alexander Hamilton. Seeking safety, he followed Thomas into the house.

"Barricade the door," Hamilton urged. "Quickly now, Robert, for I was told that the sergeant leading the pack knows where you live. He is a strapping giant of a fellow."

His voice reflective, Morris said, "I need to reason with the men."

Johannes, Robert's Negro, running in from the back of the house, breathed, "Suh, you once told me how you outsmarted those bloodthirsty pirates on that French island in the Caribbean. Suh, I know you will do the same here tonight."

Acknowledging the Negro's advice with a nod, Morris quickly dispatched him to get boards, square nails, and a hammer. Willing blew out each of the candles. With help from Johannes, Morris, Willing and Hamilton set to work boarding up the door. At Johannes' suggestion, they then turned their attention to the first floor windows that looked out onto Sixth Street, promptly nailing boards across them. Stumbling around in the darkened room, amidst the furniture of artisans-crafted Philadelphia highboys, birdcage and game tables and Chippendale chairs, the defenders succeeded in shutting out the invading light from the gas lamps in the street.

His mind in sync with the worsening situation, Morris dashed up the stairs, followed by Johannes. Opening his second story bedroom window, Morris peered out to see columns of men rounding the corner two blocks distant. Many were carrying torches. The dancing shadows of the flames eerily covered the buildings the men marched passed. The multitudes kept coming in a steady and frightening stream, muskets in hand. "Thank heaven, Molly and the children are away at Hill House," Morris said out loud to himself. Johannes nodded his agreement.

From below, Hamilton called, advising Morris he was going to go out the back door and fetch Washington, predicting with hopeful certainty, "The General will calm the men."

As Hamilton opened the rear door, they could hear the callous voice of the leading sergeant, now much closer. Though Willing quickly closed and locked the door, the gravelly voice of the militia leader penetrated the house. Now shouting from the front, the sergeant bellowed, "Mr. Morris! Come out here and give us our back pay, or else we're going to come in there and empty your strong box!"

Johannes vaulted down the stairs, unlocked the back door and ventured outside where he ran around the house and confronted the sergeant. The Negro held up both hands, frantically commanding the renegade brigade to halt. "Listen to what my master has to say," he pleaded to the militia mob.

Someone yelled, "Shoot the Negro!" Right away a pistol pop sent a pellet over Johannes' head. He screamed a Gullah obscenity from his Carolina childhood.

From upstairs, Morris heard a second shot. Simultaneously one of his upstairs windowpanes shattered, shards of glass spewing over him. To Morris' thinking, the two shots delivered not only a grim warning but also a burst of confidence. His resolve rising, the concept of a plan surged in his mind. With his mental sketchpad racing, he realized he needed more moments to refine his nascent idea. Maybe, just maybe, he could offer a solution. As Johannes had reminded him, based on his Caribbean island episode of years ago, there was a time in which to eschew fear and take action. That time was now. His plan beginning to dance in his mind, the choreography writing itself, Morris opened the upstairs window. Leaning out so those gathered below could see him, in his loudest voice he shouted, "My fellow men of Pennsylvania, allow me to let you in on where money matters stand."

The crowd noise subsided a notch. Then, upon a silencing command from the sergeant, the rumbles fell to a few murmurs.

Morris announced, "General Washington will be here momentarily."

Several cheered loudly, "Hooray for our General." One fired his pistol into the air.

The sergeant called out, his tone an order, "Men, be quiet." Silence followed. He told the men, "We came to hear what the respected Mr. Morris has to say."

The word "money!" followed by "our money!" was heard repeatedly from the ranks. For emphasis, another pistol fired into the starry night sky.

An alert Thomas Willing now stood by the side of Morris, showing his pistol to the crowd. Tension filled the air. Hand-held torches blazed. Shadows bounced off the bricks of houses, sketching a flickering and ghostly scene. Morris imagined Dante's layers of hell as, waiting in agony, he hoped for quiet from the men below.

The militia veterans looked up at Morris' open window, focusing on the man they recognized as the newly appointed powerful Superintendent of Finance.

One was heard to say, "If anyone can get us paid, Mr. Morris is the man."

In the fleeting moments, Morris debated with himself as to how he might express his freshly devised scheme. One miscue could set off a riot, perhaps the storming of his house. For a brief moment he envisioned the men's buckets of tar and their baskets of feathers. He wondered what it would be like to be tar and feathered and paraded along the streets of Philadelphia. Clearly embarrassing and worse, painful, and yes, even life threatening. The episode would be accompanied by demeaning jeers from the soldiers. Worse for him would be the diminution of his personal reputation and the eroding of confidence in the Revolution itself.

Yet the scenario was simple. The men wanted to be paid. They did not come all this way to enjoy the discomfort of one Colonial gentleman, namely himself, on this surreal night. They had left their families, their farms, their shops to rally for payment due them. Money. They wanted it before they would go into another battle against the British. Yes, that was the rumor Betsey had told him about: Washington's impending and hopefully decisive military campaign against General Cornwallis.

Morris realized the soldiers had been told that they would be getting orders to march into the Battle of Yorktown. And they have decided, en masse, patriotic as they may be, that they will not go because of not having been paid for months. Fighting for a cause— yes. But getting paid to do so, for they had forsworn their usual sources of income in order to join up and fight. Was that so wrong? Morris reminded himself that he would not have become a merchant without the prospect of being rewarded financially, compensated for taking the risks, not of dodging bullets, but for facing monetary loss, along with the possibility of being wiped out, not physically, but financially. Rewards. These men want their financial rewards. Obviously. Was it not that simple?

Trying to capture the moment, Morris began by addressing the riled-up men in a calming tone. He projected his voice out over the throng who were impatient, hoping, and craving their pay. As they nervously shifted back and forth and fingered their muskets, Morris told them, "You will each be paid. Let me assure you."

Someone yelled, "When, Mr. Morris?" At the top of his voice, another joined in, "Yes, when? We've gone months without pay." Another shouted, "We have trusted you."

Morris shouted back, "You still can trust me. Trust is all I have in this world." He paused before emphasizing, "I understand your situation. The General understands. We all understand. In fact," he went on, "as Mr. Willing told you, General Washington will be here soon to reassure you that he sympathizes with you and to assure you that you each will be paid."

The veteran fighters grumbled to each other and impatiently looked to the sergeant for orders. The sergeant acted unconvinced.

Quickly Morris' loud voice resumed control of the evening. "Let me tell you a story that will explain the events each of us has experienced in our struggle for independence."

A din of discontent filled the night air.

The sergeant held up both arms and bellowed, as only sergeants can do, "Men, let Mr. Morris speak." The discord was so great that he repeated his command three times before attentive silence awaited Morris' further words.

In a voice filled with companionship, Morris began, "Only a few years ago, 13 Colonies sought redress from a distant and hostile King and an unsympathetic Parliament. The Colonies wanted no part of paying taxes without having a say in the matter and without representation in a legislative body that met some 2,000 miles away. And met without their input or any interest in responding to their pleadings."

"Yeah, yeah, that's no story. We know that," one disgruntled militia member shouted.

Ignoring the interruption, Morris went on, "Let me continue with the story."

Grumbles, but attention.

Morris continued, "By today, as the chapters in this story have unfolded, we find ourselves on the verge of gaining independence from that oppressive and distant yoke. One more successful battle will achieve our goal to govern ourselves."

The men's attention focused more intently on Morris, as he spoke in a loud and clear voice. "But, Men, I want to tell you that in our story each of the individual Colonies has resisted our pleas for money, money for food, money for weapons, and most importantly, money for your pay. The Colonial governors and their legislatures remain in the mood to not levy taxes. Without taxes collected, the Colonies have no source of money to pay its soldiers—you brave men."

Morris paused, allowing his words to sink in. Then he continued. "The Colonies are holding out from paying me as Superintendent of Finance the necessary funds that I need to pay you. Believe me, I have made every effort and repeatedly so—letters after letters to every governor, to every legislative body in each of the Colonies—imploring them to do their duty in this struggle, to tax their constituents so we can pay for your efforts to fight for liberty for all of us."

Morris picked up random sheaves of paper from his nearby desk. He waved the thick stack at the throng, suggesting, "See, here are copies of my letters to each of the Colonies." Next he waved only two sheets of paper at the crowd. "And here are the only answers I have received, each one telling me in no uncertain terms that their state's legislatures cannot and will not levy taxes on their citizens to collect the funds to pay you." Emphasizing his movement, Morris shrugged his shoulders several times. "What can I do?" he asked the crowd. He waited agonizing moments to allow for their answers, a questioning look on his face.

Someone yelled, "Then we won't fight." Many more murmured their agreement.

"But you must fight!" Morris implored. "The entire American Revolution depends on you. Think of those brave men who have died for our cause. We cannot betray them. We must not ignore their sacrifices. They are calling out to us to continue the holy crusade, to not falter at this critical and, hopefully, final fight."

From below, the sergeant yelled, "But Mr. Morris, Sir, what can you do to help us get our pay that is so long overdue, plus the pay we'll earn if we continue the fight and march with General Washington to Yorktown?"

Thomas Willing looked in anticipation at Morris. Johannes idolized his master, waiting. Alexander Hamilton had not returned in company with the General. The air seemed filled with the uncertainty of a young country's history, which seemed about to crumble into oblivion.

From the cobblestone street in front of Morris' house, all eyes looked upward at Robert Morris. All thoughts were directed toward him. The hopes of the multitude were transmitted upward.

Morris broke the silence but not the pervasive mood of anticipated hope. "Men, I want to tell you that our esteemed friend, the honorable Silas Deane, is due back from French Martinique and Spanish Florida any day now. He will be carrying an amount of coin given to him in Martinique. In addition he will have collected hard coin from our Spanish allies in Florida. Mr. Dean will deliver these coins to me, and I will distribute them proportionally as a token payment toward amounts you have coming. I will personally make certain everyone receives a portion of their fair and due amount. This coin of the realm will tide you over."

Some in the crowd cheered. Morris promptly appended with more details of his plan. "As for the rest of your pay, as well as your pay to march with General Washington and Lafayette to fight General Cornwallis, who I have heard is cornered down there in Yorktown, my message to you tonight is as follows:" He waited for silence, then announced, "I will personally guarantee that each one of you will be paid in full."

"But you are offering only a token payment."

"That will be up front and in French and Spanish coin," Morris reminded loudly and emphatically.

The sergeant demanded, "How, Sir, will you pay us the rest of our money? And when?"

Morris waited for their full attention before replying. With all eyes directed his way, he told the men in his strong voice, "Within a week."

Cheers rose.

Morris told them, "Here is what I will do, and how I will do it, and how you will get your money." In a slow deliberate tone, he revealed his plan. "I will give each of you my personal notes. These notes will have a series of due dates specified on them, dates on which you will be paid—and with interest. The dates will begin three months from now. Each of these notes will be individually signed by me. They will represent my own personal obligation to you and to anyone to whom you might sell or pledge the notes."

"Morris Notes," one man yelled in a positive and upbeat tone.

The sergeant said it all on behalf of the men, "Mr. Morris, Sir, your credit and your reputation is all we need to be assured of receiving our pay."

"Yes," shouted several of the men from the rank and file.

At that moment Alexander Hamilton came running down the street, gesturing with one arm to the men and the other pointing behind him. There, each and everyone saw off in the dim distance a white horse with a stately rider up.

"The General!" rang out a growing chorus of military respect and reverence. Cheers rose.

"Yorktown!" cried out several men. Others echoed, more now calling out cries of "On to Yorktown" and "Victory for our Revolution!" Louder cheers soon rose across the Philadelphia night, as the militia members, one by one, saluted the General as he, returning their salutes, rode past.

# CHAPTER FORTY-SEVEN:
## SIGNING HIS PERSONAL NOTES

Philadelphia was home to only one professionally trained engraver, Amos Van Airondak. He was known to tell people who came to his shop on Fourth Street with their engraving needs how busy he was. "Six months at the earliest," he was known to tell a prospective customer. So, the next morning when Robert Morris called upon him, he was not surprised when Amos barely looked up from his tedious work and mumbled only a cursory recognition of the Revolution's Superintendent of Finance."

Morris wasted no time, for there was no time to waste—the Revolution, indeed the future, so he believed, was coming down to Amos performing his skill and doing so at once. Morris was quick to advise Amos that the 13 Colonies and the entire world was this day looking to him, an immigrant from Holland, to perform his artistic craft, for which he had apprenticed in Amsterdam, and to do so both professionally and quickly.

From his years of commercial experience in the New World, Morris knew that, on the important matters on people's minds, engraving was way down the list, if present at all. For the craft was usually performed in isolation by a recluse whose ability to tediously inscribe a steel pen into a metal form was one of the least exciting and certainly unglamorous tasks—below milking a cow, plowing a field, or harvesting a crop—all necessities for survival in any of the Colonies. Engraving was not one of life's pressing necessities— except now. For the task that Morris was going over in his mind was to produce a form—an engraved currency much like a bank note—to be printed with his personal image, and to which, individually on tens of thousands of copies, he would personally sign his name with a quill pen—making his personal guarantee to pay the holder of the note an exact amount of money at a future time specific. And this promise—which would be regarded in the minds of the fighting men to be good as gold—would pay them to fight and bring down the curtain on British rule in the 13 Colonies. With this final and decisive military victory, their force would assure the birth of the new United States of America.

Morris was pleased when Amos, having been told of his personal importance in his prioritized engraving mission, looked up, and to Morris' surprise, actually smiled. Perhaps he has never felt himself to be such an important man, Morris concluded, as he emotionally described this new job opportunity to the Dutchman. Satisfied he had enlisted Amos in the urgency and the importance of the Revolution's engraving demands, Morris went on to explain to the engraver in detail the critical task at hand.

*     *     *

Later in the City Tavern, a curious Morris asked Betsey, "Who are these two young men here with you this evening?" He looked at them more closely. "Why, they resemble you, Bets."

Betsey beamed. Proudly she introduced her two sons, now grown and quite obviously Colonial handsome. "They heard about the Yorktown campaign and have joined up with the militia," she announced. To the tallest, she gestured. "His name's Luke. And this here's his younger brother Mark."

The two young brothers and the gentleman shook hands. Morris smiled and said to Betsey, "Your letter got delivered to them, after all."

"Our letter," she corrected. "Yes, finally. Three years, at least, maybe longer. But yes."

Morris whispered, "And their father?"

Betsey turned to Luke. "Tell Mr. Morris, Luke."

Luke spoke up. "Sir, Mr. Morris, Sir, my father was shot by another settler who over the years had been continually harassing us, claiming the land we had cleared, planted, and were farming all those years was actually his land. Mark here thinks—"

"—I know so," Mark interrupted.

Luke continued, "It seems our father had bought the same tract of land as did the other man—bought from that same land salesman who came through Philadelphia when we were little boys. But out there on the frontier, there was no government for us to turn to for a settlement or for justice after my father was shot and killed. Our stepmother of sorts, the Delaware squaw Spring Robin, got scared and left. I guess she went back to her tribe. Me and Mark finally got our Mother's letter. By then we could read a little, and we decided to come home. On our way, we heard about the Revolution. Being lost as to what to do with our lives, we decided to sign up to fight at Yorktown alongside that French marquis, Lafayette, and our great General Washington."

Morris smiled at the boys and said, "Do you want to play a role right now? Start tomorrow and play a vital role in the Revolution?"

Betsey looked surprised, even fearful. Morris calmed her. "No guns, Bets, just bank notes."

"What you mean, Robert?"

"You know Amos Van Airondak?"

Betsey said, "Weird man, a recluse."

Morris smiled and nodded "But patriotic. Today he has begun engraving my personal bank notes. Very soon I will need someone to pick them up, package by package, at his shop and carry them to my warehouse office so that I can begin signing each and every note. I estimate there will be thousands and thousands. I will need help to deliver them to the paymaster of the Continental Army. And he will need help in distributing them to each of the fighting men. These tasks need to be accomplished within the next few days. Amos says he will work day and night in engraving the notes, and I will do the same in signing them."

Luke said, "Sir, Mark and I will work day and night to help you."

Betsey hugged each of her sons. "I'm proud of you both."

Morris shook their hands once again, this time empowered with the firmness of their mutual commitment.

# CHAPTER FORTY-EIGHT:
## "RESIGN YOUR COMMISSION"

The Hessian Major sat opposite Haym Solomon at a trestle table in a corner of the City Tavern's great room. At the Major's left was Robert Morris. Haym looked across the table dividing the German military man from himself—an Ashkenazi Jew from Poland, Portugal, England, and lately New York where he had twice been locked away in a British prison. Staring intently at the Major, Haym proposed, "Here's to all the good soldiers from Hesse-Kassel who have abandoned their units to remain here in the Colonies and seek new lives."

Robert said, "Yes, Haym, after Washington's surprise early Christmas morning victory at Trenton when the Hessians surrendered, many mercenaries, having become prisoners of war, soon elected to stay here and not go back. In return for their written promises, they were freed." Morris raised his glass to touch Haym's. Robert's gesture made sure the clink was noticed by the Major. Yet Major von Lowenstein sat in stone-like silence. Was he reluctant to participate in a toast offered by a Jew? Robert wondered if a salute might violate his military oath to his pure-Teutonic Hessian Prince. Yet it was apparent to the others that the Major was troubling over a restrictive emotion. Perhaps he realized it was ingrained and not learned. Yet this was the New World where new thoughts and new ideas were there for everyone to consider.

Observing the Hessian, Robert instead guessed that Haym was reviewing the Philadelphia chapter in his life. Despite his efforts and even his monetary contribution to a nascent building fund, Haym had not been able to establish a proper temple where people of his faith might worship. He understood it was a problem having to do with the liturgical conflicts between Jews from Poland and Jews from Germany. While they were of the same faith, they could not agree on doctrine.

Robert was about ready to ask Haym about the synagogue when Haym reached out verbally across the divide. "Tell me, Herr Major, what do you see in your future, now that the role of your Hessian troops has become more or less irrelevant?"

Startled, the Major harrumphed in a haughty tone. "You speak nonsense, Sir." But he immediately grew contemplative. He stroked his dark moustache. The fencing scar that ran vertically down his cheek twitched. In seeming uncertainty, he stuttered his response, "I will go home...of course. Yes, I shall go home."

"Why?" Haym's question conveyed a hint of some other possibility.

"Because," the Major began, then blanched.

Robert suggested, "Ours is now a free country. With opportunities for a man to make his fortune, to prosper, to provide security and happiness for his family."

The Major acknowledged. "Yes, I have so observed."

"Then," Haym urged, "resign your commission, send for your family back in Hesse-Kassel and join the tens of thousands of immigrants who are helping to build America."

The Major mused, "Well, if I were to do such a thing then...well...I would not have to report my findings to my Landgraf, now would I? That would be a relief, for I'm not sure what I would be saying were I to report back to him, that is, the answers to his queries that sent me here in the first place, as well as to questions I have come up with on my own while pursuing his royal assignment."

"What might you say to him were you there now standing in his presence?" Haym asked.

The Major reflected. "Well, I would say to him that the mind is an unexplored continent, much like the New World in that it is just beginning to open up. As such our first impressions may be correct, on the other hand they may be subject to further research, both in depth and over time."

"Meaning what?" Haym pressed.

Morris suggested, "The Major by now may think he knows what is in my heart and my mind. Perhaps he does, that is, to a degree, but maybe neither he nor I really know or understand. If there is still doubt remaining after our conversations, then think of the vast horizons of uncertainty that remain as to the contours of the minds of men and women."

"Precisely what my report would stress, were I to give it." The Major stood to toast. "To the minds of men," he offered.

Robert raised his glass, touching Haym's and then meaningfully reaching toward the Major's tankard. Glasses were poised in mid-air, waiting for the words hoped for from the Hessian mercenary.

Struggling with himself, the Major seemed to be mulling his instilled military code of conduct and his personal values. He soon clinked his glass to Robert's and Haym's in a sound heard 'round the tavern. He saluted his tablemates with, "To my esteemed fellow Americans!" Drinking heartedly, he said with vigor, "Yes, I, too, will stay here in America!"

# CHAPTER FORTY-NINE:
# THE DANCE AND BENJAMIN FRANKLIN

Yellowish candlelight flickered from multiple candelabra, radiating outward through the Carpenters Hall's round-arched windows. The warm welcoming light sparkled the crystals of rain that blew across the Colonial carriages as they decanted the finest-dressed of Philadelphia society. Impeccably uniformed slaves, along with free black servants, raised sheets of sailcloth above each passenger as men, women, and couples scurried to escape the wetness outside for the hall's dryness inside. The women hoped their hats and hairdos could be kept dry, along with their fashionable dresses, the latest from Paris' finest sartorial salons.

But lacking social courtesy, the tempest insisted on descending on the attendees exiting their carriages and entering the hall, there to satisfy their curiosity as to who were the other invited guests at this most important social gala.

As the rain persisted, it seemed undecided as to whether it was blowing in from off the Atlantic Ocean and crossing New Jersey, or if its storm force was streaming north from off Chesapeake Bay. For its direction of origin oscillated from one direction to the other without waiting for a meteorological explanation, leaving the trees in its path undecided as to which way to bend. The rain gusts of wind added exclamation points to the evening's deluge, rendering more dramatic the cries of angst from the ladies fearful of being beauty-spoiled by their inescapable wet greeting. Their muffled screams of angst with each new wind gust offset their giggles of delight at having been invited to this first social event of the season designed to dedicate the newly constructed Carpenters Hall.

They asked: why did the gods have to rain on such a delightful event? The dampness caused them to fear if, in the story of the new country, this evening's weather was a precursor of tomorrow's troubles. Was this stormy night at Carpenters Hall a disruption to their New World dream? Would the awakening morrow prove even more devastating? Or would the sun, again, shine on their lives and their new nation?

As Molly and Robert Morris entered the Hall, a sort of hush at noticing their presence fell across the multitude of guests, allowing the soft viola de gamba music to be better heard. The female Negro slave who was playing the instrument remained expressionless even as more of the guests, focusing on her playing, openly admired her talent and realized she had likely benefited from the coaching of a white woman. Some asked if a woman so talented could actually be a slave. How could that be so?

Molly and Robert greeted Alexander Hamilton, John Jay, and Benjamin Rush and then, turning to Anne and Thomas Willing, exchanged damp hugs.

Champagne in hand, Thomas said, "Thank heaven we have so many expert carpenters and brick masons in Philadelphia. Otherwise, this magnificent center piece of our city's architecture would not have been completed in time for tonight's opening."

Robert said, "I am glad to see that many of our craftsmen are present as invited guests. Rightfully so, I say."

Looking around the ballroom, Anne Willing exclaimed, "The dancing is about to begin."

Conversations ebbed as a hush fell across the hall. Philadelphia's important people, their servants, their slaves, and free blacks, as if in commanded unison, looked toward one figure entering the dance floor. Benjamin Franklin, his eyeglasses seeming to smile a Colonial camaraderie to all present, was carrying a contraption, which he carefully stood upright on the floor as a slave brought him a chair. Franklin sat, gently placing his cane by his side. He adjusted his distance to be a bit closer to the device so that both hands were resting atop what all could see was an ivory keyboard. The guests then observed that his black leather shoes touched upon a treadle underneath the musical instrument.

Molly whispered to Robert, "This is Ben's night to show us his new invention. He has named it a 'glass armonica'."

Responding to Robert's inquisitive glance, Anne explained, "There is a spiral of glass within that contains dripping water. When Ben activates the treadle and plays on the keyboard and changes the force in his fingers, we will hear sweet harmonic music."

Thomas whispered to Robert, "Anne's had a private demonstration. You know, she plays several instruments."

Molly smiled. "She does especially well playing for family and friends on the harpsichord. All while raising 13 children." Molly added with admiration, "Six more than Bob and me."

Anne interceded, "But you, my dear Molly, are the social leader with the many parties you and Mrs. Bingham put on. The two of you set a standard none of us can come close to matching."

Molly blushed, smiling demurely.

Ben Franklin started playing.

The dancing began.

Anne commented to her companions that Ben was playing a Mozart piece written specifically for his glass harmonica. The instrument's lilting music filled the hall as couples' dance steps followed the beat. Smiles and curtsies on the part of the ladies mixed with the answering polite nods of the handsomely attired gentlemen as Colonial Philadelphia enjoyed its evening of dedication to the carpenters and masons who helped create the new pulsating community hall.

New Music. New ideas. New times. For those who themselves or their parents had crossed the ocean, a sea change in the philosophy of government loomed on the horizon as they listened to the notes from Ben's magical musical invention. For tonight, despite the storm howling outside, many taking part in this Colonial festive occasion sensed the presence of an enigmatic future and a conundrum of change.

Compared to previous social occasions, the dance steps this evening seemed to Robert to be more vibrant, more anticipatory. The milieu of the moment suggested the impending end to the howling wind from a place afar and a cessation to the loud pummeling rain from heaven, each assuredly to be followed by the arrival of an enlightening dawn.

Perhaps, he pondered, personal profits would piggyback.

# CHAPTER FIFTY:
# BUY LAND, LOTS OF LAND

Staring up at Robert Morris from atop his felt-covered plank table was a map, albeit crudely drawn, of the western lands of the New York Colony. His gaze shifted back and forth from Lake Ontario on the north to Lake Erie on the west and then to the Colony's southern border with Pennsylvania. He ran his fingers across the vast expanse of unoccupied land making up most of the map's vaguely defined landmarks—rivers, swamps, rolling hills, forests of virgin timber, valuable salt deposits, the beaver dams and lakes (weren't beaver hats the epitome of male style in Europe?). Except here and there were shown Native American villages and the range of their roaming traditional hunting grounds. He reasoned that with clever negotiating and offerings of trinkets, the Indians surely could be convinced to give up the previous treaties and sign new treaties. Then they would move on to "glorious new hunting grounds" farther, and then even farther west, allowing European settlers free range.

Yes, Morris beamed, Western New York was all his! He had agreed to buy it from an estate in Scotland, whose caretaker manager had been instructed to sell. He wondered if the Scots had lost the enticing glow of the economic opportunity shining from the New World. Anyway, for whatever reason, they were selling, and he was buying. Why Not? The millions of his purchase money were not due to be paid—after the token down payment—until off in the future. Besides, the so-called money the Estate had agreed upon was to be paid in Colonial script, which had so depreciated in value as to render the actual purchase price to be a shadow of the agreed-upon amount. But to European investors—yes, they would be scrambling to own a piece of the New World.

Meanwhile…was not his colleague, Silas Deane, in France re-cultivating his many personal contacts from when he had placed all those orders for armaments? Over there, he was shuttling from one investor to another, with instructions to tout the riches they could accumulate by acquiring parcels of this western New York land. Silas was already playing to their greed while calculating his earned share of the many purchases he would entice to be made by Old World land speculators.

Robert took up his quill pen, dipped it into the ink well and jotted the anticipated sales prices of the almost unlimited number of parcels that Silas would surely sell. The total coming into his personal coffers, so Robert totaled, surpassed the entire purchase price by a factor of—yes, the gain for him was incredible, the gleam of potential profit blinding his vision of the map's uncharted details.

Silently he toasted himself before spreading out his next map of the Georgia Colony. It stretched all the way west to the great river called the Mississippi. He examined again his contract to acquire, with a token down payment, the orange grove plantation of some half million acres, though its borders were crudely defined.

With the institution of slavery surely to be preserved in any constitution drawn up for the Colonies, the cultivation and farming of such huge tracts of land offered coin of the realm riches. Extolling such a story to European investors, Silas would again prove his mettle as a salesman as he emphasized parcels thought to be desirable due to either location on navigable waterways, rich farming soils, or vast stands of virgin timber.

Indeed a second toast was in order, and Robert poured another ale into his glass as he examined the next map, this one of Western Pennsylvania as Thomas Willing entered the office, saw the maps, and queried, "Robert, why do you keep adding to your land holdings? You are deviating from ocean commerce, a trade we both know and well understand. With it, we are comfortable with the many risks and its lucrative rewards, all of which make it a known quantity. Now you are into land speculation—something you and I know little about. I for one feel uncomfortable with such schemes. Robert, I fear you are changing course, giving up a known quantity, while substituting a list of unknowns."

Robert said, "A number of our Founding Fathers have spotted the same shining stars of opportunity."

"I see an eclipse of the sun, Robert, and maybe even the moon."

Entering, Major von Lowenstein saw the maps and asked Robert to explain the purpose of his many land purchases. "Why, Robert—"

"—Exactly my question," Thomas said, interrupting.

The Major said, "What is in your mind, Sir?"

Robert rallied his resolve. "Gentlemen, I am responding to reality."

"Which, in your mind, is?" the Major asked.

Morris said, "We have a new nation. We have voted the Declaration. With the victory at the Battle of Yorktown, we have won the war against the Crown. From now on, we will write our own laws and pursue our own opportunities. We will enjoy a clear path to profit for those of us who see the horizon as clearly as I do. The future, gentlemen, is ours to exploit as we take advantage of the many benefits of being alive in these exciting times."

Thomas showed contemplation. "I am comfortable with my present position, with my family and the prospects for finalizing our independence from an oppressive monarch."

The Major nodded his understanding and then asked, "And what, Robert Morris, Sir, are you comfortable with?"

Robert didn't hesitate. "My enthusiasm."

"Which comes from?" the Major wanted to know.

Robert showed annoyance.

"Sir," the Major began. "I—"

"—This is no time for humility," Robert shot back.

"What's wrong with humility?"

"It veers you from your chosen path."

The Major asked Morris to explain.

"Sir, I believe that, if in your own best judgment, you define an objective, you must pursue it. Is not that the course you military men follow in battle? Such is the course I have charted for my life."

"Take me through that course, Sir," the Major implored, his tone inquisitive.

Thomas took out his pipe and filled it with Virginia tobacco. He lit it from the tip of a pointed stick he had inserted into the fireplace. He puffed and waited for Robert to say more.

"My father brought me here from off the docks of Liverpool to learn merchant commerce and pursue my goal of building my fortune. His shadow and his spirit of hard work have encouraged me onward. I have followed his lead, while lamenting his untimely death—as you, Thomas, have lamented your father's untimely death."

Thomas nodded.

Robert went on, "Although I was able to spend only a little time with him, his image, his honor, his values have guided me."

The Major asked, "And they are?"

"To take pride in your word and cherish the confidence of your business associates. Your honor and your reputation make up your soul. I have employed those principles in helping to finance the Revolution. It has worked. Of course, I have had valuable assistance in working with others, especially Haym Solomon in procuring funds from France. But my point is, I have nurtured a strong conviction in my abilities to finance, not only the Revolution, but also my own future and to further enhance my fortune. Today I see the future in the value of all this land stretching westward across the continent."

"Speculation," Thomas said, his tone judgmental.

"Label it what you will. Read what Adam Smith says about the value of land in his book The Wealth of Nations. Many of us have read it. Land, capital, and productivity—that is the picture I see on the horizon, in my future and in the future of this new continent where I want to continue to be out front, as I know I have been during our Revolution."

# CHAPTER FIFTY-ONE:
# THE SHERIFF NABS ROBERT

As time went by and unpaid debts for his land purchases continued to come due, piling up one after the other and coming at Robert Morris like unceasing ocean waves, he could find no relief from the incessant demands of creditors. He told himself that debts, in themselves, are not onerous—that is, assuming the debtor has the financial means of payment, but as of now, being unable to devise a visible means of payment, the debts consumed his thoughts, dictated his evasive actions, dominated his emotions and, worst of all, eroded the fading hope of solution.

That was the situation in which Robert Morris found himself. To his dismay, Silas Deane, reporting in letter after letter, advised that he had been unable to sell any of the plats of his land in New York, Georgia, or Pennsylvania to European investors. Why was that so? Morris agonized in the return letters he dispatched to Deane.

In Deane's replies, Morris read stories of those investors who had been approached in France, Holland, and England. Almost in unison, they complained that the boundaries of the parcels being offered were so ill defined that they did not understand the precise parcels of land in which they were being asked to invest. Morris, of course, understood the truism that no investor likes uncertainty. But now, adding to investor worries were rumors that land values in the New World would plummet because there was so much land available and, unfortunately due to the uncertainties, and with so few buyers willing to part with their money, these two adverse factors were drying up any willing investor funds.

Matters grew fearful. Morris, along with those other Colonial leaders who had also speculated in land, found themselves in similarly distressed circumstances: no sales, and yet payments on their land coming due and now, with the passing of time, were past due. In conformance to the law, the court was issuing warrants for the arrest of debtors in response to the many legal pleadings of creditors and their lawyers.

To avoid meeting any of these insistent creditors who knew him—and most of them did—Morris hid in his house during the week so as not be seen by them or the sheriff. That dreaded man was bound by the law of the land to arrest anyone for whom a court order had been issued for non-payment of debts. With that document clutched in his hand, the sheriff was obliged to unceremoniously apprehend and promptly escort the delinquent debtor to prison.

However, on Sundays the Sheriff rested, or did whatever sheriffs do on Sundays, allowing Morris and his similarly circumstanced friends the freedom to walk the streets of Philadelphia, to greet their friends and, unimpeded, to enjoy the fresh invigorating air of the new nation.

$$* \qquad * \qquad *$$

Ludwig Hess had been a corporal in the Hessian mercenary ranks. He had deserted on the first opportunity following his division's landing in North America. Thereafter, he heard stories of untold numbers of jobs available in cities in the New World and, being a wanted man back home—for stealing a goose from a farmer—Ludwig knew he dare not return. Not wanting to get himself killed fighting for the British, the choice for his future had become crystal clear.

He learned English from a fraulein he took up with outside Trenton, where captured mercenaries had been interred by the Continental Army. Ludwig blended into the scene and, when he felt confident of his language skills, he made his way to Philadelphia. There, with an introduction from men in the German community, he applied for the job of Sheriff, the previous lawman having joined up with the Colonial militia and been killed in battle.

Adhering to his own set of strict standards, Ludwig decided that once a court order had been duly issued, it was his job, regardless of the day of the week, to enforce that order. An order is an order, he reasoned. If there was protest from the man apprehended, the local judge, who secretly shared Ludwig's values, was known to look the other way, allowing apprehension and prompt imprisonment of the debtor.

On this particular Sunday, Ludwig was on the prowl along Philadelphia's cobblestone streets searching among the day's strollers for any man for whom arrest warrants had been issued. He soon spied Robert Morris walking along Sixth Street as he was passing by the house where Thomas Jefferson and his colleagues drafted and re-drafted the Declaration of Independence. Approaching Morris, holding high with one hand the authorized red-wax-affixed court warrant, and with the other hand his pistol, Sheriff Hess confronted the Revolutionary financier.

With his fellow citizens observing, Morris had no choice but to allow the lawman, at pistol point and with arrest warrant in hand, to march him forthwith to the Prune Street Debtors' Prison.

## CHAPTER FIFTY-TWO:
## DEBTORS' PRISON

As Major von Lowenstein and Dr. von Hogarth sipped ale in the City Tavern, warmed by the log fire in the gaping stone fireplace, they watched President George Washington ascend the stairs to the second floor. His gait conveyed the assurance of a personage in charge of everything and everybody. His manner connoted leadership. The look in his eyes seemed, or so the Major commented, to connote the necessary discipline to monitor military maneuvers. "See, his facial expression reflects the battlefield challenges of both defeat and victory. I've seen that demeanor in battle-hardened cohorts." The Major gestured up the stairs and asked, "What's going on up there?"

"It is the Society of The Cincinnati," Dr. Hogarth replied. "They are meeting. As always, our General will be in charge."

The Major asked about the society's name.

"Named after the Roman general and emperor whose virtuous behavior became a model for a ruler." He paused. "Like Machiavelli, I suppose. The exclusive membership in this new organization, so I am told, is restricted to Continental and French Officers who fought the British."

"Lets me out," the Major quipped and chuckled.

The doctor nodded. "Me, too, but I have heard that the General intends the organization to continue on into the future—the far-off future—to be one of the traditions of the new nation."

"Tradition can be a powerful force," the Major suggested. "It has been so in my Hesse-Kassel." Musing and sipping more ale, he asked, "Are these 'Cincinnati' officers the ones with answers for how the future of the country will unfold?"

The doctor chuckled, "Answers depend on the questions."

"Are you saying, my good doctor, that if I pose the burning question that has brought us together here today, you may have the answer?"

"No guarantee, Major, but proceed."

The Major straightened his posture, his Teutonic military bearing enhancing his aura. The doctor puffed on his pipe, the misty smoke not concealing the joint curiosity that had brought the two together. The Major began. "Yesterday, I thought about visiting Robert Morris in debtors' prison on Prune Street. As you know, he has been confined there for some weeks."

"Pity," the doctor lamented. "No way for him to have continued to dodge the Sheriff—except to pay his creditors the mountainous sums he owes, which he is unable to do."

"So I understand. But, Doctor, how did such a humiliating fate befall such an important man? He was revered in the Revolution. Now the court in the country that he himself helped create is punishing him with an indefinite prison sentence. I do not understand such a society as this, nor do I agree with its verdict of confinement simply for money matters. He has committed no crime."

"I do not understand either." Dr. Hogarth sipped his ale and asked, "Is money the highest value of the land, or is happiness the zenith of our existence here on Earth?"

The Major reflected, "My Prince—my former Prince, that is— would say that military discipline and loyalty to one's Prince or King are most important, for those guiding lights have shown the way in our culture for centuries."

"But where does one's personal reputation fit? I mean, I value what my fellow citizens think of me as a doctor, as a person. How people regard me is important to my self esteem."

"Good thoughts, from your patients and colleagues, yes, but lasting only as long as you pay your bills," the Major suggested, sarcasm coloring his tone. He added, "In this new country of yours, now mine, the popular value scale ranks money uber alles. Will it always be that way?"

Dr. Hogarth reflected. "Many things are new in this land, so perhaps prevailing human values will evolve in tandem with the new form of government, and we will enter into a culture with more lofty values."

"You Sir, are a romantic—a trait with which I am not familiar."

The two men sat in contemplative silence until the Major prompted, "My question, Sir? You said—"

"—Ah, yes…you asked about why our friend Morris has been confined in debtors' prison for debts he is unable to pay. I will pass along the explanation given to me by Mrs. G the other day. Well actually, I overheard her discussing it with Arnold, her Negro slave. You see, she arranged for him to be my patient." Dr. Hogarth paused, doubt creeping into his countenance. "Perhaps I will be betraying doctor-patient privilege if I tell you."

"Mrs. G? Her slave?"

"Arnold. He is quite bright, literate, self-educated, of course, learned from General Gates—by osmosis, perhaps. He is patriotic, told me about his hero, Crispus Attucks, the Negro who fought for independence. He was the first American to fall to British gunfire in the Boston Massacre, and is idolized by Negros, slave and free, as the first martyr of the American Revolution."

"Yes, slaves are indeed real people. They do count."

"Only by two-thirds in the census." The doctor shook his head in disbelief. As to his own ethical question, he said, "I guess it is within the limits of my oath as a doctor to tell you." He went on, "The former slave is free now. Mrs. G's husband gave him liberty in tribute to the Continental victory at Yorktown."

"What did the former slave Arnold say is the explanation for Morris' fate?"

"Major, I am a doctor, not a man of finance. My explanation my be imprecise."

"Allowances made."

"Well, our Mr. Morris agreed to make a multiple number of land purchases, ranging from New York to Georgia—huge tracts there and in Pennsylvania."

"He was speculating on rising values of land, I suppose."

The doctor nodded. "Logical, I suppose. Over time, land values will certainly rise with a growing population. But the problem with his speculation was not the idea, the farsightedness, his looking to the future."

"What then was the problem?"

"The amounts of money he agreed to pay for the land purchases…the notes he signed were denominated in the new money of the country, which at the time was being discounted to a tiny fraction of its face value. In other words, Morris agreed to pay in what he thought would be pennies on the dollar."

"Clever…I suppose."

"Yes, if the value of the dollar remained low."

"And it did not?"

The doctor held up an index finger. "Quite so, Major."

"So, what happened?"

The doctor replied, "The new country's credit rating—its financial integrity, that is—was not well regarded." The doctor sipped his ale. "But then something happened, something that changed the whole game of land speculation and paying the debts incurred."

"And that was?"

The doctor repeated what the slave Arnold told him. "Surprise to all, Congress voted to actually pay its debts by raising real money from the states, from tariffs, taxes, and other sources. As a result, the value of the new American credit instruments—called the dollar—rose. Suddenly American money became regarded as being worthy of investor merit—its value rose to par and was being honored at face value by creditors around the world."

The Major scratched his head. "So?"

"So, now Morris had to pay his debts—instead of pennies on the dollar—with 100 cents on the dollar."

"Which meant?"

"That he could not come close to paying, for all along he had expected to pay only a few pennies." The doctor paused. "There are two more factors at work."

"Which are?"

"First, Silas Deane was supposed to sell land tracts in Europe, tracts carved out of Morris' purchases. Well, Deane may have sold a few, but the tracts were ill defined, their borders uncertain, and in some cases contested. European investors became skittish. Morris' hopes of bailing himself out by Deane pulling off massive European land sales foundered."

"And the second?"

"This is more basic. In the Negro's judgment—and I suspect they do have judgments now and again—our revolutionary hero shifted his attention and his skills from something he knew well—perhaps better than any other man, with the exception of Thomas Willing."

The Major said, "You mean, he shifted from ocean commerce to land speculation. Like going from water to dirt?"

The doctor nodded. "Yes, for example, it would be like me changing from medicine to running a tavern." He chuckled. "Indeed, I would be trying to make a living in strange waters. It was as if Morris found himself aboard a ship in a storm, and the storm overcame him and the ship struck the rocks. And the Sheriff..."

"Yes, the Sheriff came calling." The Major lamented. "And now Robert Morris languishes in Prune Street Debtors' Prison."

"Yes, a pity, for he is one of only three men to sign all three of the deciding Revolutionary documents: the Articles of Confederation, the Declaration of Independence, and the Constitution."

The Major asked, "But what went on in his mind? Beyond what Arnold told you. I really must know, Doctor, if I am to understand the mind of this American Revolutionary."

The doctor suggested, "Perhaps you and I have made that discovery."

Uncertain about the nature of what the doctor was calling a "discovery," the Major ordered another ale for himself and one for his medical companion. Following a pinch of the barmaid's backside as she turned to leave, the Major directed his breath through his teeth in a high whistle as he asked the doctor, "Don't we want to know what the barmaid thinks when I do that?"

The doctor laughed, "Are you serious? You and I don't care...or do we?"

"Does she care?" The Major waited. "Do we care what Robert Morris thinks about this unfortunate situation of his?"

"A pinch is praise, as far as the barmaid is concerned. She knows we are interested in her."

"Exactly my point, Sir. I want Robert Morris to know that I...and you...are interested in what he has to say, what is in his mind...now...and when he got himself into this financial predicament. I want to know why he allowed himself to do it." The Major paused, adding, "And I want to know if the slave, I mean the former slave, Arnold, is correct in his assessment of what has taken place in Robert Morris' life."

The doctor said, "In that case, I will pen a personal note to the warden, explaining that I am a doctor, and that I want to be assured of my client Robert Morris' well being, and that I wish to visit him tomorrow, along with you, Major, his old friend."

# CHAPTER FIFTY-THREE:
## ROBERT MORRIS CONFINED

Philadelphia's Debtors' Prison at 6th and Prune Streets loomed ahead like the entrance to hell, the Major thought as he and Dr. von Hogarth approached the grim edifice. The gray clouds overhanging the city served only to color the already dismal building a deeper shade of gloom.

Drawing closer, they were confronted by a set of vertical black iron bars framed by sturdy iron posts, preventing entry or exit without an enormous key being inserted in a shield-shaped lock of immense proportions. Beyond, through the bars, loomed an arched double entry gate painted in even bleaker shades of gray.

No one was in sight. A string of sleigh bells on a leather strap hung from a hook by the iron bars. With vigor, the doctor whisked the sleigh bells back and forth until a grim-looking man attired in a black tri-cornered hat and a long and soiled dark coat appeared, having first opened one of the two entry doors, its hinges sounding the reluctance of rare use.

The Major whispered to the doctor, "I have seen the Hesse-Kassel military prison, but this place is more hostile, more...well, more forever in your face and, worse, in your mind."

The guard hoarsed, "My warden is expecting you, Doctor...." He led them inside where he pointed down a long stone corridor, its floor moist, its walls covered with mildew. It was as equally bleak as the spot where the darkly clad warden stood, a gatekeeper waiting, challenging, hostile. Everywhere was a lack of color, even in faces now allied with the all-present gray stone. The visiting duo asked themselves what must be the hideous strength that debilitates one in the sameness of inhuman moment after inhuman moment, where confinement trumps free spirit, where the absence of hope rules, where there appears to be a lack of imagination, where creativity is continuously crushed.

The place seemed to the Major to be, by and in itself, punishment enough—for a human being simply to be subject to the awful negative forces at work here. He asked his medical companion, "How could a man's spirit continue to exist, being locked away in such a place as this?"

The doctor said, "I am reminded of Dante's Divine Comedy, for which the faithful lithographer, Gustave Dore, in his work, noted the inscription above the gates to Hell, 'Abandon all hope, ye who enter here'."

Trying to be upbeat, the Major said, "There is always hope, I suppose. You know, doctor, I think Congress should outlaw these sorts of prisons. What ever happened to the word "happiness" as stated in the Declaration of Independence as an imbued right of all men?"

"Who are created equal," the doctor added. And I add, women, too. And, yes, I shall add slaves, as well—those men and women who should no longer be slaves. Where is our Congress on those issues, I ask?"

Their deliberations were interrupted by the gruff voice of the warden, "Morris is this way." He set off, expecting the two visitors to follow. At a small wooden door, the Warden pointed. "The prisoner is expecting you."

"Does he receive many visitors?" the doctor asked.

"His wife." The Warden added with no show of interest, "She comes with his dinner several evenings a week."

"Anyone else?"

The warden's clenched grimy fist struck the wooden door, announcing visitors. He turned to look at the two men, "General Washington was here a week ago." He added without feeling, "They dined together."

The Major evidenced a traditional Germanic exclamation point by blowing softly but meaningfully through his teeth.

The guard added, "And then there was that younger good looking woman—her name was...ah...Polly."

The doctor repeated the name in a questioning tone.

"A daughter, I think," the guard said, further information fading into the rusty creak of the confining prison door as it opened.

Robert Morris, appearing tired, not beaten, remorseful perhaps, bored definitely, happy to see them for sure...ah, possibly...the Major surmised upon imagining himself, a mercenary major, being the prisoner herein.

Seemingly lost in memories. Morris' eyes darted back and forth as if searching for the next ship appearing on the horizon coming up the Delaware from Chesapeake Bay. The Major surmised that his mind might be mentally calculating the cargo sailing off or the cargo about to be unloaded. Yet the Major detected a hint of anger from Morris' look, perhaps echoing from the bleak stone walls of his cell and, yes, surely directed at his unjust and debilitating confinement.

The sole doorway allowed an opening to an austere room. Through this opening stepped the two guests, who were now allowed to join Morris and experience along with him a taste of day-to-day unforgiving stone confinement.

"Mr. Morris, Sir," the Major offered, his voice firm, upbeat, respectful, friendly, reflecting a certain awe for the Revolution and those who acted the story that by now had been written into volumes of world history.

In a slight motion of acknowledgement, Morris nodded. Slowly his hand reached out, shaking first the Major's, then the doctor's. He said, "I trust you did not bring the Yellow Fever with you." Morris smiled, as if the statement was an attempt at humor, albeit humor with a diseased and deadly vein. "Many in here have died," he added, his voice as cold as the walls encircling them. He gestured to the outside, "The prison for criminals is just the other side of that low wall outside. The fever can easily jump across and sicken us in here. The fever is all over Philadelphia...my son Robert III...perhaps you have heard."

Dr. von Hogarth said he hadn't heard about young Robert and offered his condolences. The Major said he was sorry at the news, his thoughts whisking across the great distance to his own sons in Hesse-Kassel.

The prison room was furnished with three wingback chairs, a smallish wooden dining table, its legs looking rickety, and a side table Morris seemed to be using as a desk. Clothes hung on pegs awkwardly driven into gaps between stones in the wall. The only opening, a small glass window, offered a view through the thick stone wall out onto Prune Street.

Morris half-heartedly motioned to the meager furnishings and commented, "Donated by the local charitable Quaker Relief Group. They have taken pity upon me.

Looking around and recalling Morris' orderly and efficient office in the Willing & Morris Warehouse on the Philadelphia wharf, the Major's uneasy feeling consumed him with discomfort, perhaps even pity, unusual emotions for a military man. Yet he managed to pose the question he had come here to this disagreeable place to pose: "Will you please tell me, Sir, what goes through your mind about this new direction in which your career has unfolded, not the end, that is, not the final end, for sure. Tell me about your feelings concerning your moments here in this...ah...place."

Morris' demeanor didn't change. Contrary to the Major's hope, Morris didn't seem to contemplate or deliberate or even mentally debate a deep and thoughtful reply. Instead, after a moment, a long moment in the Major's sense, Morris spoke, his voice clear. "Major von Lowenstein, Sir, one does what one is inspired to do at any moment, or sequence of moments, given the circumstances prevailing. I am proud that I endeavored to respond to the needs of our Colonies and benefit the Revolution."

"And yourself, as well?" Very quickly, the Major wished he hadn't added that comment for he observed that Morris began to take on a look of hostility. The Major tried to change the subject, asking, "But then...afterward, you...you...."

Morris' countenance reverted to resignation. He nodded. Slowly he said, "The Epilogue is not necessarily the story, Sir. Only an appendage, and like the human appendix, it is not a benefit to our true self, yet it, or its counterpart, can easily debilitate us, as it has me and, to my regret, my dear family."

The doctor looked around the small room and saw upon the wall a framed etching of a sailing ship. He gestured toward it and asked, "Is that one of your merchant ships, Sir?"

Looking at the slough longingly, Morris told them it was once one of his ships. "My portrait artist drew it...sketched it...as a favor. Named for my son, Robert III—studied in Germany, you know." Before ethnic camaraderie could consume the moment, Morris said, "But, of course, I am English by birth, but American now."

The doctor remarked, "As are we all…now."

Morris pointed to the other two chairs, "Sit there. It is where George Washington and Alexander Hamilton sat." He added, "By the way, three of my Revolutionary colleagues are also herein ensconced for not having paid their debts."

Seated, the guard having departed, the three men each filled their glasses from the bottle of cognac the doctor extracted from his great coat.

"Tell me, Sir," the Major began, "What is it like for you to be confined here in this…." He wanted to assign a label, a negative label, to the prison, but he refrained from doing so for fear a chosen adjective might color the response to his question. He again ended his query with the word "place."

Morris didn't reply right away. He downed his cognac in one gulp and smiled. "Beautiful," he said, gesturing lovingly at his empty glass. Turning reflective, Morris suggested, "There is beauty around us everywhere." He added, "Here, I feel an isolation from nagging creditors. And I enjoy fellowship among colleagues. Each of us is adrift in the same abandoned ship, but of course without a sail to capture a welcome wind to move us onward to a safe and welcoming harbor."

The Major asked, "So, you sense satisfaction with your life, perhaps a new and certain tranquility?"

Morris nodded slightly, almost absently, the thoughts in his mind seeming to transcend the surrounding stone barriers.

"Where are you?" the Major pressed Morris, almost too insistently, the doctor thought, a growing sorrow for the revolutionary hero overtaking his emotions. Uncontrollably, he grasped Morris' arm and squeezed. Morris repelled a bit, then looked intently at the visitors. Slowly he requested, "Please do not show sympathy overtly, for such displays are rare in each of our cultures. We three here today do not enjoy the closeness of family."

The cell turned silent until the Major managed to ask, "And if we were? Family, that is?"

Morris took the cognac and replenished his glass, this time allowing one slow sip. "Then I would confide to you as I did the other day with my daughter Polly."

"Polly?" the doctor repeated the name, intoning a question.

Not replying at first to the doctor, Morris started on a personal story, but then stopped to reply, "From early on in Oxford. I promised her mother, a most beautiful young woman, that I would care for our daughter, and I always have…until now, when I can no longer do so. But we remain close. We are family."

The Major nodded his understanding, as did the doctor, who then prodded, "You grew up in—"

"—Yes, as a boy on the docks of Liverpool. I saw how the world of ocean trade works. As a young man on the wharfs of Oxford and then on the docks of Philadelphia, I lived the opportunities. When the King and Parliament became oppressive, curtailing the opportunities I saw lying ahead for me in this New World, I shared my vision of making my personal future with the visions I, along with many others perceived to lie ahead for this new land and all the lands lying to The Westward. These visions soon merged to become a new country."

The Major nodded. The doctor waited. Morris went on, "Only then did I allow my appetite for fortune to shape my life, its fragrant flavors luring me on toward a monstrous financial feast of real estate opportunity. I may have been a hundred, maybe two hundred, more likely three hundred years too soon for the land to rise in value and my dream of unlimited wealth to be realized. Therein lies my mistake, a vision blurred by the opaqueness of time. Unlike Washington Irving's Rip Van Winkle, I could not go up into the hills and sleep for 40 years, wake up and return to enter a future with new opportunities." Morris appended, "You see, Gentlemen, I followed my mind to those places of fascination where it led me. I now enjoy the resultant rewards of satisfaction and endure the angst of monetary setback."

"And Polly?"

"And my father?" Morris nodded. "Yes, Gentlemen, were they here with us now, they would laud my life."

"How about Molly, your wife?" The Major asked. "And your seven…ah…six other children?"

The doctor interjected, "They have also lost, or so I suspect. The money, your money, I mean."

Robert Morris did not reply for a while, the two visitors soon shifting uncomfortably in their wingbacks. Then, by his facial expression, the Revolutionary hero seemed to gradually accept the question. He looked at the doctor and then at the Major, as he began to formulate a reply.

Through the little window cut through the thick stonewall came a brighter and more mellow light from the setting sun, now breaking through the day's pervasive cloud cover. A sudden burst of sunshine illuminated Morris' aging face. In an eerie hue, his skin showed the paleness from a lack of sunlight, and his wrinkles were highlighted. Yet his eyes sparkled with what each of his visitors later remarked were a glow of Revolutionary importance. It was then that the Major saw what he thought were tears forming in Morris' eyes, and a feeling of compassion must have overcome the military man, for he, too, dabbed at his eyes.

At that point, Morris rose, his action suggesting they should leave. As they stood to do so, Robert Morris slowly nodded his agreement to the conclusion. But then as they were handshaking their good-byes, in a considered voice, Morris said, "Gentlemen, we are each on a short fuse to eternity, and we have only so much time before the spark dies out. I have spent my spark."

As they turned to exit, Morris added, "What we have done here on these shores of the Atlantic transcends any one individual patriot's efforts. It also exceeds any possible purse of property or prosperity, for our combined endeavors at achieving independence is wealth enough. My personal fortune, once so dear to me in my plans for my future, has given way to the realization of a Revolution that in itself will, or so I foresee, provide both material wealth beyond our imaginations today and intellectual opportunities that, in today's world, would overwhelm us."

# THE END

# EPILOGUE

Robert Morris spent four years in Prune Street Debtors' Prison. In 1800, Congress voted the Bankruptcy Act, the new nation's first consumer protection law. Morris' creditors finally wrote off his debts and, as the new century blossomed and the new law took effect, he was released in December 1801. He wrote to his son who had been elected to Congress that he was "a free citizen of the United States without one cent that I can call my own." Living on charity and penniless, Robert Morris died in 1806.

"Molly" Morris became a popular hero of the American Revolution. She passed away in 1827 in Philadelphia.

*Screenplays (available only in eBook format)*

**Painted Waters**
a Zuni Pueblo portrait artist meets a
cyberspace evangelist and an Irish journalist

**A Nuclear Tide**
Nuclear waste storage

**Marathon, My Marathon**
Adapted from the novel

**Time to Retire**
Adapted from the novel


*Current Fiction by Jon Foyt*

**Time to Retire**
Mystery and romance in a retirement community lifestyle

**Marcel Proust in Taos**
A Los Alamos physicist retires to Taos and finds romance

**The Sculpture of Time**
Shakespeare's "The Winters Tale" set in California

# ABOUT THE AUTHOR

*photo by Helen Munch, Victoria, BC, 2013*

Striving for new heights on the literary landscape, Jon Foyt began writing novels with his late wife, Lois, while living in Manhattan in 1992.

Their earlier published novels range from offshore trusts to a story set in Albania, the untold account of the Erie Canal, to a faux biography of a socialite leading WACs into Normandy in WW II. Jon's most recent novel, Time To Retire, is set in a fictionalized active adult retirement community.

A distance runner, Jon has completed 60 marathons. His degrees from Stanford are in Journalism plus an MBA. He completed the Historic Preservation degree program at the University of Georgia.

Jon is active in the 10,000-strong retirement community of Rossmoor in Walnut Creek, California.

Website: http://www.jonfoyt.com      email: jonfoyt@mac.com

# BIBLIOGRAPHY
*The Mind of an American Revolutionary*

*The Diary of Elizabeth Drinker, Vol 1*, 1758-1795, Northeastern University Press, Boston, 1991, Elaine Forman Crane, Editor

*Financial Founding Fathers*, Robert E. Wright and David J. Cowen, University Of Chicago Press, 2006

*The Selected Papers of John Jay, Vol 1*, 1760-1779, Elizabeth M. Nuxoll, Editor, University of Virginia Press, 2010

*Memoirs of Benjamin Franklin*, Written by Himself, Derby and Jackson, New York, 1859

*Common Sense*, Thomas Paine, 1776

*The Unknown American Revolution*, Gary B. Nash, Viking Penguin, 2005

*Rebels Rising, Cities and the American Revolution*, Benjamin L. Carp, Oxford, 2007

*Patrick Henry, the Voice of Freedom*, Jacob Axelrad, Greenwood Press, Westport, Connecticut, 1947

*Alexander Hamilton, a Biography*, Forrest McDonald, W. W. Norton, New York, 1979

*America's Women in the Revolutionary Era: A History through Bibliography*, Eric G. Grundset for the National Society Daughters of the American Revolution, Washington, DC, 2011

*In the Words of Women, the Revolutionary War and the Birth of the Nation*, Louise V. North, Janet M. Wedge, Landa M. Freeman, Lexington Books, 2011

*Women of the Republican Court, or American Society in the Days of Washington, revised*, Annie Turner, Rufus W. Griswold, D. Appleton and Company, New York, 1856

*The Papers of Robert Morris*, 1781-1784, E. James Ferguson, Editor, John Catanzariti, Associate Editor, University of Pittsburgh Press, 1973

*Robert Morris, Revolutionary Financier, with an analysis of his earlier career,* Clarence L. Ver Steeg, University of Pennsylvania Press, 1954

*Benjamin Franklin, Autobiography, Poor Richard, and Later Writings, Literary Classics of America, New York,* Jay A. Leo Lemay, compiler, 1997

*Thomas Willing and the First American Financial System,* Burton Alva Konkle, University of Pennsylvania Press, Philadelphia, 1937,

*Benjamin Franklin & Music of the 18th Century,* Philadelphia Museum of Art CD (Computer Disc)

*Eighteenth-Century Colonial American Merchant Ship Construction, A Thesis* by Kellie Michelle Van Horn, Submitted to the Office of Graduate Studies of Texas A&M University in partial fulfillment of the requirements for the degree of Master of Arts, 2004

*The Colonial Homes of Philadelphia,* Harold Donaldson Eberlein and Horace Mather Lippincott, J. B. Lippincott Company, Philadelphia and London, 1912

*Abraham Clark as the Quest for Equality in the Revolutionary Era,* Ruth Bogin, Fairleigh Dickinson University Press, London and Toronto, 1982

*John Jay, The Making of a Revolutionary,* unpublished papers, 1745-1780, edited by Richard B. Morris, Harper & Row, 1975

*Silas Deane, Revolutionary War Diplomat and Politician,* Milton C. Van Vlack, McFarland & Co, Jefferson SC., 2013

*The Confidential Correspondence of Robert Morris,* Stan V. Henkels, Auction Commission Merchant, Jan. 16th, 1917 Catalogs, Philadelphia, inherited by Mrs. Edward Waln, granddaughter of Robert Morris

*Life of Robert Morris.* The Great Financier, pamphlet, Desilver, Publisher, 1841

*Pennsylvania History, Volume V,* 1938, University of Pennsylvania Press, Philadelphia, Robert Morris and the Provisioning of the American Army during the campaign of 1781, Victor L. Johnson

*Robert Morris and the "Art Magick,"* John Dos Passos, American Heritage, The Magazine of History, October, 1956

*Robert Morris, A Sketch*, Charles Henry Hart, The Pennsylvania Magazine of History, 1877

*"Thomas Willing [An Account of his Life,]* from the collection of Mary Helen Cadwalader, 1890

*Financing the American Revolution*, Udo Hielscher, Museum of American Financial History, New York, 2005

*A History of Psychiatry*, Edward Shorter, John Wiley & Sons, New York, 1997

*Thomas Paine*, Craig Nelson, Penguin Books, New York, 2006

*Revolutionaries*, Jack Rakove, Houghton Mifflin, New York, 2010

*Pennsylvania*, 13 Colonies Series, Raintree Press, Chicago, 2005

*The History of Psychiatry*, Franz G. Alexander, Rowman & Littlefield, London, 1995

*Robert Morris, Audacious Patriot*, Frederick Wagner, Dodd, Mead, New York, 1976

*The Founders and Finance*, Thomas K. McGraw, Harvard University Press, Cambridge, MA, 2012

*Robert Morris, Financing of the American Revolution*, Charles Rappleye, Simon& Schuster, New York, 2010

*Puritan Boston and Quaker Philadelphia*, E. Digby Baltzell, The Free Press, New York, 1979

*With the British Army in Philadelphia, 1777-1778*, John W. Jackson, Presidio Press, San Rafael, CA & London, 1979

*A Hessian Diary of the American Revolution*, Johann Conrad Dohla (1750-1820), translated and edited by Bruce E. Burgoyne, University of Oklahoma Press, 1990

*The Hessians, Mercenaries from Hesse-Kassel in the American Revolution*, Rodney Atwood, Cambridge University Press, 1980